FIR[illegible]

Once again, his tong[illegible] this time, she respond[illegible] playing her own tongue against his, [illegible]ping and praying she was doing it correctly. A deep, almost soundless moan rumbled in his chest, reassuring her that he was aroused by her kiss. He tightened his embrace, and her worries fled as new, compelling sensations surged through her own body. Pleasure such as she had never experienced, and yet somehow she wanted more. . . .

"Juliette! *Juliette*!"

Madame Bouchard's shrill voice suddenly penetrated Juliana's awareness. Burning, she pulled back from Lord Dare, panicking to see that many of the dancers had already left. But she could not run off, and let Dare think his kiss had overset her. She summoned up the courage to look back at him.

"Why, thank you, milord Dare," she said. "You kiss well . . . for an Englishman."

SIGNET

REGENCY ROMANCE

COMING IN DECEMBER 2003

FINE FEATHERS and
THE MAKESHIFT MARRIAGE
by Sandra Heath 0-451-20963-X

For the first time in one volume, Signet Regency Romance presents one brand-new Regency and one beloved classic from an author with "a rare talent for crafting unusual but intriguing tales...which amuse and beguile readers" (*Romance Fiction Forum*).

THE WAGERED HEART
by Rhonda Woodward 0-451-21021-2

Miss Juliann Alard must cut short her season and return home—where she'll concoct an elaborate plan of revenge against the rougish Duke of Kelbourne. Little does she know, however, that the duke also has some plans up his rakish sleeve.

AN ENCOUNTER WITH VENUS
by Elizabeth Mansfield 0-451-20997-4

When he was seventeen, George Frobisher caught a glimpse of his sister's best friend emerging for a bathtub...*naked*. In the ten years since that fateful day, however, the Earl of Chadleigh hasn't heard a word about the dazzling Venus—until now.

Available wherever books are sold, or
to order call: 1-800-788-6262

The Redwyck Charm

Elena Greene

A SIGNET BOOK

SIGNET
Published by New American Library, a division of
Penguin Group (USA) Inc., 375 Hudson Street,
New York, New York 10014, U.S.A.
Penguin Books Ltd, 80 Strand,
London WC2R 0RL, England
Penguin Books Australia Ltd, 250 Camberwell Road,
Camberwell, Victoria 3124, Australia
Penguin Books Canada Ltd, 10 Alcorn Avenue,
Toronto, Ontario, Canada M4V 3B2
Penguin Books (N.Z.) Ltd, Cnr Rosedale and Airborne Roads,
Albany, Auckland 1310, New Zealand

Penguin Books Ltd, Registered Offices:
80 Strand, London WC2R 0RL, England

First published by Signet, an imprint of New American Library,
a division of Penguin Group (USA) Inc.

First Printing, November 2003
10 9 8 7 6 5 4 3 2 1

Printed in the United States of America

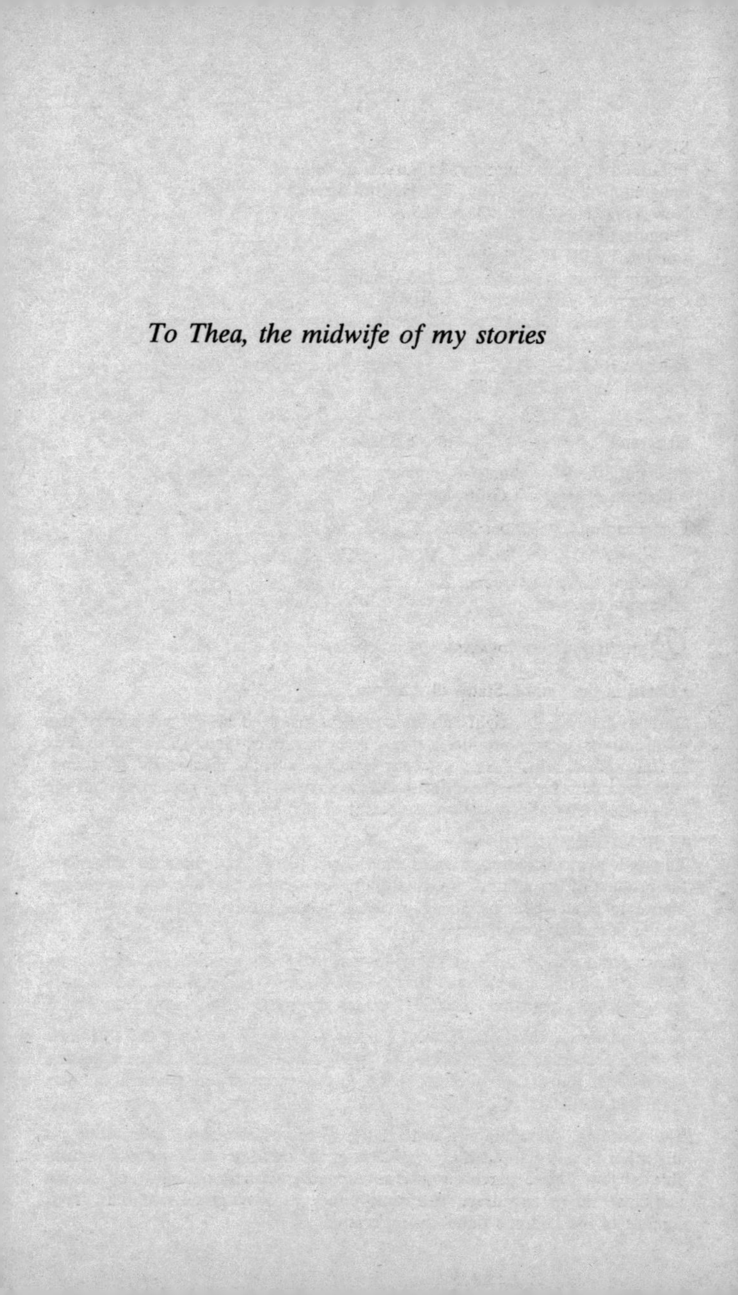

To Thea, the midwife of my stories

Chapter One

Marcus Redwyck, seventh Earl of Amberley, slumped at his desk for a moment and gazed out of the window. The prospect from his study was usually a cheering one: a lawn sloping gently down toward a stream bordered by several fine willows. But the drab light of a rainy day in March muted all colors to a dull gray-green and robbed the stream of its sparkle. After a few moments, Marcus straightened and looked resolutely back at the neat columns of numbers before him. No, there was no mistake. He never made mistakes with figures.

It was a relief to hear the familiar sound of Critchley clearing his throat.

"Lord Plumbrook is here to see you, my lord."

Despite the start that this form of address still gave Marcus, he gave a perfunctory smile to the elderly butler, who had served the Redwycks of Redwyck Hall as long as he could remember.

"Show him in, and bring us some sherry, please."

He rose from his chair and flexed muscles stiff from prolonged sitting, and forced yet another smile for the portly, middle-aged gentleman who entered his study a few moments later.

"Good day, sir," he said.

"Good day, Marcus," said Lord Plumbrook. "Or Amberley, as I should call you now. And no need to call me sir, either. You know you outrank me."

Marcus grimaced at the mention of his title. "Very well. You must forgive some lapses, though. You have been my good friend and advisor for so long I'm afraid it has become a habit with me."

He waved Lord Plumbrook to a chair covered in worn, cracked leather, and took the other beside it, away from the desk with its neat stacks of account books and papers. Critchley poured the sherry and left, his tread slow and painful. No doubt he was suffering a relapse of his gout, but Marcus knew better than to say anything. The one time he had expressed the wish that he could provide Critchley with a comfortable pension, the loyal old retainer had behaved as if his pride had just been dealt a mortal blow.

"Demmed fine stuff, this," said Lord Plumbrook, as he leaned back in his chair and savored his wine. "Whatever his faults, your uncle did have a discerning palate."

Marcus made no answer. At the mention of his uncle, anger, guilt and helpless frustration coursed through him, feelings that had been mounting ever since he had received word of the previous earl's sudden death and begun to learn the extent of the disaster left behind. In his careless way, Uncle Harold had always been kind to Marcus and his family, readily offering them all a home when Marcus's own father died over fifteen years ago. Even in the depths of gloom, Marcus found it difficult to hate him.

"That bad, is it?"

Marcus recognized the kind intent behind Lord Plumbrook's gruff question, and answered with equal candor.

"I'm afraid it is worse. Bentwood holds the mortgages on our lands, everything except Redwyck Hall itself."

"Bentwood! That greedy upstart!"

Marcus was not surprised by the revulsion in Lord Plumbrook's voice at the mention of Sir Barnaby Bentwood, infamous throughout the Cotswolds for both his grasping ways and his shortsighted treatment of his tenants. No doubt Lord Plumbrook did not relish the idea of Bentwood as a neighbor. Marcus had his own reasons for detesting the man.

"I had hoped the sale of the town house would enable me to meet the next few payments," he continued. "That was before I learned that the town house is mortgaged as well. I have wracked my brains for a way to meet the next payment, and failed. By midsummer, Bentwood will be in a position to foreclose. I do not expect he will exercise any forbearance in the matter."

"Good God! Did your uncle have any plan to meet his obligations?"

"I believe he hoped to restore the family fortunes with some lucky investments," Marcus replied, unable to keep a bitter note from his voice.

"So the fool was gambling on the 'Change as well as at the table. And the curricle race? I suppose he hoped to win a handsome sum off that?"

"Quite possibly," said Marcus, with a wry smile. He remembered feeling shock, but also a guilty sense of relief, at the news that his uncle had broken his neck. At the time he had thought there was still some hope of halting the family's headlong plunge into ruin. Now he knew better.

"So what do you plan to do now?" Lord Plumbrook asked, looking at Marcus keenly from under his bushy eyebrows.

"I must find a tenant for the Hall. It is a fine old place, so perhaps I can find someone willing to take it, ill-furnished as it is. With any luck, the rents should enable me to set Mama and Lucy up in a small house or cottage somewhere."

"And as for yourself?"

"I shall seek employment."

"Where? To do what?"

"The only thing I'm fit for. I shall seek a position as a steward on some gentleman's estate."

"A *steward*? I'll admit you are qualified, what with having tried to keep this ramshackle place in order while your uncle played ducks and drakes with the family fortune. I've never seen anyone with a better head for figures. But who do you think would employ an earl as their steward?"

"I shall revert to calling myself Mr. Redwyck. If that does not answer, perhaps I shall go to America, or India, or somewhere where I am *allowed* to pursue gainful occupation."

Lord Plumbrook sat back in his chair, swirling the dregs in his glass for a few moments, his brow furrowed.

"I admire your fortitude, lad," he said after a moment. "I do think I have a better plan to offer you. It's something I have been thinking about for some time now."

He paused again, as if seeking the right words to make a ticklish suggestion. Marcus thought he knew what his friend was about to say.

"If you are thinking of offering me a loan, sir, I'm very grateful, but I cannot accept. It would be many years before I could repay you. I could not put you in such a position."

"No, I was not thinking of a loan."

Marcus felt curiosity and the faintest stirring of hope at Lord Plumbrook's words. Perhaps he did have some scheme in mind—but what could it be?

"Have you given any thought to marriage?"

"You are thinking I should pay court to some heiress?" Marcus tried to keep the revulsion out of his voice as he asked the question.

"That's exactly what I think."

He sighed. "I suppose such marriages are a Redwyck tradition. But time is short, and I am not acquainted with any heiresses. I'd hoped to find more honorable means of restoring the family fortunes."

"Well, it so happens I have someone in mind. It's a Miss Juliana Hutton. She is the granddaughter of Josiah Hutton. He's a Cit but very respectable, and could buy and sell twenty estates like yours. Years ago, when I was a young fool and ran aground, he lent enough money to get me afloat again. Never demanded a penny of interest, but when his granddaughter was born he asked if I would act as her godfather. Poor girl was orphaned a few years later. Parents lost at sea while sailing along the coast of Scotland. Now she's all Hutton has left, and his dearest wish is to see his great-grandson a lord."

"So Miss Hutton is to be induced to fulfill his ambitions? Or does she share them?" Marcus didn't know which was worse: an unwilling bride, or one who would accept him for a title alone.

"Who can say what's in a young chit's head?" asked

Lord Plumbrook. "Miss Hutton has never confided in me. You know I don't care for London, only go up once or twice during the Season when m'wife needs me as host for her parties. But Lady Plumbrook took the girl about last spring, and says there is nothing in her speech or manners to put you to the blush. Hutton made sure she was educated at a most select school. And don't be thinking she's any sort of antidote! She's quite lovely, yellow hair, blue eyes, all that sort of thing."

"I am surprised such a paragon still remains unwed." Marcus could not keep a touch of skepticism from his voice at Lord Plumbrook's unmitigated praise of Miss Hutton.

"According to Amelia, she's had a dozen offers, but refused them all."

"If Miss Hutton has turned away so many suitors, why do you think she would consider *my* suit?"

"You outrank all of them, for one thing." Lord Plumbrook must have seen Marcus wince, for he instantly added, "I expect it's Hutton who is impressed by your title. No doubt Miss Hutton is like most foolish chits of her age, and has some romantic fancies of marrying for love."

"What, are you saying I should deceive her by pretending to fall in love with her?"

"No, no, nothing so extreme! Just get to know the girl, talk to her, and see where matters progress from there."

"I'm afraid I'm far better versed in sheep breeding and crop rotations than in gossip or fashion. I shouldn't know what to say to her."

"Come, come! You Redwyck men have always been able to win the favor of any woman you choose to pursue. Handsome, smooth-tongued devils, the lot of you. If the first Baron Redwyck could turn Queen Elizabeth up sweet, there's no reason you can't do the same with Miss Hutton, if you would but try."

Marcus frowned. Whatever history said, he had no reason to believe in the legendary Redwyck charm. If the trait truly existed, it must have skipped his generation.

"Do you think she would be willing to overlook my . . . my disfigurement?"

"What, that paltry limp? No doubt she will find it romantic. A few years ago they were all out of their minds over that poet fellow. Byron, you know. And his limp was far more pronounced than yours."

"I doubt she'd find it romantic if she knew I had broken my leg falling through the attic floor while searching for family heirlooms to sell," he said, remembering another young lady who had quite certainly not seen anything romantic in his plight.

"So you don't tell her. You may not like the idea of an arranged marriage, but this is a golden opportunity. Don't pass it up. I'm not just saying this because I don't fancy the thought of Bentwood as a neighbor. Damn it, I'm fond of you. I should hate to see strangers living at the Hall. I had rather see you here, with a wife and a bevy of brats around you to carry on the name." Lord Plumbrook paused to draw breath, and continued, "Think about it! You'll be able to restore the Hall to what it once was. You'll be able to arrange for Lucy to be brought out in style."

"Lucy would not thank you for that suggestion," he replied, with a glimmer of a smile at the thought of his hoydenish little sister. "But you are right. Very well, I will court this heiress of yours, to the best of my ability."

"Good lad! I thought you'd see reason." Lord Plumbrook's cheeks puffed out in a satisfied smile. "I'll write to Hutton immediately, and arrange for you to introduce yourself."

Lord Plumbrook remained only a few more minutes, discussing the projected meeting, before taking his leave. Marcus saw him out, then paused on the steps to gaze out at the undulating hills and woods that surrounded the Hall.

He wished Lord Plumbrook had been able to tell him more about Miss Hutton. Did she perhaps rebel against the fate decreed for her? He felt a twinge of pity for the girl. If she proved unwilling, he would have to withdraw his suit and deal with the consequences.

However, it seemed more likely that she was merely being selective in her choice of husband, knowing her grandfather's wealth would outweigh her lowly pedigree in the eyes of many an impoverished peer. Perhaps she looked for not only a title in her suitor, but also fashion and elegance. Marcus remembered what Lord Plumbrook had said about her education, and immediately the image formed in his mind of a coldly ambitious young lady, trained from birth for marriage into the upper echelons of the aristocracy. What would life be like with such a companion?

He chided himself. It was not the time for second thoughts; in a few hours Lord Plumbrook would be penning his letter to Miss Hutton's grandfather. There was a multitude of matters to arrange before he himself left for London, but somehow he felt too restless to start. He thought of going to the stables, but the prospect of a ride down muddy lanes under dripping trees held little appeal.

Abruptly turning on his heel, he crossed the entrance hall and swiftly walked down a long corridor, ignoring the pain as his leg protested the sudden exertion after too many hours of inactivity. A few minutes later, he reached his destination, the long gallery containing the only paintings remaining at Redwyck Hall. All of the landscapes and still lifes had been sold long since to pay servants' wages and defray pressing debts, but here the images of his ancestors still remained.

He slowed as he entered the gallery. Tall windows to one side let in a feeble ray of sunshine as the clouds parted momentarily, lighting up the portrait of Harold, first Baron Redwyck. A sea captain, privateer and reputedly one of Queen Elizabeth's favorite courtiers. Despite his mustache, his pointed beard and the stiff lace ruff that framed his face, the first Baron Redwyck seemed uncannily familiar. The brown hair, the forehead, the aquiline nose, all were just what Marcus was used to seeing in the mirror each morning. The eyes. . . . It was difficult to see their exact color in the two-hundred year old painting; Marcus thought it likely to be the same hazel as his own. There was a bold light in his ancestor's eyes, and the hint of a triumphant smile about his mouth, too.

Damned pirate, Marcus thought, and moved on, past more portraits of gentlemen and ladies, and the occasional family grouping. All the gentlemen bore the same aristocratic visage, with the same hint of roguishness.

There was Marcus, the first Earl, reputed to have won the charming Nell Gwynne's favors before she decided to bestow them on King Charles II. Attired in the rich red of his state robes, wearing a jeweled chain around his neck, his dark brown hair in long, luxuriant curls, Marcus's ancestor had that same cursed devil-may-care expression in his eyes.

Damned popinjay!

Marcus limped on, past bewigged and powdered gentlemen, and smiling ladies whose dresses seemed in imminent danger of slipping off their curved, white shoulders. There, finally, was Sir Joshua Reynolds's portrait of Marcus's grandfather, Charles Redwyck, the fifth earl, in his powdered wig, and with the same arrogant look in his eyes. Marcus had no memory of the fifth earl, but as a boy he had thoroughly enjoyed reading through his grandfather's account of all the adventures he'd enjoyed on his Grand Tour.

Beside his grandfather's portrait was a smaller one of Uncle Harold. Marcus gazed for a moment into those languidly smiling hazel eyes.

"Damn you all," he said, aloud this time.

They had all gone their own ways, pursuing pleasure and adventures as they wished, losing and regaining fortunes with equal recklessness and fathering who knew how many bastards. Had they ever worried about them? Had they ever wasted a thought on any of those whose livelihood depended on them, on their tenants, the laborers who worked the land, generations of loyal servants? Marcus doubted it.

Several times some head of the family would bring them all to the brink of ruin, then a successor would win royal favor through extraordinary valor on the battlefield, or avert disaster by a brilliant investment or even more brilliant marriage. And the cycle would begin anew.

Ever since Marcus had realized that Uncle Harold was a confirmed bachelor, he had known it was his turn to restore the family fortunes. While his friends set off for Oxford or Cambridge, he had followed an aging bailiff around the estate, studied crops and fertilizers and sheep. While other young men were busy chasing lightskirts or placing bets at Tattersall's, he had buried himself in agricultural reports and account books, and done what he could to improve the estate.

All for naught!

Now, the fate of the Redwycks depended on his ability to woo a fastidious heiress, and he had no idea how to go about it. His one previous attempt at courtship had failed. Although in hindsight he knew he had made a lucky escape, still he had no idea what a woman would want . . . or need from him.

His gaze swept back across the long parade of his ancestors. *They* had known.

However, they had left nothing of their knowledge behind, except for that special collection in the library. Marcus had found it while in his teens: stacks of treatises, manuals and even memoirs dealing with the amorous arts. He'd devoured them at the time, even though the illustrations in *Aretino's Postures* had seriously disturbed his sleep for months. Before too many years passed, however, he had learned of the disastrous consequences of his forebears' devil-may-care behavior, and had resolved not to follow in their footsteps.

He turned on his heel, suppressing the guilty envy he felt whenever he thought of his ancestors' adventures. The fact remained that they had left him nothing of use; nothing about flirtation or courtship, nothing to tell him how to succeed where so many others had failed.

But succeed he must.

He would find a way somehow.

"Damn you all," he repeated softly, and left the gallery.

Chapter Two

"I received some good news from Lord Plumbrook today."

Juliana thought she detected a hint of stiffness in her Grandfather's manner, and wondered at it. He did not often dine with her and her companion, Mrs. Frisby. Instead, he usually dined with his associates in the City, and was too occupied with business to spend many evenings with her. It was a rare treat to join him in a game of chess here in his favorite room, and hers. She loved being here, loved the oriental carpets on the parquet floor, the fine paintings dramatically displayed against deep red walls, the mahogany display cases containing treasures from around the globe. Even more, she enjoyed matching wits with her Grandfather in a harmless game. She had hoped to enjoy the evening, but now she felt apprehensive.

"How is Lord Plumbrook, Grandpapa?" she replied, cautiously moving a skillfully carved ivory pawn. "And is dear Lady Plumbrook in good health?"

"Yes, yes, they are in good health, both of them," replied her grandfather, making his own move with his usual deliberation before looking back up at her, his blue eyes piercing under thick eyebrows that were as white as his neatly trimmed hair. "Her ladyship is all eagerness to return to London, and has graciously offered to take you about with her again this Season."

"She is kindness itself," Juliana replied sincerely, while hiding her disappointment at the news.

"She has been more than patient with you, granddaughter."

She bit her lip at the accusing note in Grandpapa's voice. Lady Plumbrook had indeed been more than kind. Juliana knew Lord Plumbrook was under some sort of obligation to Grandpapa, but Lady Plumbrook had not shown any reluctance in repaying the debt. She had taken Juliana under her wing and treated her as the daughter she never had, using all her resources to procure a number of respectable invitations for her. She had braved the snubs of Almack's patronesses who had persisted in denying her protégé entrance to their exclusive club. She had not even uttered a single word of reproof when Juliana rejected one offer after another from the fashionable, if impoverished, gentlemen she had introduced to her.

"I trust you do not intend to disappoint Lady Plumbrook *this* Season," continued her grandfather.

Juliana stifled her annoyance at the warning in his voice, instead pretending to be absorbed in her next move. It was ever a chess game with Grandpapa. She could not afford to show her feelings; he would call her a foolish child.

"In fact, it is that very subject that Lord Plumbrook addresses in his letter."

Juliana paused in the act of moving her knight.

"Lord Plumbrook writes that his good friend and neighbor, the Earl of Amberley, is eager to make your acquaintance."

An earl! she thought, releasing the chess piece. *How perfectly dreadful.*

"I suppose it is the usual tale," she said aloud. "Gaming debts, estates mortgaged to the hilt, rapacious creditors?"

"There is no need to be so cynical, child."

"I am sorry, Grandpapa. But do you truly wish me to marry a gamester, someone who will fritter away whatever you choose to settle on me within a year, and be a parasite on you ever after?"

She watched him carefully for signs of weakening. This argument had been very effective last year. Now it seemed not to be working at all. A triumphant smile stretched Grandpapa's thin, wrinkled face as he moved his bishop. *Drat!* she thought, looking down to see him challenge her queen.

"Of course not, my dear granddaughter. Lord Amberley is no gamester. He has only recently come to the title, and a burden of debt accumulated by his uncle. Lord Plumbrook says *this* Lord Amberley is a most conscientious young man. He has been seeking to restore the family fortune through better management of his estate, and it is only with the greatest reluctance that he has conceded that he must make an advantageous marriage as well."

"How condescending of him," she muttered, moving at random.

"Don't be impertinent!" he said, a touch of anger in his voice. "You should be grateful for such an opportunity. Checkmate."

She looked down at the chess pieces, realizing she had been distracted and outmaneuvered. She could not let him goad her into further betraying herself.

"Forgive me, Grandpapa," she said, hiding her clenched fists under the table, "but you know I do not wish for marriage."

"Pshaw! All females wish for marriage. You are merely being fastidious. I expect you'll feel differently once you have met Lord Amberley. Lord Plumbrook says he is very handsome and amiable, and will make you a charming husband."

"Then perhaps when I refuse him you will finally believe that I do not wish to marry."

Grandpapa glared at her, a vein pulsing in his high forehead. She had the satisfaction of knowing he was at least attending to her words now.

"You are not still cherishing that foolish plan you broached to me last year, are you?"

She looked him in the eyes and nodded.

"Yes, I am."

"I thought you'd outgrown such folly. A Grand Tour! A green girl like you, junket about the world by yourself? Bah!"

"Mrs. Frisby would come with me. You cannot say she

has no experience of travel," said Juliana. Mrs. Frisby, the widow of one of Grandpapa's sea captains, had accompanied her husband on many trips to both the East and West Indies.

"I should never have engaged her services," he said, frowning. "Most likely it was *she* who put these insane notions into your head."

"Please, you must not blame poor Mrs. Frisby. She did not put any notions in my head; I have always wished to travel."

"Hmmph! That must be why you attended to your French and Italian lessons at Miss Stratton's school, and little else."

"Both Monsieur Dubois and Signor Bonelli said I have an aptitude for languages. So you see, I shall be able to go on splendidly—"

"Splendidly? You are more likely to end up like Lady Hester Stanhope, cruising about the Mediterranean with her lover, her reputation in tatters!"

"I do not wish for romantic entanglements. Particularly not with adventurers interested in my fortune. I met enough of *them* in the polite drawing rooms and ballrooms of the *ton*."

Grandpapa frowned. She almost thought she had scored a hit, but he came back staunchly. "You say that now, granddaughter, but you do not know how clever some of those rogues can be. Besides, you would run into debt within a sennight. I know the troubles Mr. Coutts has had to endure."

Juliana winced at the reference to Lady Hester's banker. "Grandpapa, *I* would not run into debt. You know I have never exceeded the pin money you give me. Moreover, you know I have managed the household accounts this past year and more, since *I* discovered your old housekeeper was cheating you."

"You have done very well, my dear," he said, with an indulgent, patronizing smile that set her teeth on edge. "The experience will hold you in good stead when you are mistress of a large household of your own. Lord Amberley has a fine home in the Cotswolds. Redwyck Hall, I believe it is called."

He sat back, half-closing his eyes, and Juliana could see he was already imagining her the chatelaine of a vast ancestral seat, surrounded by a horde of his great-grandchildren. She shuddered. She'd spent half her life here, in Russell Square, and the other half within the confines of Miss Stratton's select school for girls. Now Grandpapa seemed set on dooming her to live the rest of her life in dreary domesticity, subject to the whims and demands of an unknown husband and as many children as were necessary to ensure the succession of the earldom.

Once again she clenched her fists in a desperate attempt to control her frustration, while she sought words to explain herself.

"Grandpapa, you have surrounded yourself—and me—with such wonders. Can you not understand why I wish to travel?"

She jumped up and went to stand by one of her favorite paintings, a view of the Grand Canal in Venice, by Canaletto himself. She gazed up at the luminous sky, the crisp details of domed churches and the gracefully curved prows of the little boats that plied the sparkling canal. Then she turned back to her grandfather.

"I should like to see Venice for myself," she said.

She went to one of the display cases, where priceless bowls and vases from China gleamed, their colors and patterns exotic and mysterious in the flickering candlelight.

"I should like to see where these were made."

Going to the other case, she waved toward a set of carved ivories depicting palm trees and elephants.

"I should like to see a real elephant, with my own eyes."

"Are you mad?"

She jumped as Grandpapa slapped the game board with his fist. Turning around, she saw that bright red color suffused his pale face. She'd miscalculated terribly. He did *not* understand. Guilt overcame her anger as she watched him struggle to his feet. He looked dreadfully frail despite the anger blazing from his eyes. She ran to help him, but he shook off her hand.

"With all your opportunities, with all that Lady Plumbrook and I have done for you, is this all you can say?" he demanded. "That you wish to gawk at outlandish animals in strange, heathenish countries?"

"Better *that* than to suffer through yet another Season spent gossiping about who has a *tendre* for whom, or discussing the latest style in sleeves! Or to make idle conversation with some fool who has parted with his fortune and now hopes to use my dowry for his clothes, his gaming, and his—his mistresses!"

"Is that the fate you think I wish for you, girl?" he demanded.

"No, Grandpapa. But can you not understand that I do not share your dreams for my future?"

"You are too young to know your own mind," he said curtly. He cleared his throat, then continued. "In two weeks' time, you will meet Lord Amberley, and I expect you to greet him with courtesy, amiability and above all, an open mind."

He turned and hobbled out of the room. She watched, not knowing whether to scream or cry. Instead, she paced about the room. Part of her wished to go and make her peace with Grandpapa. But how could she, without giving in to his plans?

As she strode past the display cabinet containing the china, it rattled slightly, and she slowed her pace. Agitated though she was, she could not risk damaging any of the objects Grandpapa had so lovingly collected. She left the room and headed for the small conservatory at the back of the house. Though potted palms, camellias and other plants lined the walls, there was room to walk there.

She closed her eyes, basking in the warmth of the room. For a moment, she pictured herself standing in the Piazza San Marco in Venice, bathed in sunshine. Then a gust of wind brought rain to tap against the windows, reminding her that she was in London, and that it was not yet April.

She thought of Lady Hester, riding across the desert on camels or fine Arabian horses. She herself had never even ridden a horse; Grandpapa judged it too dangerous. A gentle walk in the conservatory or the park was the only exercise permitted her.

She reopened her eyes. A feverish energy coursed through

her body. No, a sedate walk was not enough. She lifted her arms and began to waltz, as she had been taught at Miss Stratton's school, although as yet she had not been permitted to do so in company. She circled the room, to an ever-increasing tempo, adding an occasional pirouette or leap such as she had seen on the stage of the Opera House. Finally, she came to a stop, breathing quickly, her heart pounding.

But it was useless. She felt more restless than ever. She would have to find a way to win over Grandpapa, or she would, indeed, go mad.

The next day, Juliana arose early. She went to the window, and was cheered to see that the clouds were high and pearly, not threatening imminent rain. She would be able to go to Green Park as she had planned to walk with her friend, Miss Penelope Talcott.

Pen had been one of her closest friends at Miss Stratton's, part of a threesome the teachers had dubbed "The Three Disgraces." She had just returned to London from Sussex, along with her uncle and aunt, Sir Ralph and Lady Talcott, who had taken her in after her parents' deaths. Juliana had not seen Pen since the end of the previous Season. Now that Catherine, the third of their group, had married and lived in Cumberland, Pen was the only friend whom Juliana could trust as a confidante.

An hour later, after breakfast with Mrs. Frisby, she alighted from Grandpapa's carriage at the entrance to the park. A brisk wind blew up, making her glad she had donned a warm, dark blue wool pelisse with a matching bonnet, and insisted that her maid Polly dress in warm clothes as well.

A short distance away she spied Pen, wearing a fawn-colored pelisse and accompanied by her aunt's maidservant. As Juliana ran toward her, Pen turned and smiled in greeting, her hazel eyes sparkling, her red locks curling around her face under the brim of a bonnet trimmed with pink and yellow flowers. It seemed Lady Talcott's taste in clothing had not improved; certainly Pen would not wear such an unbecoming hat of her own choice. Though of course,

Pen would not have protested, not wishing to seem ungrateful.

Moments later they embraced.

"Oh, how I have missed you, Pen," Juliana said, holding her friend's slight figure tightly for a moment.

"And I you. Seeing you again is by far the best thing about coming back to London."

They linked arms and began to walk, their maids following behind, closely enough for respectability and just far enough for privacy. Juliana looked down at her friend. Despite the hideous hat, there was a pretty color in Pen's lightly freckled cheeks. She also seemed to be in far better spirits than Juliana would have expected. Their last Season had been a trial for both of them. Many in the *ton* had looked askance at Juliana because of her connections with Trade, while Penelope's family had never quite found their niche in London society either, despite regularly overspending their income to create a false impression of greater wealth than that afforded by their modest estate in Sussex. Juliana could not imagine that Pen looked forward to yet another Season.

"How was your journey, dear?" she asked. "You don't look tired at all."

"Actually, we have been in London for several days now. Aunt Mary insisted we go shopping the first day back. She bought me this hat." Pen rolled her eyes upward expressively.

"It *is* dreadful," agreed Juliana. "I suppose you could not persuade her to let you choose for yourself?"

"How could I, when it is so important to her to purchase all the latest fashions? Besides, hats like this will serve my purpose very well."

A mischievous smile played around Pen's mouth.

"What are you planning, Pen? Do you think if you repulse enough suitors you will be sent home in disgrace?"

"No, although that would be lovely. The bluebells will be coming out in another few weeks." Pen sighed, then continued. "I have no scheme. It is merely that I have become resigned to the prospect of another Season."

"I see how you are smiling. You cannot fool me. What

is your plan? Let me guess. You have a suitor back in Sussex, and you hope that ugly hat will repel any London beaux whom your relatives might favor."

A telltale blush appeared under Pen's freckles, but she shook her head.

"Come. Am I in the right of it?"

"We—there is no understanding. He has not offered for me, or anything like that."

"But you think he will. Tell me. Who is it?"

"It is Mr. Welling, the curate. He will likely obtain the living at our parish once the present rector retires, which we think he might do next year. I trust that by then my aunt and uncle will have resigned themselves to the fact that I will not make a better match."

"I am sure all will be just as you wish." Pen, who had been raised in a country vicarage, had often said she wanted nothing better than to return to such a quiet life, surrounded by children and pets.

"I know the life I wish for sounds dreadfully dull to you," said Pen earnestly. "I wish you could understand how delightful it can be just to be part of a family. But your parents died so young, perhaps you cannot remember such things."

For an instant, vague memories of a soft voice, a playful touch, stole over Juliana.

"No, I do *not* remember," she said, shaking her head. "So don't feel sorry for me, Pen. Grandpapa has always cared for me, and provided all the nursemaids and toys I wished for."

"That is not at all the same thing," said Pen, frowning.

"In any case, I do not wish for marriage, or children. Of course, Grandpapa has far different ideas," she said, as they entered the shelter of a grove of trees.

After she had told Pen about the match Grandpapa had arranged for her, her friend wrinkled her brow.

"I think this Lord Amberley sounds very amiable," she said, after a pause. "You cannot blame him for wishing to care for his tenants, and his family."

"Yes, yes, he is so virtuous he is even willing to marry a lowly tradesman's daughter to save the family fortunes. Well, I have no desire to be part of such a sacrifice." Juliana caught herself walking too quickly, then slowed to accommodate Pen's shorter stride.

"If you find he is truly odious of course you should refuse him. But perhaps, once you become acquainted, you may find him more agreeable than you expect. You might even fall in love."

"You are too romantic! I do not believe I shall ever fall in love. In my experience, there are two kinds of men in the world: those like Grandpapa, benevolent tyrants who would manage women's lives as if they had no will of their own, and the second sort, who merely take advantage. Think of poor Mrs. Frisby, whose husband spent all his wages before she saw a penny of them, and left her destitute. And think of what happened to Catherine. She wanted to escape her family, but made the mistake of asking help from that scoundrel Lord Verwood. He must have deserted her, for why else would she have allowed herself to be buried in the country with a gentleman farmer, of all things?"

"I think you are wrong. I believe she loves Mr. Woodmere. She writes that she is happy beyond all her expectations, and he is everything that is good and kind. Now they are expecting a dear little baby." Penelope sighed wistfully.

Juliana could not share Pen's feelings. Her heart felt heavy as she thought of Cat, forced to live in the distant north, bound by marriage to the unknown but undoubtedly rustic Mr. Woodmere. No wonder she wrote often, urging them to visit her.

"She has written the same to me, but I am convinced Cat is merely putting a brave face on her troubles." Juliana decided not to voice her worst fears. Cat's mother had died in childbirth. What if the same happened to Cat, before either of them could even see her again?

Pen shook her head. "I think Cat is happy with Mr. Woodmere. Why do you persist in thinking that men are all such tyrants? My own papa always confided in my mother, and asked her advice on every matter of importance. They were totally devoted to one another."

"Such men are rare. Besides, I find the mere thought of being kissed or . . . or touched by a man thoroughly disgusting."

"I have always felt that to be kissed by a man who loved me would be one of the greatest joys imaginable." Pen's impish smile returned.

"Well, I expect you will enjoy it very much when Mr. Welling kisses you. *I*, however, have already been kissed. Twice, and both times the *gentlemen* professed to be in love with me. The first was that toad Augustus Twickham, one of Grandpapa's clerks, who thought to advance his career by wooing me."

"That must have been unpleasant."

"He tasted of stale cabbage soup."

"Ugh!"

"Oh, and then there was that fool Charles Bentwood, whom I met this summer in Brighton. I admit, I was foolish enough to find him attractive on our first meeting. The next time we met, he found an occasion to seize me in his arms. He then proceeded to do a fine imitation of a bear intent on devouring me."

"That sounds more passionate."

"Not a bit of it. He stepped on my foot."

Penelope giggled. "Oh, I am sorry. I should not laugh. What happened then?"

"When I cried out, he relaxed his hold slightly, which gave me the opportunity to slap his face as he deserved. Polly came to my rescue soon after, at which point he had the audacity to claim that only the deepest ardor had tempted him to pass the line. It was clear enough what had happened. Grandpapa must have refused his suit, since he is a younger son, and his brother is only a baronet. So he decided to see if he could compromise me into marriage."

"That was certainly dreadful, but dearest Jule, you must believe that there are men who will value you as they should."

"I do not depend on it. My choices are to marry one of those fools, or remain an old maid in Grandpapa's household."

"Lord Amberley does sound better than your other suitors."

"I am sure he is quite dreadfully respectable. If I marry him, no doubt he will expect me to live quietly in the country, so as not to embarrass his family with my vulgarity, and of course, he will expect me to bear him numerous children to ensure the succession."

"So you still hope to travel?"

"Yes, but Grandpapa will not hear of it. He is convinced that only marriage with a peer of the realm will secure my happiness. I cannot think of a way to persuade him otherwise."

Pen squeezed her arm. "I know. It is difficult to know what to do."

"Perhaps I shall run away," Juliana said lightly.

"You are not serious, are you?" Pen stopped and stared at Juliana, her eyes wide.

Juliana had spoken half in jest, but as they resumed their walk, she considered her words. "Perhaps. But this is different from the pranks we played at school. If I merely steal the housekeeping money and hide for a week or so, Grandpapa will only make Mrs. Frisby and the servants keep a stricter watch over me. No, I must think of a disguise, and also some way of supporting myself until he relents."

"Where would you go? What would you do?"

"I do not know."

"Well, I think you should just stay, and meet Lord Amberley."

"That certainly would be the sensible thing to do," Juliana replied, seeing that Pen looked upset. Perhaps Pen was thinking of Catherine, who had gotten herself in so much trouble by trying to run away with a rake. Whatever she did, Juliana would not repeat Cat's mistake of trusting a man to help her out of her predicament. She would prove to Grandpapa that she knew how to resist the advances of unscrupulous males.

"Can you guess who I saw yesterday while Aunt Mary and I were shopping at Grafton House?" asked Penelope, in an obvious attempt to divert Juliana's mind.

"No, who?"

"Madame Bouchard. Do you remember her?"

"Of course," said Juliana, smiling at the memory of their old dancing mistress who had once graced the stage of the Paris Opera House. "How is she? I always wondered what happened to her after Miss Stratton dismissed her. And I still do not believe she ever carried on an *affaire* with Monsieur Dubois."

"We don't know for certain that was why she left, Jule. Anyway, she now teaches at one of the dancing academies, and also lets out rooms in her house in Half Moon Street, mostly to opera dancers, I think. She seems to be well and happy."

"I am glad. She was always so kind and patient with us, when we must have irritated her beyond anything at times."

"You did not. You were the best dancer among us. I never could master any of the ballet steps she taught us, before Miss Stratton put a stop to it."

"Yes, all because the author of *The Mirror of Graces* lamented that 'chaste minuet is banished, and, in place of dignity and grace, we behold strange wheelings on one leg; stretching out the other till our eye meets the *garter*,' " said Juliana, placing wicked emphasis on the last word.

" '—and a variety of endless contortions, fitter for the zenana of an eastern satrap, or the gardens of Mahomet, than the ballroom of an Englishwoman of . . . of quality and virtue,' " Pen concluded primly.

They both laughed.

Arms linked, they continued to stroll, enjoying each other's company and the fitful sunshine just beginning to pierce the gray veil overhead. But as they talked, a new idea began to revolve in Juliana's head. She made no mention of it to Pen, knowing it would make Pen very uneasy. But by the time her carriage arrived to take her home, her plan was nearly complete.

It seemed adventure beckoned her, after all.

Chapter Three

"You are going to London to court an *heiress*?"

Marcus had not had much to smile about in the past weeks, but he could not stifle a grin at the deep revulsion in his sister's voice.

"Yes, Lucy, I *am* going to London. Lord Plumbrook has very kindly arranged for me to meet a young lady who happens to be an heiress. I am engaged to visit them in about a week, so that she and I can become better acquainted."

"Mama, tell him he must not!"

"Marcus, my darling, is this truly necessary?" his mother asked.

They both gazed at him intently, their dark brown eyes alight with curiosity and concern. Thus far he had managed to withhold the worst of the news from them; perhaps he could still soften the blow.

"I am afraid it *is* necessary. You are both too intelligent not to understand our circumstances."

"I thought we were going to save the family fortunes by breeding hunters. I never thought you would resort to such a paltry scheme," said Lucy.

Marcus watched in fond amusement as she jumped up and paced restlessly about their dimly lit library, dusky curls bobbing, the skirt of her old blue dress swinging to a long, mannish stride. No doubt Mama had insisted she change for the evening; left to her own devices, his fifteen-year old sister would surely have spent the entire day in her riding habit. However, there would probably come a day soon when she would find other interests besides horses, and perhaps wish to make her entry into society. He only hoped that he would be able to provide her with the means to do so, and also with a respectable dowry.

"Lucy, I am afraid such a plan would take too long to prosecute," he replied. "In fact, I have already sold Apollo to Lord Plumbrook."

"Apollo! We had such hopes of him. How could you?"

Marcus tried not to think of the lively colt he had bred and trained himself into one of the finest hunters in the Cotswolds, or of their plan to begin breeding from him. Like all his other plans for improving the estate, it would not bear fruit quickly enough to do any good.

"Lord Plumbrook offered me a very generous sum for Apollo, which I need in order to present a creditable appearance in London."

"Present a creditable appearance? I suppose you will have to dress like a dandy, and say all sorts of stupid flattering things to her!"

"Something like that," he said with a smile.

"Well, this Miss Hutton sounds perfectly odious. Mama, you cannot wish Marcus to marry such a stupid chit?"

"Lucy dear, please sit down and mind your language. Not that I do not agree with her," said Mama. "I cannot like the thought of you offering for a woman whose only desire is to marry into the peerage."

Marcus glanced over toward his mother. Tall, slim and vivacious, she could almost have been taken for their older sister. Only a certain grace of demeanor and a silvering in her nearly black hair betrayed that she was past forty.

"Lord Plumbrook says Miss Hutton is quite pretty, and not at all vulgar in her manners or her speech," Marcus offered.

"She still sounds odious to me," said Lucy.

His mother made no response, merely leaning back gracefully on the sofa, closing her eyes in concentration. It was a pose he knew well, though it seemed hardly the time. . . .

A moment later, her eyes flew open.

"I have it! A sea monster will do quite nicely!"

"Or perhaps a giant octopus?" asked Marcus, trying to suppress a chuckle.

She sat up, waving her hands enthusiastically. "Can you not picture it, darlings? A sea monster will attack the evil duke's ship after he steals Francesca away, and he will drown, while she washes up on shore, clinging to a plank, only to be found on the beach by her lover, Alonzo. He has been suffering agonies since she was torn from his arms. At first, he believes she has died, but she awakens in his arms, and—"

"Mama, it is not the time for your stories. Marcus is in trouble!" Lucy interrupted, with a frown.

"Don't you see? Now all I need to do is write several more chapters, send it off to the Minerva Press, and I am certain *The Perils of Francesca* will make quite a hit!"

Marcus closed his eyes momentarily, touched and amused. Mama's outlandish stories certainly enlivened their fireside, and no doubt helped to reconcile her to a quiet existence in the country. Perhaps *The Perils of Francesca* would even engage the interest of the editors at the Minerva Press, but it was ludicrous to think the proceeds would lift one-tenth of the debt currently facing their family.

With only a slight tremor in his voice, he replied, "Thank you, but I would not wish you to rush your creative endeavors."

"For you, I shall make the effort."

Marcus shook his head and tried to smile, though his heart ached at his loved ones' naive schemes to forestall his courtship of Miss Hutton. Perhaps it was time to let them know how matters stood; it would at least prepare them for the possibility that his courtship of Miss Hutton would not succeed.

"I am afraid matters are too desperate for that," he said. "I hoped to conceal this from you, but Sir Barnaby Bentwood holds the mortgage on our lands. If matters do not improve quickly, he will be in a position to foreclose by the end of next month."

"Dearest, I would rather live in a cottage than have you make such a sacrifice of yourself," said his mother. "I had always hoped that both of you would marry for love."

Lucy rolled her eyes at Mama's romantic words, but added her objections. "Marcus, please do not marry Miss Hutton on *my* account. If you are thinking of using her dowry to finance my come out, you may be perfectly easy. I have no wish to enter into society, and will be quite happy to live in a cottage. Even if we have to sell *all* our horses!"

"You would not wish our lands to pass into Sir Barnaby's hands, would you? You know what that would mean to our people?"

Both Lucy and his mother paused at that, struck by this argument, as he had known they would be.

"So you see, I have no choice but to do my best to win Miss Hutton's hand. I only hope I can succeed."

"I have no doubt that you shall," said his mother. "For all you have been obliged to live such a quiet life, poor boy, you *are* a Redwyck, and as handsome as any of your forebears. I only wish you could use your charm to woo someone more worthy of you."

She sighed, but Lucy snickered in true sisterly fashion.

"Have you a scene to read to us tonight, Mama?" he asked, seeing his mother preparing to reprimand his little sister.

As his mother began to read the latest installment of *The Perils of Francesca*, Marcus watched them both from his shabby wing chair. He could not take his mother's praise too seriously. She was too fond a parent to be a judge of his assets. Only time would tell whether he would be able to win Miss Hutton's hand and provide for these two, his nearest and dearest.

"Please remain still, my lord. Do not try to help me."

Marcus restrained his impatience and obediently waited as Pridwell carefully drew the new black coat up over his shoulders. Unused to any more assistance than what was required to pull off his riding boots, Marcus had found it rather a trial to be obliged to sit quietly while his hair was painstakingly combed into a Windswept style, and to endure a lengthy lesson in the art of tying a cravat. Fashion was certainly a fatiguing business.

Marcus reminded himself that winning Miss Hutton's hand might depend on his ability to strike just the right balance of respectability and elegance. He must forever be grateful to Pridwell for his assistance. The elderly valet had served Uncle Harold for over thirty years, but few younger men would have shown such zeal. He had guided Marcus to the most elegant tailors' and bootmakers' establishments, and through the arduous task of selecting from a bewildering variety of wares.

"There, my lord," said Pridwell, smoothing a wrinkle from Marcus's sleeve. "I trust my work meets your approval."

Marcus surveyed himself in the mirror in the corner of the room. He had to admit the black coat did look rather elegant, perhaps even justifying the hole its purchase had made in his purse. He supposed the discreet Mathematical Tie and the subtle gray brocade of his waistcoat would also strike the correct balance between elegance and mourning. Then he looked down at the new, smoothly fitted pantaloons. Their subdued dove gray matched the rest of the ensemble. However. . . .

Looking abruptly back at Pridwell, he was shocked to see tears in the valet's eyes.

"Whatever is the matter, Pridwell?" he asked. "You have done your best; it is not your fault if you cannot make a silk purse from a sow's ear."

"Oh no, my lord," said the valet in a shaking voice. "If I may say so, you look splendid. Why, even my late master—God rest his soul—though a fine figure of a man, even in his prime he was not your equal."

Marcus stared at the man. Perhaps Pridwell had gone senile? Aloud, he asked, "Are you quite certain Weston measured me correctly for this coat? It seems rather tight, as do the . . . the pantaloons."

Pridwell straightened, reassuming his dignity. "Not at all, my lord. The loose-fitting coats you have been accustomed to wearing do not do justice to your lordship's shoulders. If I may presume to say so, I have never seen a finer pair on any gentleman. As for the pantaloons, they are all the mode. And might I add"—he coughed discreetly—"although of course they do not speak of such matters, the ladies are not at all averse to the sight of a well-muscled, er, thigh."

Marcus grimaced. Pridwell spoke with the authority of one who had served a fashionable rake through all the vicissitudes and adventures of his amorous career. Marcus ought to be grateful that his valet, like all of Uncle Harold's servants, would do anything to help him win Miss Hutton's hand and secure all their futures.

"Thank you, Pridwell," he said, as he put on the hat and gloves held out to him. "I shall do my best not to disappoint you."

"My lord, you cannot but succeed. You are, after all, a Redwyck."

Marcus left the room, wishing he felt some of the same confidence. He descended the staircase to the marble-tiled entrance hall, and out the door toward his awaiting coach. It would not do to be late for his first meeting with the Huttons. Just as he started down the steps, he nearly collided with a young gentleman ascending them.

"Hallo, Marcus! Good to see you." The young gentleman's round cheeks puffed out in a smile, and his eyes twinkled.

"Hello, Jerry," said Marcus, recognizing Mr. Jeremy Plumbrook, Lord Plumbrook's only son. Although they had not spent much time together of late, it seemed Jerry had not forgotten their boyhood friendship.

"Aren't you slap up to the echo! I almost didn't recognize you," said Jerry, admiring Marcus's attire. "M'father said you were coming to London. You should have called on me!"

"I'm afraid I have been rather busy the past week."

"Getting ready to court the Hutton girl? Papa wrote as much."

Marcus nodded. "In fact, I was just setting out to call on her and her grandfather. Do you know Miss Hutton?"

"Not particularly. You know I'm not much for the *ton* parties. Too many chits on the catch for husbands, and I'm just not ready to get caught in the parson's mousetrap. Not yet anyway. There's better fun to be had in town. A shame you're to be leg shackled yourself so soon. But that reminds me why I came here. I've invited some of m'friends to come to my lodging this evening. Just a little picnic, some wine and cards. You're more than welcome to join us. All our pockets are to let, so don't worry that we'll play deep."

"Thank you, Jerry, but I can't promise I'll come. If the Huttons invite me to dine with them. . . ."

"Yes, I understand," said Jerry, nodding sympathetically. "Come if you can. Good luck with the heiress!"

As Uncle Harold's glossy town coach took him away, Marcus reflected that he might need more than luck. Soon, he ascended the steps to the Huttons' home in Russell Square. It was a respectable residence, decorated with elegance but without vulgar ostentation.

The butler conducted him to a richly furnished study, all gleaming mahogany against deep green striped hangings. From one of a pair of leather-upholstered armchairs, a thin, white haired gentleman arose and bowed. Bright blue eyes gleamed from his pale, wrinkled face, looking Marcus over with keen interest, but there was a slight tension in the man's demeanor.

"Good day, my lord," said Mr. Hutton, a slight quaver in his voice.

"I am delighted to make your acquaintance, Mr. Hutton," he said, extending his hand.

Hutton shook his hand, his fingers bony but still firm in their grip, his gaze not wavering from Marcus's face.

"Please be seated, my lord. Do you care for some sherry? Or other refreshments?"

Marcus declined the offer, and took a seat adjacent to the older gentleman's. No doubt Hutton wished to acquaint himself with Marcus before introducing him to his granddaughter. It was an awkward situation. Marcus decided only a straightforward approach would do.

"I believe Lord Plumbrook has acquainted you with my circumstances," he began.

"Yes, he has told me you must make an advantageous marriage, and quickly."

Marcus rather liked the man's businesslike manner.

"I appreciate your candor, sir," he replied, meeting Hutton's eyes. "I trust you will permit me to pay my addresses to your granddaughter. I promise you that if she accepts my suit, I will do everything in my power to ensure her happiness."

"Plumbrook did say you would make her a fine husband."

"Lord Plumbrook is very kind."

"I've found him to be a fair judge of character. As am I. I have to admit, I like the look of you. You do not appear the sort of man who would gamble away his fortune, or neglect his wife in pursuit of opera dancers."

"Of course not," said Marcus, wondering a little at the undertone of anxiety he heard in Hutton's voice. Had the old gentleman heard reports of the rakishness that was the trademark of the Redwycks?

"Sorry if I've offended you, my lord. Earl or not, I have to think of my granddaughter's happiness."

"Quite understandable," he replied, relaxing slightly. It appeared he had crossed the first hurdle. Although there was still a shade of unease in Hutton's voice, apparently he approved Marcus's suit.

Hearing a slight cough from the doorway, Marcus turned his head, and saw that the butler had returned.

"I thought you would wish to receive this, sir."

Hutton nodded quickly to the butler, who advanced into the room to hand Hutton a folded slip of paper before bowing himself out again.

"Please forgive this interruption, my lord," said Hutton, sounding genuinely distressed. "I have been awaiting some important news."

Marcus nodded, wondering what could be important enough to interrupt their discussion. Hutton's hands trembled slightly as he opened the letter. As he quickly perused it, the lines in his face softened, and he relaxed slightly in his chair.

"I hope all is well?" Marcus asked as the older gentleman refolded the letter and tucked it into his waistcoat.

"As well as I had expected."

Hutton sounded relieved, but there was still an undercurrent of annoyance in his manner. Perhaps some matter of business was not progressing quite as well as the man wished. However, Hutton's tone did not invite further questioning. It was time to return to the purpose of their meeting.

"Is Miss Hutton at home? I should very much like to

make her acquaintance," said Marcus, gathering his resolution.

Hutton hesitated before replying. "I regret to say, my lord, my granddaughter is indisposed."

Indisposed? Or just indisposed to see him?

"Nothing serious, I trust?" he asked, aloud.

"Just a touch of the influenza. I expect she will be better in a week or so."

Marcus observed Hutton's tight jaw, and the deepening anxiety in his eyes, and wondered if Miss Hutton's illness was more serious than her grandfather implied. Did she have a frail constitution? Or was she merely avoiding this meeting?

"I trust Miss Hutton is not suffering from aversion to my suit," he said.

"I am not coercing her into marriage," said Hutton, not quite meeting Marcus's eyes. "You shall meet her, and soon."

"I wish her a speedy recovery, then," said Marcus, rising up to take his leave.

Hutton escorted him to the hall, and they made their farewells. As Marcus rode back to Amberley House, he mentally reviewed his brief meeting with Hutton. He had liked him; Hutton seemed both honest and scrupulous, and sincerely concerned with his granddaughter's welfare. However, it was clear he was hiding something. Marcus could not rid himself of the suspicion that for some reason, Miss Hutton wished to avoid meeting him. If so, all his plans might be in vain.

He wished there were more he could do while he waited for Miss Hutton to recover from her indisposition, whatever it was. Time was passing quickly; in another month Bentwood would gleefully demand the next payment of the mortgage. Marcus cursed the fate that put his future, and the future of all those who depended on him, in the hands of a temperamental heiress.

By the time the coach reached Grosvenor Square, Marcus's mood reflected the cloudy skies overhead. Once inside the house, he was surprised to see Barnes, Uncle Harold's butler, coming forward to relieve him of his cane.

"My lord, we were not expecting you home so soon."

A note of anxiety threaded through Barnes's usually expressionless voice. Marcus realized that Barnes, as head of the London staff, wanted to be the first to learn how he had fared with the Huttons. The butler was undoubtedly disappointed to learn that Marcus had not stayed long, let alone been invited to dine with them.

"Miss Hutton is suffering from the influenza. I could not stay long under such circumstances," Marcus replied, hoping his voice sounded reassuring. "I trust I shall be able to make her acquaintance next week."

The butler's brow cleared. "Yes, there has been much influenza about lately. Once the young lady has recovered she cannot help but rejoice in making your acquaintance, my lord."

Marcus winced inwardly. Poor Barnes and the rest of them, so certain that one smile from him and the heiress would fall into his arms!

"When will your lordship desire dinner?"

The butler's question drew Marcus back into the present. The prospect of a solitary dinner held little appeal.

Then he remembered Jerry's careless invitation.

"I shall dine with Mr. Plumbrook, Barnes."

"Very well, my lord. At what hour will you wish the carriage to be brought round?"

"There is no need. I shall walk."

Barnes looked shocked. "You would not so demean yourself, my lord."

"I'm not a cripple, Barnes. I shall be surprised if it takes more than ten minutes to get there. I shall walk."

"Very well, my lord. You will at least change your attire?"

Marcus yielded to the pleading note in Barnes's voice, and nodded. He didn't wish to offend Barnes, or Pridwell either, since both of them had his interests so closely to heart. Up in his uncle's bedroom, he repeated the story of his visit to the Huttons to the anxious valet. Having exchanged his coat for another that Pridwell insisted was more suitable for evening, his gray pantaloons for an equally tight-fitting black pair, and his gleaming Hessian boots for shoes, he finally set off for Jeremy's apartments, breathing a sigh of relief at his escape from overly solicitous servants.

Ten minutes later, a slovenly manservant admitted Marcus into Jerry's sitting room. Marcus looked about curiously, noting several umbrellas and riding whips leaning against the wall near the door, stacks of newspapers and sporting periodicals on every chair and the sofa, and a jumble of quills, ink bottles, a snuffbox, a decanter of wine and a half-empty glass on the round table in the center of the room. So this was how Jerry lived in London, thought Marcus, feeling envious of the cheerful chaos.

"That you, Marcus?" Jerry sauntered out of his bedchamber, wearing a bright blue dressing gown over his shirt and trousers.

"Have I mistaken the evening?" Marcus asked.

"No, not at all. You're just a trifle early. I forgot you're used to country hours. George and Oswald are coming in another hour or so. Hickman, you lazy lout! Clear us some room and pour us some wine."

The grinning manservant cleared some chairs by moving their contents to the sofa, poured wine into two dusty glasses and then left, sped on his way by further insults from his master.

Marcus sat down and sipped the burgundy. It was not so fine as Uncle Harold's stock, but potent enough to soften the edges of his depression, as did Jerry's unquestioning welcome.

"So how'd you fare with the Huttons?" asked his friend.

Marcus took another sip of the wine before replying bluntly. "Miss Hutton was indisposed."

"You don't think she's trying to avoid you?" asked Jerry, with a flash of his father's shrewdness.

"I can't rid myself of the suspicion."

Jerry looked at him sympathetically. "I've heard she's refused a lot of fellows. It seems the chit don't want to marry. Odd, ain't it? I thought that's all females want. But who's to guess what's in their pretty heads?"

"Not I, more's the pity."

"Perhaps she'll come round," said Jerry in a consoling tone. "Still, it's no wonder you look blue-deviled. We'll have to think of something to cheer you up. Maybe after dinner we'll go to the Opera House. Just the thing!"

"I didn't know you were fond of music."

Jerry looked appalled. "Good God, no! Who wants to listen to all that screeching and caterwauling?"

"Then why do you go?"

"Lord, Marcus, you're such a greenhead!" Jerry laughed. "We go to see the *ballet*, of course. Actually, the dancers. Give you my word, you won't see more ravishing women anywhere. There's a new one you must see—Mademoiselle Juliette Lamant. The loveliest, sauciest creature you could imagine!"

"You . . . consort with an opera dancer?" Marcus did not know whether to be shocked or envious. The latter, he thought.

"Lord, no! I'm not nearly wealthy enough to afford such a highflier. She flirts with me—with all of us—but it's only a matter of time before some rich lord snaps her up," said Jerry philosophically. "Still, it's grand sport to go to the Green Room and watch her and the others practice their steps. Say you'll come with us. One look at the divine Juliette and you'll forget the Hutton chit. For an evening, at least."

"Thank you, Jerry. I wish I could come, but . . . I cannot," said Marcus. He did not even want to think about such things. There was no use imagining he could live like Jerry or his friends, or indulge in the same amusements.

"Oh, don't be such a sobersides! What's the harm in it?"

"More than you can imagine. If the Huttons learn that I've so much as talked to an opera dancer, it would be the end of all my chances."

"You may be right. Cits are so devilishly straitlaced." Jerry paused, looking thoughtful, then his eyes twinkled. "I have it! Just go by a different name. No one here knows you, and we won't even tell George or Oswald who you are."

Marcus hesitated, not wanting to get caught up in Jerry's excitement. It was a ludicrous scheme, of course, but. . . .

"Come on, Marcus. It'll probably be at least a week before you can see the Hutton chit again. What's the harm in having some fun in the meantime?"

Jerry refilled Marcus's glass, and Marcus tossed it down recklessly, letting the warmth of the wine steal through him as he pondered Jerry's suggestion. After all, what could be the harm in just going to see this famous Juliette? It was not as if he would do more than look.

"Come on, Marcus. I dare you to do it," said Jerry.

Marcus smiled at the echo from their boyhood. He had never been as impulsive as Jerry, but where had all his discretion gotten him?

"Oh, very well," he said, setting down his wineglass. "I'll go along."

"Splendid!" Jerry grinned, and refilled both their glasses. "Hmmm. . . . Now we must think of a new name for you. Something dashing, and not too common sounding. I have it! You shall be Lord Dare."

"Would I not attract less attention as a mister?"

"No. If we're going to do this, why do it by halves? Lord Dare you shall be. You are new to the London scene, just having returned from several years on the Continent," said Jerry, holding a hand to his head as if to aid his imagination.

"Who's going to believe such a tale? I—"

Marcus paused, hearing a knock on the door.

"Ah, they're here," said Jerry, jumping up from his seat.

Marcus stood up and blinked as Jerry let his friends in. There could be no stronger contrast between two young gentlemen. The first sauntered in, tall and thin, wearing a brown coat that was already out at the elbows, and a cravat that seemed intentionally askew, as if he wished to proclaim to the world his total indifference to fashion and propriety. He was followed by an even odder apparition, wearing baggy trousers, a green coat and a waistcoat in a startling shade of salmon.

"Marcus, this is George Dudley, and Oswald Babbinswood," said Jerry. "George, Oswald, this is my friend Lord Dare. He's just arrived in London. We used to hunt together before he went off to the Continent for a few years. Diplomatic affairs, the Congress of Vienna, and all that. You must not expect him to talk of it too much, though." Jerry winked at Marcus.

"I am delighted to make both your acquaintances," he

said, obediently falling in with Jerry's tale. He took several steps forward and bowed, wondering who could be gullible enough to believe he had actually played a covert role in the intrigues surrounding the Congress of Vienna. Then he saw the awed expressions on the faces of Jerry's friends.

"I assure you, my part in the Congress was of the very slightest nature," he said, unnerved by their blatant belief in the story.

"Ah, we understand," said Oswald, nodding his head wisely. "We won't breathe a word to anyone, we promise!"

"No, really—" Marcus began, only to be interrupted by the thin one called George.

"Don't worry, Dare. We will keep your secret, even under torture," he said, gazing down at Marcus's limbs with what was clearly intended to be a brooding look. "I see you have been wounded. I myself am no stranger to pain, having taken part in any number of duels. Just last month—"

"Well, now that's settled," interrupted Jerry briskly. "Lads, Dare don't fancy cards tonight. I thought maybe after dinner we'll go to the opera."

"A famous notion!" said Oswald, his protruding eyes shining in anticipation as he looked up at Marcus. "Has Jerry told you about Mademoiselle Juliette? Or have you already seen her, on the Parisian stage?"

"I cannot say I have had that pleasure," said Marcus.

"Then you're in for a treat. What a face! What a figure! And what a dancer she is!"

Jerry chuckled. "What a dancer indeed!"

"Do you dare to disparage the Incomparable Juliette?" demanded George, rounding on his friend. "She is perfection itself, and I will challenge anyone who thinks otherwise!"

"Give it up, George. I'm not going to fight you," said Jerry. "But I will wager either of you five Yellow Boys she makes her first mistake before she's been on the stage for as many minutes."

"Done!" chorused the other two.

Jerry turned to Marcus, smiling. "Actually, it wouldn't matter if she came out and fell over her feet every night.

She's so beautiful half the bucks in London are head over heels in love with her, though so far no one seems to have won her favor. Don't know why she bothers with any of us, really."

"Perhaps she appreciates the attention of a man of action," said George loftily.

"Don't flatter yourself that she likes you best!" said Oswald. "I am certain Mademoiselle Juliette prefers consorting with gentlemen of taste and refinement."

"If so, you'd best change that waistcoat of yours," said Jerry. "Those Petersham trousers are bad enough without that damned pink thing. My eyes hurt just looking at it."

"Pink?" said Oswald. "This is pink? I thought it was yellow."

"As if that would be better," groaned Jerry. "You know you can't tell one color from another. Why don't you just let your man choose your clothes? Come, I'll find you something."

"Your clothes are all too big for me," protested Oswald, but the other two dragged him off into Jerry's bedroom.

Marcus sat back down, amused by the sounds of argument issuing from the other room. A few minutes later, the trio emerged, Oswald wearing a white waistcoat and a peevish expression. A glass of wine did much to cheer him. Soon after, Jerry's manservant arrived bringing their dinner.

Marcus found himself enjoying the meal, despite the fact that the mutton was overdone and the potatoes the opposite. It was impossible to wallow in melancholy while talking to Jerry's friends, even if at times they made him feel about a hundred years old. Drawing on what he'd read in his grandfather's journals, he had little difficulty satisfying their curiosity about life on the Continent, although clearly they were disappointed by his vague replies to their frank questions about the antics of Frenchwomen. Several times, his eyes met Jerry's over the table and both men nearly succumbed to laughter.

After dinner and several more bottles of burgundy, they all piled into a hack and set off for the opera. The cool night air sobered Marcus, enough to make him remember his resolve to behave discreetly. Perhaps he ought not even enter the Green Room; surely he would get quite a satisfactory look at Mademoiselle Juliette on the stage.

They soon alighted in the Haymarket, and Marcus looked about curiously, never having seen the King's Theatre before. He received only a brief impression of a long colonnaded facade as Jerry and his friends hurried in thc main entrance.

As they purchased their tickets, Marcus noticed the bill announcing the evening's entertainment.

"*La Molinara.* The miller girl?" he asked, hazarding a translation.

Jerry and his friends looked at him in amazed respect, then George and Oswald nodded to each other knowingly. Marcus stifled a chuckle, imagining their disappointment if they ever learned that he had acquired a smattering of Italian, and a bit more French, through helping Mama in her attempts to teach Lucy the basic feminine accomplishments. In truth, Marcus had learned more than his rebellious sister, though he doubted it would ever be of use to him.

They climbed the grand double staircase and entered the auditorium. The opera being already in progress, they quickly made their way to the pit and found seats on the end of one of the benches. Marcus looked about surreptitiously, trying not to appear too amazed. He had never seen so many chandeliers in one place, casting their light over the fashionably dressed occupants of the many boxes, or such a vast, elaborately painted ceiling. He could not but be impressed.

Perhaps he was indeed a hopeless rustic, for he thought the rural scene depicted on the stage quite lovely, and the music itself even more engaging, its melodies easy and pleasant. He listened closely to the words, catching the sense of them enough to laugh at the occasional joke, while most of the audience seemed oblivious. The masculine crowd in the pit, in particular, seemed not to be attending very closely at all. Some barely applauded at the end of the first act, though their gazes were attentively focused on the stage for the first time.

"Ah! There they are!"

In response to Jerry's loud whisper, Marcus looked back

toward the stage. Involuntarily, his jaw dropped. Now he knew why the *ballet* was so popular with Jerry and his friends.

Eight young women had come onto the stage, and the dance they were performing looked to be inspired by folk dances, as did their costumes. However, Marcus doubted any peasant girl had ever worn quite such an ensemble. Low cut, tightly-laced bodices in rich colors and voluminous, knee-length skirts tantalizingly displayed more feminine charms than Marcus had ever beheld. All he could think was that the engravings he had seen in the library at Redwyck Hall did not do the faintest justice to the beauty of the female form.

Hoping no one would notice his flush, he watched first one dancer, then another. Each seemed lovelier than the last. Then his gaze alighted on a tall girl, positioned near the back of the group, perhaps because of her height. He looked a silent question toward Jerry.

"Yes, that is she. Juliette," Jerry whispered her name dreamily, his eyes fixed on the tall dancer.

Now that Mademoiselle Juliette had caught his attention, Marcus found himself entranced. The lamps around the stage transformed her red-gold hair into a fiery coronet, in striking contrast to the tiny, blue-green bodice that lifted an enticing expanse of creamy, rounded flesh to view. As she danced, her frothy skirt swayed, revealing long, shapely limbs that gave rise to all sorts of wild and wicked thoughts.

Good God! What was he thinking? Even if he were not pledged to pursue another woman, he should not waste his time dreaming about such a Bird of Paradise. No doubt there were scores of wealthier and more sophisticated bucks vying for her favors. He chided himself for being a fool, but still found himself unable to drag his gaze away from the tall dancer as she joined the others in a circle. Some measures later, they all reversed directions, except for Mademoiselle Juliette, who bumped into the adjoining dancer before hastily changing her direction as well.

Marcus's trance was momentarily interrupted by her slight mishap, and by the noise Jerry and his friends made as they settled their wager. He looked back again at their idol, but found he could not be an impartial judge of her dancing. He thought her graceful beyond anything, and the look of intense concentration on her perfect oval of a face rather attractive in contrast to the bold smiles of the others.

Perhaps her mistake was only due to her newness to this company of dancers. Or perhaps he was already besotted, just like the rest of them. It didn't matter; he only knew that when his friends urged him to accompany them to the Green Room to see thc divine Juliette more closely, he would not be able to refuse.

Chapter Four

Despite its several fine arias and duets, Marcus found it more difficult to concentrate on the second act of the opera. Soon enough, however, it was over and he followed the others out of the pit. As they strolled down Fops' Alley, Marcus found himself the target of bold, inviting glances from several women that frequented the corridor through the pit. He whispered a question to Jerry, and flushed hotly at the reply. He'd heard of such women, but he had not seen one before. It seemed shocking that they could ply their wares so boldly in one of London's most prestigious theatres.

"Don't stare, Marcus," said Jerry. "Come along. Those tarts are not half so pretty as Mademoiselle Juliette, and they won't flirt with you as she will."

A few minutes later, they reached the entrance to the Green Room. Marcus put a hand on Jerry's arm to detain him as George and Oswald rushed ahead of them.

"Jerry, you need not introduce me, you know. I really had better just stay back and watch."

"Oh, very well," Jerry grumbled. "If you're determined to be such a dull dog, I won't stand in your way."

They both entered the large, candlelit room. Marcus paused on the threshold, briefly overwhelmed by the mingled scents of perfume and perspiration, the warmth of the crowded room and the colorful chaos of costumed singers and dancers, punctuated by the darker attire of the gentlemen who came to ogle the dancers. Then he noticed Jerry and his friends heading toward a small knot of gentlemen near the end of the room. Above their heads Marcus could see the top of a large, gilded mirror, and surmised that the fascinating Juliette must be practicing her steps before it.

Suddenly, the group parted to allow Jerry and his friends to come closer. Marcus noted disappointed and puzzled expressions on the faces of the displaced gentlemen as Mademoiselle Juliette smiled a bright welcome to his own friends. Awkwardly, he stopped to stand a short distance behind them. The hum of conversation around him made it impossible to hear what his friends said to the dancer. It didn't matter. All he wanted to do was to gaze at her.

Poised on one foot before the mirror, lifting an exquisitely turned leg into the air behind her, she at first put him in mind of some exotic bird or butterfly; a bright yet elusive creature with her glorious flaming hair and peacock blue bodice. Then she turned to stand facing Jerry and his friends. Marcus took a step closer, and was a little disappointed when he gazed at her face. Her cheeks and lips were quite heavily rouged, making her seem both more sophisticated and older than her lithe, youthful figure suggested.

Marcus froze as she looked past Jerry and his friends, meeting his own gaze. She must have used something to darken her eyelashes, but there was nothing at all artificial about the deep, brilliant blue of her eyes. It reminded him of the intense hue of the sky on a clear, crisp day in autumn. Catching a look of doubt in her face, he looked away in embarrassment. Why did she seem ill at ease with his scrutiny? Surely she was accustomed to such admiring stares.

He was close enough now to hear the tinkle of her laugh as she responded to one of Oswald's elaborate compliments.

"Ah, you are a flatterer, Meester Babbinswood," she said, in a delightfully accented voice. Her eyes sparkled with amusement as she smiled at Oswald. "You are looking verry handsome this evening. Is this—this stunning *ensemble* in my honor?"

Oswald bowed deeply, and beamed from ear to ear at her praise.

"Ah, I would do far greater things in your honor, my goddess," said George, turning to sneer at Oswald before transferring an adoring gaze back toward Mademoiselle Juliette. "*I* am no fashionable fribble. You may count on me if you should ever require the defense of a *real* man. Only last week I came close to sustaining a wound that might have taken me from this world forever. Allow me to show you," he said, putting a hand up to his already untidy cravat and baring a portion of his neck.

Mademoiselle Juliette drew back, in temporary astonishment at his bizarre offer, but she recovered quickly.

"*Mon dieu!* You might have been killed!" she said in an admiring tone of voice, but Marcus saw her eyes were dancing.

"He cut himself shaving!" interjected Oswald.

"Ah, but I know Meester Dudley is very brave," she said, bestowing another of her fascinating smiles on George.

"I have sustained far graver wounds, fair Juliette, but I could not show them to you except in private," he responded hopefully.

Her full lips twitched a little, but Mademoiselle Juliette's voice was steady as she replied. "*Non, non!* I could not bear such a manly display; it would be too overwhelming for such a frail creature as I am."

Marcus chuckled quietly at her quick-witted response.

"You must be tired of all this nonsense, Mademoiselle Juliette," said Jerry, claiming her attention. "I can offer you something more pleasant. Perhaps you would care to join me for supper after the performance?"

"I thank you for your so kind offer, Meester Plumbrook," she said. "But I must get my sleep. We rehearse a new *ballet* tomorrow morning."

Jerry and his friends eagerly plied her with questions about the upcoming performance, asking if she had been offered a solo role. Her eyes gleamed with humor again as she gently deflated their hopes, insisting that she was no *soloiste* and was quite content with her humble position in the *corps de ballet*. Marcus listened quietly, enjoying Mademoiselle Juliette's tactful handling of her admirers. It was clear she was no feather-witted beauty. It was very good-natured of her to flirt so kindly with Jerry and his friends.

Perhaps it was time for him to leave. He began to feel foolish standing behind his friends, like a skeleton at a feast, with his somber attire and lack of conversation. Yet he could not summon the will to leave, fascinated as he was by Mademoiselle Juliette's animated expression and delicious figure. He could not help wondering how it would feel to put an arm around that slender waist, to kiss those ripe lips. To untie the laces that held the tiny bodice closed and kiss that white skin, and learn for himself if it was as soft and dewy as it looked. . . .

Too late, he realized that Mademoiselle Juliette had dismissed Jerry and his friends. He found himself staring once more into her questioning blue eyes. Was she blushing, or was it a trick of the candlelight on her painted face?

"*Monsieur*, I asked your friends to leave so I may practice my steps," she said, a hint of reproach in her voice.

He flushed in response. He knew he should just bow and leave, yet he felt a desperate urge to retrieve his blunder in a more graceful manner. Perhaps she would enjoy being addressed in her native tongue.

"Excusez-moi, Mademoiselle," he said, and continued in the same language. "Forgive me. I was lost in admiration of your beauty."

Where had those words come from? he wondered. He would not have dared to utter such a compliment in his native English, but in French the words had come tripping right off his tongue. Perhaps it was all the Burgundy he'd drunk at dinner.

"Ah, you are a Frenchman?" she asked, and he stared at her in shock. Was his accent *that* good?

"No, I am desolated to admit I am not a countryman of yours," he replied, having paused just long enough to remember the persona Jerry had devised for him. "I have just completed a prolonged sojourn on the Continent."

She seemed to stiffen, and he wondered why.

"Did you see much of France, monsieur . . . monsieur? I believe you have the advantage of me."

"My deepest apologies, mademoiselle. I should have introduced myself. I am Lord Dare, at your service." He bowed, hoping he did not cut too clumsy a figure.

"I am delighted to make your acquaintance, milord," she replied, sweeping him a slow courtesy, extending a gracefully arched foot in a dainty slipper and giving him an enticing view of her décolletage.

"I hope you are enjoying our performance, milord," she said, straightening up.

"Very much. I have seen nothing so wonderful before."

Her eyebrows rose. "I am certain you are accustomed to far superior performances at the Paris Opera House."

"Unfortunately, I had little luxury of indulging in such pleasures," he replied, hoping to retrieve his slip. "I am sure nothing could be more lovely than what I have seen tonight."

"You flatter me, milord. But now you must permit me to continue practicing. Soon I must partake in the *divertissement*."

As she looked up at him, Marcus thought her smile seemed different from the ones she had bestowed on his friends. Had she enjoyed their banter, or was it merely the wine befuddling his brain? Was it his imagination, or did her eyes seem even larger, her lips redder and fuller than before? No doubt those lips had been kissed countless times before, but they were no less tempting for all that.

"Milord, what must I do to convince you to leave?" she asked. She looked at him pointedly, but her voice sounded intriguingly breathless.

"Kiss me."

The words slipped from his lips before he could stop them. What had come over him, to be so bold? Good God! He'd never kissed anyone before. He was bound to make a laughingstock of himself. But he might never get such a chance again. It was worth the risk.

Juliana looked up at Lord Dare, at a loss for how to deal with him. She'd been uneasily aware of his presence as he had hovered, silent and mysterious, outside the circle of foolish admirers she cultivated as a shield from more dangerous bucks. With his height, his broad shoulders, lean frame and darkly elegant attire, Dare looked more rakish than any gentleman she had yet encountered in her impulsive masquerade.

As he took a step toward her, she noticed he walked with a slight limp. Had he been injured during his sojourn on the Continent, perhaps in a duel with a bitter Bonapartist? Although he seemed not to be out of his twenties, there were faint lines around Dare's eyes and mouth that spoke of pain and experiences she could only imagine. There was no doubt that he had traveled widely. It was alarming to have met someone so fluent in the French tongue.

Equally alarming was the look of keen intelligence in the aristocratic, sculptured lines of his face, and the intensity of his gaze. At first his eyes had seemed green, but now that he stood quite close Juliana saw they were an intriguing hazel, a mixture of blue and green, with flecks of golden brown about the rims of his irises. Colors of adventure, of the land and sea and sky, she thought for a mad moment, heart pounding wildly at his proximity.

She reminded herself that he might be a real rake, unlike Jeremy Plumbrook and his friends, who only pretended. She had to find a way to repel his advances without ruining her disguise. A light approach would probably serve best.

She assumed what she hoped was jaded air, and said, "Ah, but I am weary of kisses. You cannot wish for one so badly."

"I assure you, Mademoiselle, that having received one kiss from your lips, I would die a happy man," Dare replied, his husky voice caressing each word.

"But I do not wish any man's death on my conscience!" she parried.

"Ah, but I think I shall die if you do *not* kiss me," was his instant reply. An earnest note in his voice seemed to belie his theatrical words. He was nothing like the fools who had kissed her so clumsily in the past. Perhaps his kiss would be different. She had wanted experiences, adventures. Why not seize this one?

"Come, you cannot begrudge me just one kiss."

Awaiting her reply, he stood so close that his pantaloons pressed the full, short skirt of her costume back against her limbs. She saw desire in his eyes, a look of determination about his firm-lipped mouth. Why not let him kiss her?

Mademoiselle Juliette Lamant was an abandoned woman already, with no reputation to be smirched. Theirs would be a kiss without consequences. It was too tempting.

"Very well, milord," she said, lifting her chin. "You may have just one kiss."

He expelled a deep sigh, as if he'd been holding his breath. Did he desire her so much? she wondered. It was intoxicating and a little frightening to have such power.

He put his arms around her and drew her gently toward him. Gradually, he tightened his embrace, one arm around her waist, the other caressing her bare shoulders, the very hesitancy of his movements enhancing every sensation. When was he going to kiss her? Oh, he was wicked indeed to tease her so, prolonging the moment, making her more and more aware of her own scanty raiment, and of the ebb and fall of his breath as the crisp linen of his shirt and the smooth silk waistcoat pressed against her bare skin, his warmth pervading her whole being. This was nothing like Charles Bentwood's hasty assault.

Belatedly, she remembered to return his embrace. It was strange, but exciting, to encircle his firm, masculine body with her arms. She hoped she did not seem awkward. Finally, Dare lowered his face down to hers, and brushed her lips with his. His mouth was warm, and tasted of wine. She pressed her own lips up against his, savoring the unexpectedly pleasant sensation. A moment later, seemingly by accident, his tongue slipped between her parted lips, and as quickly withdrew again. She gasped with surprise, and then pressed her mouth back against his, in a frantic attempt to hide her shock. She had not realized one could kiss so, but it would be fatal to let him know.

Once again, his tongue penetrated her mouth, and this time, she responded, curling and playing her own tongue against his, hoping and praying she was doing it correctly. A deep, almost soundless moan rumbled in his chest, reassuring her that he was aroused by her kiss. He tightened his embrace, and her worries fled as new, compelling sensations surged through her own body. Pleasure such as she had never experienced, and yet somehow she wanted even more. . . .

"Juliette! *Juliette!*"

Madame Bouchard's shrill voice suddenly penetrated Juliana's awareness. Burning, she pulled back from Lord Dare. He seemed flustered, his eyes bright and his hitherto perfect neckcloth slightly rumpled. She looked away so he would not see her blush.

"Have you lost your mind?" cried Madame Bouchard, echoing Juliana's own thoughts. "There are less than five minutes before you must be on stage again!"

Juliana slipped quickly out of Dare's loosened hold, panicking to see that many of the dancers had already left. But she could not run off, and let Dare think his kiss had overset her. She summoned up the courage to look back up at him.

"Why thank you, milord Dare," she said. "You kiss well . . . for an Englishman."

"I am glad I did not disappoint," he said, and made her a stiff bow. Had she gone too far, and offended him?

"And now I must go. Adieu!" she said, making him a little courtesy before leaving with Madame Bouchard.

However, she could not resist one backward glance before leaving the Green Room. Jeremy Plumbrook and his friends had surrounded Dare, slapping him on the shoulder, their eyes filled with awe and admiration. Rage surged through her at the sight. Had they made some sort of wager? Was that what his kiss was all about?

She hurried along, only half listening to Madame Bouchard's scolding, even though she knew she deserved it. She should have known better than to allow Lord Dare to make a plaything of her. She knew what men were, and Dare's charm and skill only made him more dangerous. But how could she have guessed how wonderful it would feel to be caressed by such a man?

They reached the backstage, and Juliana forced herself to mentally review the figures of the *divertissement* that followed the opera. She had a dance to perform, and more challenges to face before she could end her masquerade. Now that she knew the perils and temptations of this life, she would learn to resist them.

Head held high, back straight, she followed the other dancers onto the stage.

* * *

Marcus watched Mademoiselle Juliette as she hurried away with the older woman. Her casual words stung him, but he composed his features as Jerry and the others came to his side.

"Well done!" said Jerry, beaming generously, looking almost as pleased at Marcus's feat as if he had managed to accomplish it himself.

"How I envy you, Dare," Oswald breathed, eyes wide with hero worship. "What it must have felt like to have that glorious creature in your arms! You must tell us all about it. *All* about it."

Marcus shook his head. He was not about to satisfy Oswald's lewd curiosity, even if he could find the words to describe the rapturous moments before Mademoiselle Juliette had made it quite clear that the kiss that had affected him so powerfully had meant less than nothing to her.

"I for one wish to know how you induced her to do it," said George, scowling. "If I find that you used any sort of coercion on that lovely creature—"

"Stubble it, George!" interrupted Jerry, and winked at Marcus. "Dare's too *charming* to have to resort to coercion. He probably just told her she was beautiful in her own tongue."

George and Oswald stared at each other, arrested expressions on their faces, then they looked back at Marcus and Jerry.

"Where does one find a French tutor?" queried Oswald eagerly.

"Yes, where?" echoed George, dropping his martial stance.

"Oh, I don't know. There must be some impoverished emigrée that might be induced to teach you dolts," said Jerry. "You can find out tomorrow. We'd better hurry or we'll miss the end of Mademoiselle Juliette's performance."

George and Oswald hurried out of the nearly empty room.

"I think I shall go home, Jerry," said Marcus, following. "You know I am not accustomed to town hours."

"Suit yourself," said Jerry. He paused and looked at

Marcus with friendly curiosity. "You're not by some chance falling for that coquette, are you? You do know this is just a game?"

"Of course. I'm not a fool."

However, as Marcus rode home in a bouncing old hack, Mademoiselle Juliette's words echoed through his head.

You kiss well . . . for an Englishman.

The words rankled. Holding her warm, supple body in his arms, feeling her quickened breath, tasting her lips was the single most glorious, transcendent experience of his hitherto boring existence. He had even thought he'd succeeded in pleasing her as well, since she had returned his kiss with what felt like true passion.

But no, it was probably just the practiced response of one accustomed to flattering her admirers. She clearly had legions of them. Lovers, too, probably. Why should he expect that *his* kiss meant anything more to her than a minor diversion?

As he entered his town house, he wondered why his desire for Mademoiselle Juliette had only grown, instead of dying when she had so easily dismissed him. In his room, he found Pridwell waiting up for him. Although he did not want the valet's assistance or his company, he allowed Pridwell to help him out of his clothing and into his nightshirt, and even to pour him a glass of brandy. After Pridwell left, he sat up in the bed and sipped at the brandy, telling himself he ought not to let his mind dwell on Mademoiselle Juliette, or her words.

You kiss well . . . for an Englishman.

Vous embrassez bon pour un Anglais.

He set his glass down abruptly. Now he knew why he could not get her words out of his head.

The lying minx! It was a good thing she had mentioned that there was a rehearsal tomorrow. It appeared that another visit to the King's Theatre was in order.

Chapter Five

"Again."

Obedient to Monsieur Léon's command, Juliana took a deep breath, and launched herself once more into the *jeté*.

"Your head up, and shoulders back, Mademoiselle. Can you not understand me?"

Juliana tried not to allow herself to be rattled by the dance master's impatient tone. Again, she concentrated on the challenging leap, trying to remember everything Madame Bouchard had drilled into her.

"Again."

Three more times she leapt into the air, ignoring aching muscles that protested the unaccustomed discipline, until finally Monsieur Léon nodded.

"It is satisfactory," he said curtly. "But do not forget to smile."

He gestured for the other dancers to rejoin them, and relief flooded through Juliana. Even to have gained such lukewarm approval from the exacting dance master was an achievement. Neither the grudging tone of his voice, nor the looks of sympathy or superiority from the other dancers could mar her satisfaction.

She continued to put forth her best efforts during the rest of the rehearsal. She even managed to avoid further censure from Monsieur Léon, although she was under no illusion that her dancing was anywhere near the standard normally expected from a member of the *corps de ballet.* Last week she had even overheard an argument between Monsieur Léon and Mr. Waters, the manager. Monsieur Léon had expressed his wish to find someone to replace her, but Mr. Waters had argued that attendance, particularly in the pit, had increased noticeably since her first performance. It was a bit mortifying to think that it was her looks alone that drew an additional masculine crowd, but she was relieved to know she had not detracted from the success of the theatre.

When the rehearsal was over, Juliana took advantage of the empty stage to practice a little more. Finally exhausted, and satisfied that she could do no more, she prepared to leave. As she exchanged her slippers for half boots and buttoned a warm pelisse over her thin dress, Juliana reflected that if she had ever seriously dreamt of a career on the stage, her experience here would have brought her back to earth quite quickly. The life of an opera dancer involved more gruelling work than she had ever imagined, and even so, few attained the success of the famous Armand Vestris or the graceful Mélanie Duval.

In truth, she would not be too sad when this masquerade was over. Surely Grandpapa would relent within the next few months, by which time the injured dancer whose place she had taken would have returned to the King's Theatre. But for the time being, Juliana could not help but savor the pleasure that bubbled up in her at having somewhat mastered the *jeté*. Even the ache in her muscles was a good ache, achieved through hard work that brought her more restful nights than she'd ever experienced in her own ornate bed at Grandpapa's house. Earning her own keep, moving freely about London without a chaperone, all these things were part of an experience she would always savor.

She had to admit that even her encounter with Lord Dare last night had been a glorious part of the adventure. Warmth spread through her as she remembered how he had taken her into his arms and kissed her with such slow, spellbinding thoroughness. She reminded herself that she should court no more of his kisses in the future. At least she'd had the good sense to give Lord Dare a rebuff which should prevent any further advances from *him*.

As she left the theatre she braced herself, leaning into the wind as she headed down the Haymarket toward Pall Mall.

"Mademoiselle Lamant."

She stopped and found herself looking up and into Lord Dare's hazel eyes. Today, there was no soft desire shining from those eyes, only a look of determination that made her vaguely uneasy.

"Milord Dare," she said with an inclination of the head, and prepared to walk around him.

"I wish to speak to you," he said, his broad shoulders blocking her way. She wondered why he spoke English rather than his excellent French, even as his tall, immaculately dressed presence beside her caused her pulse to leap.

"Pourquoi?" she asked. "Did you not win your wager last night, or has a new one been proposed?"

"My—my wager? Did you think I kissed you to win a bet?"

"You did not?"

"I kissed you because I wished to, and for no other reason."

The fierce sincerity in his voice sent a shudder of excitement through her. She looked down, only to gain an excellent view of his muscular thighs, encased in tightly fitted pale gray pantaloons. She looked back up, hoping he did not see her blush. She could not let this continue.

"I am flattered, milord," she said lightly. "But I am afraid I find repeat performances most fatiguing."

His shoulders stiffened visibly under his closely tailored black coat.

"I am not asking for another kiss, *Mademoiselle Lamant.* I am asking for the truth."

"Whatever do you mean, milord?" she asked, looking away from him as she summoned up a carefree smile.

"I mean that I know you are not what you seem," he said, lowering his voice.

She looked back up at him, but did not dare say anything.

"This is too busy a place to talk," he said. "Come stroll with me in the park."

She nodded and accepted his arm. It felt dangerous to

walk beside him so, but she had to learn how much he knew or guessed of her masquerade. In silence, they walked to the juncture of Pall Mall and Cockspur Street, turned left and wound their way toward St. James's Park. Juliana's mind raced the whole way. Why had he emphasized her name so? Had he guessed her identity? But how could that be? She was quite certain they had not met before, and he was far too handsome and dashing to be someone Grandpapa had hired to find her.

As they passed under the first trees of St. James's Park, Juliana could no longer contain her anxious curiosity.

"Now, milord Dare, you must tell me what you think you 'ave discovered," she said, meeting his eyes.

"I have learned that whatever your name is, it is not Juliette Lamant."

" 'Ow can you know that?"

"From what you were so kind to say to me last night. *Vous embrassez bon . . . pour un Anglais.*"

She looked away, assaulted by an unwelcome suspicion.

"Perhaps you meant to say, *Vous embrassez bien . . .* ?"

Blast! Monsieur Dubois, the French master at Miss Stratton's select school for girls, would be most disappointed if he realized his most avid student had allowed a stranger's kiss to rob her of her grammar. There was no convincing way to cover up such a slip. Only the truth—a partial truth—would do.

"Yes, I admit it," she said, lifting her chin. "I am as English as you are."

"But why the pretense?"

"Is it not obvious? I have made a much greater hit as Mademoiselle Juliette Lamant than I ever could have as . . . as under my own name."

"I think you would make a hit under any name," he replied, more gently.

She let out a chuckle, relieved that he accepted her explanation. "No, in truth I am not a good enough dancer."

He grinned at her in return. So he was not such a fool as to admire her dancing, although he did seem to admire *her*. Suddenly, she realized that her situation was still quite precarious. Was Dare the gentleman he seemed?

"Will you tell me your real name?" he asked. "I do not even know what to call you now."

"Mademoiselle Juliette will do," she replied. "I would rather no one knew my real name. You must realize that my position at the opera is very important to me. The wages are so much higher than at the lesser theatres where I have danced in the past, but if I lose favor with the audience, I could be dismissed. Please, will you keep my secret?"

"Of course," he replied. "Upon one condition."

She stiffened, angry and somehow disappointed. No doubt he wished to make her his mistress. What was she to do now?

"Don't you wish to know my condition?" he asked.

She could not keep the bitterness from her voice as she replied. "I suppose it is the usual. You will keep my secret, and in turn you expect me to reward you with . . . with private performances upon your request."

He suddenly stopped walking, the pressure of his hand on her arm halting her as well. He turned to face her.

"Do you think I would take such advantage of a lady?"

"I beg your pardon, Lord Dare," she said, her heart lightening at his indignant tone. "What *is* your condition?"

"You must admit you enjoyed our kiss, at least a little."

"Is that all?" she asked, relief and amusement bubbling up inside her. Then she saw from his intent expression that he was not jesting. Did he actually doubt his affect on a woman?

"Very well, Lord Dare. I *did* enjoy our kiss," she said.

A new smile broke out on his face, lighting his eyes. He had retained his hold on her arm, and now grasped the other as well. Her heart began to pound more quickly again as she battled a sudden, strong urge to take a step forward into his arms, and let him kiss her again. Madness! She could not allow herself to be beguiled once more. Hastily, she slipped from his grasp.

"You rogue!" she said, trying to smile. "You seek to entice me with your kisses, but you must believe me when I say I am *not* seeking a lover."

"Why not?"

He seemed surprised, and she realized that her words were out of character for the dashing Mademoiselle Lamant.

"Lovers can be so fatiguing," she said with a cynical sigh, as she began to walk again, this time avoiding his proffered arm. "They take all one's energy with their incessant demands, and then as often as not, abandon one without another thought."

"Surely not all gentlemen are so callous with their mistresses?" he asked. He sounded curious, but that could not be. He was probably only hinting that *he* would behave differently, should she accept a *carte blanche* from him.

On her guard, she retorted, "Possibly, but how is one to know that in advance? One of my fellow dancers has lost her position due to just such a *gentleman*."

"Would they dismiss a dancer for having a lover?"

"You know as well as I do that they would not. She could not continue dancing while in the family way."

"And he abandoned her?"

Juliana nodded. Seeing his expression, she could almost believe Dare was as disgusted as he sounded.

"I assure you, not all men are such blackguards."

"I must suppose you refer to yourself, my lord," she said.

His mouth twisted into a rueful smile. "I would never treat a lady so, but I am not in a position to take a mistress. I was only shocked to hear you speak so cynically. You seem so young."

"I have seen enough to make me wary of your sex."

"You may trust *me*."

They walked in silence for a few minutes. Juliana wondered what he would think if he knew the truth about her.

"What do you wish from me then, if it is not to become your mistress?" she asked.

He slowed, an arrested expression on his face, as if he had not considered the matter. Her curiosity mounted as she waited for him to reply.

"What I wish is of no consequence. As I said, I am not free to take a mistress . . . however much I should wish to."

She should have been relieved; instead, the desire and regret in his voice struck a disturbing chord inside her.

"Shall we see you again at the Opera House?"

"I cannot say."

She swallowed, trying not to appear disappointed, telling herself it might be better not to see him again.

"It is time for me to be on my way home," she said, seeing that they were near the end of the path.

"May I escort you home?"

She considered this a moment. She did not wish to part from him; she even had a strong conviction that he would always behave in a gentlemanly manner. However, prudence dictated that it would be wise not to let him know where she lived.

"Thank you, but that will not be necessary."

Before she could turn away, he possessed himself of her hand. He lifted it to his lips and pressed a lingering kiss to the narrow ribbon of skin exposed between her glove and her sleeve.

"*Au revoir*, Juliette," he said, bowing slightly.

"*Au revoir*, milord Dare," she replied softly, then turned to leave.

As she walked away, she struggled to keep from turning back to see if he watched her. During the rest of the walk back to Half Moon Street, she could think of nothing else.

What a mystery the man presented! His elegant attire bespoke a man of fashion and wealth, but he claimed not to be in a position to take a mistress. He had cleverly penetrated her disguise, but with real or feigned chivalry, he had chosen not to take advantage of his knowledge. Perhaps he was on the verge of leaving for the Continent again. But then, why had he sought her out this morning? It was all very intriguing. She enjoyed matching wits with him, and could not help wishing to see him again, but it was a dangerous game. He was too clever and too charming; if she was not careful he could be her undoing.

Lost in thought, she nearly collided with a short, stocky man in a brown coat.

"Sorry, miss," he said gruffly, staring into her face.

"*Excusez-moi, monsieur,*" she replied, on her guard.

He passed on without further words, and she breathed a sigh of relief. She should not have allowed Dare to distract her so; a female walking the streets alone had to keep her wits about her. Moreover, the stocky man seemed somehow familiar. Had she seen him near the neighborhood of Half Moon Street before?

She walked on, more alert now. As she turned from Picadilly onto Half Moon Street, she had the distinct impression that someone was following her. She risked a brief glance over her shoulder, and saw that she was indeed being pursued. It was not the man in the brown coat, however. It was Penelope, accompanied by her maid. What were they doing here?

Juliana quickened her pace, but it was useless.

"Mademoiselle Lamant!" she heard Pen call behind her.

Reluctantly, she turned around. Penelope and the maid were close behind her. Despite the maid's disapproving frown, Pen addressed Juliana again.

"My apologies for detaining you, *Mademoiselle Lamant*," she said, her eyes sparkling fiercely. "Perhaps you will be so kind as to tell us which of these houses is Madame Bouchard's?"

Apparently Pen had recognized her, but at least she was not going to give her away in front of her maid.

"Why, this one, *mademoiselle*," she replied. "I am so fortunate as to lodge here with Madame Bouchard. 'Ave you come to visit her?"

Pen nodded, and they all entered the house together. Knowing Pen would wish to speak to her alone, Juliana summoned one of Madame Bouchard's housemaids to conduct Lady Talcott's maid to the small servants' parlor in the back of the house, while she herself offered to take Pen upstairs to Madame Bouchard's sitting room.

"Juliana, I cannot believe you—"

"Hush. Madame Bouchard's servants don't know about me," she whispered, leading the way up the stairs to the apartment she shared with Jenny Church, the opera dancer she had told Dare about. Jenny would most likely be in their sitting room, busily sewing, if she was not lying down in the bedroom. At the current stage of her pregnancy, her morning sickness prevented her going about much. Briefly, Juliana wondered what Pen, the vicar's daughter, would make of young Jenny.

They entered, and saw not only Jenny sitting on the sofa,

but also Madame Bouchard. Blonde, sweet-faced Jenny looked a little pale, as Madame Bouchard coaxed her to consume some tea and toast. They looked up as Juliana and Penelope entered.

After Penelope and Madame Bouchard exchanged greetings, Juliana introduced Jenny. Pen's eyes strayed briefly toward Jenny's middle, but she smiled kindly in response to the girl's soft-voiced welcome.

"Jenny knows all about me, Pen, so you may speak freely now," said Juliana, going to fetch two more teacups.

"Thank you," said Pen, seating herself in one of the two spindly chairs the sitting room boasted. "Perhaps you will tell me why you have entered into such a wild masquerade."

Juliana poured their tea before replying. "I think you know already. I wished to find a way to convince Grandpapa I can take care of myself, so I needed both a disguise and gainful occupation. I have few accomplishments besides foreign languages and dancing, so when Madame Bouchard told me Monsieur Léon was desperately seeking dancers to replace Jenny and another who has sprained her ankle, it seemed like the perfect answer."

"Have you thought about what would happen to your reputation if anyone found out what you have been doing?"

"That is why I have taken such pains to disguise myself. I know it would upset Grandpapa if there was a scandal. But as for myself, I do not care a whit. If I am no longer accepted in polite society it will be just that much easier for me to pursue the life I truly wish for."

"But your grandfather must be so dreadfully worried!"

"I write to him almost every day, to let him know that I am well. I will return as soon as he inserts a notice in the *Times* to let me know he has given up his plans for my future."

"What if he does not?"

"He must do so, eventually."

"Oh, you are both so stubborn!" Pen sighed, then looked at Madame Bouchard. "How could you allow her to do this, Madame?"

"*Mon petit*, your friend was being coerced into a marriage she did not wish for. What could I do but help her?" Madame raised her hands in a fatalistic gesture.

"I can see you meant well, but can you not see how dangerous this is? I have been to the King's Theatre. It is a popular haunt for every sort of rake and scoundrel. There's no telling what could happen to Juliana there—"

Pen looked at Jenny, then broke off, flushing brightly, while Jenny's already wan complexion paled even further.

"Oh, I am so sorry," said Pen. "I did not mean to imply—I meant no insult—"

"I know you did not," said Jenny, her expression sad but resigned. "I have already warned your friend to beware of the—the gentlemen who come to see the dancers in the Green Room. Now you must excuse me, for I wish to lie down."

She arose to go to the bedroom, Madame Bouchard going along clucking at her like a concerned hen, and reassuring her that the sickly phase of her pregnancy would soon pass.

As soon as they were out of earshot, Pen asked, "I hope I did not offend her. She seems like a sweet girl."

"She is. I thought you would not judge her too harshly. Things have not been easy for her; she was not born to live the life of an opera dancer. She is far too naive and trusting; in fact, she still insists that her lover had plans to marry her."

Pen looked pensive. Juliana reached a hand over and took Pen's smaller one in her own.

"I know you are concerned for me, dear, but you know I am not sentimental. I would not be so easily taken in."

"Has anyone asked you—I mean, has anyone offered you—"

"A *carte blanche*?" asked Juliana, understanding Pen's embarrassment.

Pen nodded.

"Well, there have been several gentlemen who have expressed an interest," she said, smiling as she thought of Jerry Plumbrook and his friends.

"But no one in particular?"

She hesitated, wondering how much to tell Pen about Lord Dare. She certainly could not admit how she had learned that Pen was right about the pleasures of kissing.

"Jule, there is something you are not telling me."

"Well, there *is* a gentleman who . . . who I have found rather charming, but he has not asked me to be his mistress. Nor do I wish to prejudice my plans by becoming entangled with him. And I do understand that it is the woman who must suffer the consequences of yielding to passion." She glanced toward the door of the bedroom in oblique reference to Jenny's plight.

Pen still looked worried. Juliana decided it was time to change the subject.

"So how did you find me out?" she asked.

"I started to suspect when they said you were ailing. I know you are hardly ever ill. Then Aunt Mary took me to the opera last night. I thought you looked familiar. At first I was sure I was mistaken, then I remembered how we had talked about Madame Bouchard. I decided to pay her a visit and find out, but it was only when I saw you more closely that I knew for sure. I don't think anyone who does not know you well would guess."

"I hope not. So you will not tell anyone?"

"You should have told *me*," said Pen.

"I would have, but I did not want to worry you, or put you in this uncomfortable position. You *will* keep my secret for me, won't you?"

"Oh, very well," said Pen reluctantly. "But not if I suspect you are in any trouble."

"I promise you faithfully that I will avoid all advances from suspicious gentlemen."

A worried frown still troubled Pen's wide forehead. During the rest of the visit, Juliana continued to try to reassure her friend, but with mixed success. Clearly, Pen was shocked by her masquerade, and by the knowledge that Juliana was in a position to receive less than respectable offers from numerous London bucks. Which led Juliana to wonder later why Lord Dare's advances did not offend her as they should have. Perhaps it was the way he seemed to enjoy looking at her, and how he spoke to her, as if to an equal. Or perhaps it was the fact that he wanted *her*, and not her grandfather's fortune. Yes, perhaps that was it. He had made her feel desired. It was a pleasant sensation.

One she had best not indulge in, or she would indeed find herself in trouble, as Pen feared.

Marcus took a hack home. His bad leg had not bothered him during his walk with Mademoiselle Juliette, or whatever her name was. Now it ached, a tangible reminder of his responsibilities.

He'd acted on impulse this morning, which was not like him. Somehow the determination to make her take back her dismissive words had overcome all his good sense. Even though they hadn't kissed again, he had enjoyed their encounter. Wine and candlelight had not befuddled his senses as much as he'd feared. Juliette was just as lovely and appealing by daylight, despite the excessive rouge that she wore. It was a disguise that accorded well with the false accent she had assumed. But a few times she had smiled at him openly, when she had admitted her shortcomings as a dancer, and when she had said she had enjoyed his kiss. He'd caught glimpses of what must be aspects of her true nature: honesty, a sense of humor, even a lively sense of adventure behind her flirtatious facade.

He wondered about her life, how many lovers she had had, and what had happened to make her so suspicious of men. But was he any better than them? He had hardly been able to restrain himself from clasping her to his chest again and tasting her lips, right there in St. James's Park for all to see. Perhaps he had inherited his share of the Redwyck rakishness, after all.

He reminded himself that tempting though it was, he could not continue to play at being a rake. He could not afford to see Mademoiselle Juliette again. It would be an intolerable insult to the Huttons if word got around that he had consorted with opera dancers. More importantly, it would be unfair to Miss Hutton, and hellish for him, if they entered into marriage while he obsessed about another woman. Although he had only met her twice, Mademoiselle Juliette already played havoc with his good resolutions. Further encounters would just make matters worse.

With this noble resolve, Marcus bent himself to the tedious task of cataloguing the contents of the town house. Uncle Harold had not yet sold the paintings or objets d'art that adorned the place, and if Marcus's plan to marry Miss Hutton failed, their sale would at least contribute to Mama and Lucy's comfort.

Several days passed, and still there was no word from the Huttons. Marcus wondered if he ought to send Miss Hutton some flowers, but decided that their lack of acquaintance made it inappropriate. He was glad, for it would have felt like a lie, when thoughts of Mademoiselle Juliette's smile, voice and graceful figure intruded into his thoughts at unexpected moments throughout each day.

He arranged yet another appointment with the family man of business, to discuss the possibility that Miss Hutton would refuse his suit. Mr. Willett was surprisingly sanguine, refusing to enter into Marcus's fears. He left Marcus wondering how such a practical, levelheaded man could be just like Barnes and Pridwell and the rest of them, convinced that the cursed Redwyck charm would save them all.

That evening Marcus invited Jerry and his friends to dine with him. Uncle Harold's excellent Burgundy flowed freely, as did the nonsense. Marcus found himself cheered by the company, though he was careful not to enter into the discussion of Mademoiselle Juliette. Apparently they had already begun to take French lessons, and at least George and Oswald were hopeful that this might win their goddess's approval.

On impulse, Marcus asked them about the wronged dancer that Mademoiselle Juliette had mentioned. Jerry and his friends readily supplied the details, and Marcus was happy to see they disapproved of the gentleman's shabby behavior.

Resolutely, he declined their suggestion that he accompany them to another performance at the King's Theatre, on the following night. Instead, he spent a dreary evening alone in his uncle's study, reading and drinking brandy, although thoughts of his flame-haired dancer distracted him from his book.

Playing the part of a rake had been much more fun.

* * *

Juliana looked about the Green Room. It was Saturday night, bringing a larger crowd of patrons than attended the Tuesday night performance. She smiled and waved to one of her admirers before continuing to practice before the tall mirror; it would not do to let anyone notice that her gaze was secretly roving through the throng, seeking a certain tall, dark-clad figure.

A minute later, Jeremy Plumbrook, Oswald Babbinswood and George Dudley came in the door. Dare was not with them. Juliana swallowed her disappointment. He had said they might not meet again; why had she expected anything else?

She smiled at Plumbrook and his friends, determined not to betray herself.

"Bon soir, mademoiselle," they all intoned, bowing in time with each other.

Juliana nearly lost her composure at their earnest, hopeful expressions.

"Bon soir, monsieurs," she replied, sweeping them a courtesy. *"C'est merveilleux! Vous avez appris a parler Francais."*

The threesome exchanged puzzled looks, clearly unwilling to admit they had not understood her. Juliana had to bite her lip to keep from laughing.

"I said it was marvelous that you 'ave learned French," she translated. "I can see you 'ave been studying, but perhaps you need a little practice, *n'est ce pas?*"

They nodded eagerly, and Mr. Babbinswood stepped forward.

"Vos oeufs sont comme les sapphires," he essayed.

"My eggs are like sapphires?" she asked. Seeing his crestfallen expression, she continued, "Do not despair, Mr. Babbinswood. It was a lovely thought. Have you something you wish to say, Mr. Dudley?"

"Je mariné une mille morts pour vous," he intoned grandly.

"Perhaps it is you who are *mariné*, Mr. Dudley," she said, smiling at him. "I do not wish anyone to die for me, not even once. But truly, I am touched that you have all gone to so much trouble for my sake."

"I'm afraid none of us have Dare's way with languages," said Plumbrook.

"Where is your friend this evening?" she asked, trying not to seem too eager.

"He has had much to occupy him of late—" began Plumbrook.

"Perhaps there is some plot against the Regent—" said Babbinswood, cutting off as Dudley cuffed him.

"Oswald! You know you are not to speak of it!" Dudley whispered, so that Juliana could barely make out his words.

She looked around the threesome, wondering why they were all suddenly tongue-tied.

"Are you saying milord Dare is occupied with secret matters of state?" she asked.

"We cannot tell you that," said Plumbrook, an unusually guarded expression on his round, cherubic face.

But it did not matter what he said. The looks on the faces of the other two spoke volumes.

"I quite understand, *mes amis*," she replied, smiling reassuringly. "I assure you I am not disloyal, to your King or my own, and I shall not betray Lord Dare to anyone."

They nodded, looking satisfied, but Juliana's mind whirled at this new piece of information. For the rest of the evening, she flirted and danced as usual, but all the while she pondered the question of whether Lord Dare was in actuality a spy.

It was an exciting thought, but perhaps it was just something those silly bucks had dreamt up, no more real than all the duels Dudley claimed to have fought. Still, it explained so many things about Lord Dare. His air of mystery, his command of French, even his interest in *her*. Perhaps she had inadvertently put herself under suspicion by pretending to be French, and he had flirted with her as a means of discovering the truth.

Actually, it was a lowering thought. Now that he knew she was not French, he had apparently lost all interest.

Marcus spent a quiet Sunday morning going to Mass and then walking about St. James's Park, even though he knew it was unlikely that Mademoiselle Juliette would be there.

He wondered if she had noticed his absence last night. The words she'd spoken when they had last walked together continued to haunt him. Why did she have to view all men as scoundrels? Surely she would be happier in the end if she met some man who could convince her otherwise, who would protect her as she deserved. According to Jerry, sometimes the opera dancers made decent marriages, although generally not into the aristocracy. Try as he would, Marcus found it difficult to picture the irrepressible Juliette as the respectable wife of some banker or shopkeeper.

On Monday he received a note from Mr. Hutton, indicating that Miss Hutton was feeling better, but still indisposed to receive visitors. It was a polite note; Hutton had been careful to assure Marcus that Miss Hutton would be delighted to meet him once she had recovered from her illness. A cheerful letter from his mother, telling him she had sent *The Perils of Francesca* to the Minerva Press, and that he need not worry about her and Lucy, did little to lighten his mood. He could not be so sanguine about their futures.

Both missives left Marcus in a mood of restless impatience. He had done all he could to court his heiress; he had set his affairs in order, in preparation for the success or failure of his suit. Now he was at a loss for how to occupy himself, and keep Mademoiselle Juliette's cynical words from his mind.

Later that day, he decided to take action.

Chapter Six

For the next few days, Juliana tried not to think about Lord Dare. She rehearsed as usual, putting forth her best efforts to master the new *ballet* being prepared, based on the story of Daphnis and Chloe. As part of the *corps de ballet*, Juliana would play a wood nymph. She wondered how she would dare go on the stage. Her new costume made her peasant dress from the previous performances seem positively demure by contrast. Although it did not bare a breast, as did some costumes from seasons past, the gauzy draperies revealed more than even the daring Mademoiselle Juliette felt quite comfortable showing.

As she walked back to Madame Bouchard's house after a rehearsal, she realized it was now three weeks since she had run away. Grandpapa still had not inserted a notice into the *Times* to show that he had relented. She had done her part: earned wages, avoided rakes and scoundrels, and sent Grandpapa letters by the Penny Post several times each week to assure him of her well-being. What would it take to convince him she was capable of caring for herself? Had Lord Amberley arrived as planned, and what had Grandpapa told him?

As a slight drizzle began to fall, she reflected that her enjoyment of the masquerade was beginning to pall just a little. She even had to admit that Lord Dare's departure from her life had something to do with it.

The drizzle changed to a light rain, and she increased her

pace. At the turn from Picadilly onto Half Moon Street, she once again noticed the stocky individual she had collided with last week. It had already occurred to her that he might have been someone hired by Grandpapa to find her, but either her disguise had fooled him, or he skulked about the neighborhood for some other reason. She could not like it, and was relieved when she reached the apartment she shared with Jenny.

There an unexpected sight met her eyes. Jenny sat in a straight chair, wide-eyed and nervous, her hands folded across her slightly rounded belly. Across from her, two gentlemen occupied the small sofa. The younger of the two was thin, handsome and looked as anxious as Jenny. He must be her Edward, the young man who was studying to be a barrister, and had deserted her in such a cowardly manner when he had realized she was increasing. The other, a stout gentleman dressed in old-fashioned knee breeches, looked of an age to be his father.

As Juliana advanced into the room, the younger gentleman stood up, but the other remained in his seat, looking her over with a contemptuous eye.

"Sir William, Edward, this is Mademoiselle Lamant, who shares this lodging with me," said Jenny, stammering a little. "Juliette, this is Sir William Kendal, and his son Edward."

The younger man responded politely, but his father continued to scowl. The hostility in his expression and the uneasy looks on the two lovers' faces made it clear that matters were not proceeding smoothly. Was there any way she could help?

"*Bon jour*, Saire William," she said.

If anything, Sir William's scowl intensified at her words. Clearly he disapproved of loose Frenchwomen; Juliana wondered if his distrust could be put to good account. She glanced over at Jenny, satisfied to see that her friend looked modest and demure as usual in a plain blue dress, a cap she had been embroidering for the baby still in her lap. There could be no stronger contrast with her own attire and demeanor, Juliana thought, now doubly glad she had purchased the closely tailored, dashing moss green pelisse she was wearing.

She removed her hat with its long ostrich plume and set it down on a side table, strutted into the room and boldly took the other seat at the table where Jenny sat.

"I presume you 'ave come here to make poor Jenny reparation for the wrongs that have been done her," she said, smiling brightly at the gentlemen on the sofa.

"Hmmph!" said Sir William. "Wrongs? I'll wager your precious Jenny has no proof that my Edward fathered her child. I wouldn't be surprised if he was just one of many."

"Papa, I told you it wasn't like that!" protested young Kendal. "I love Jenny, and she loves me—or did—and if she will forgive me I intend to marry her!"

"Marry her?" Juliana asked cautiously, not wishing to appear too excited over this unlooked-for turn of events.

"Of course not!" said Sir William. "It is out of the question. My son and an opera dancer? Outrageous!"

"Oh, I quite agree!" trilled Juliana. She looked at Jenny and winked, then fluttered her eyelashes before looking back at the two gentlemen. "How can you think she would wish to be the respectable wife of a barrister? No, it would be so much more amusing for her, and comfortable for you, if you would just make her a . . . a settlement!"

They all goggled at her.

"Is that not the correct word?"

"No, it is not!" said the older gentleman, glaring at Jenny. "You think to extort money from us, girl?"

Jenny quailed under his angry gaze.

"Mon pauvre," Juliana said, leaning over to put an arm on Jenny's shoulder. "Do not let him frighten you. We must make certain you receive your due. Then you will be comfortable, and buy many lovely gowns. Perhaps, once the baby is born, you may even find a new, more amusing lover, *n'est ce pas*?"

"I don't wish for another lover!" said Jenny, staring at Juliana as if she had lost her mind. "I do not wish to cause any trouble, only to—"

"But of course you do not *wish* to cause any trouble," Juliana interrupted. "*Chérie*, you must think of yourself. If they do not make reparation to you you can easily make a suit for—how do you English call it when a gentleman promises marriage and then runs off?"

"Breach of promise," supplied young Kendal.

Sir William turned his angry gaze on his son.

"Ah yes! Breach of promise," Juliana echoed.

"You will neither of you do any such thing! There is no proof other than this girl's word that Edward promised her marriage—if he ever did, which I take leave to doubt!"

"I told you, Papa, I did," said Edward, braving another wrathful glance from his father.

"But I do not wish to testify against Edward!" cried Jenny.

Gleefully, Juliana noted how Sir William's eyes darted between her and Jenny. If all went well, Mademoiselle Lamant's outrageous demands would throw a more flattering light on shy, undemanding Jenny.

"It will not be necessary if his father agrees to compensate you as you deserve," she said. "Ten thousand pounds would not be an unreasonable request."

"Ten thousand pounds! You impudent French hussy!" Sir William's face reddened with anger as he jumped up from the sofa and advanced toward Juliana. He stopped and stared at her, clearly torn between the desire to strangle her and an innate politeness that prevented him from manhandling even a woman of such questionable character.

"Yes, I think it quite a reasonable sum," she replied, looking up at him calmly. "You English would do anything to avoid a scandal."

"Stop it!" cried Jenny. "I do not wish to bring any suit against Edward!"

"You heard the girl," said Sir William, his angry color receding a little. "She does not wish to bring suit against us."

Juliana noticed his gaze soften as he looked at Jenny.

"Kindly leave us now," he continued. "This is none of your affair, and rest assured *you* will not profit by it!"

She looked at Jenny, then at him.

"Well, *chérie*, if you really wish to marry the son of such a tedious English squire. . . ." she said, raising her eyebrows.

"I do!" said Jenny, her eyes shining with tears as she looked nervously back at Sir William. "But not if it means his family will disown him."

"Hm, well, I would never disown my son," said Sir William.

He was clearly weakening. Juliana hid a smile.

"Edward tells me your birth is respectable, eh?" he asked Jenny bluntly, but his voice was gentler than before.

As Jenny recounted her sad family history, Juliana quietly arose and left the three of them. She entered her bedroom, but stayed close to the door. She listened happily as Sir William gave his permission for the young couple to wed, and even helped them make plans to keep the exact date of their marriage vague to prevent unwanted gossip. After these details were arranged, Sir William made his farewells, leaving his son to spend some time alone with his intended. Juliana moved away from the door and went to stand by the window, not wishing to eavesdrop on the lovers. Finally, she heard the door close again. She left her bedroom, and found Jenny beaming and walking about the sitting room, as if too excited to rest.

"So, is it all settled?" she asked.

Jenny nodded. "I still cannot believe my good fortune. I did not think Sir William would ever relent. Then you came in, and acted like such a . . . such a. . . ."

"A scheming French hussy," supplied Juliana, grinning. "You thought I had gone mad, didn't you?"

"Well, at first I did. But then I realized what you were doing. It answered perfectly. Thank you!"

Juliana embraced her heartily, then laughed. "It was nothing, I assure you. I had only to convince Sir William how fortunate he was to be dealing with a gentle, unassuming *English* girl. Once I had achieved that, I knew all would be well."

"Indeed, I am so happy!"

"I am so glad Edward came to a realization of his responsibilities. I had not expected it at all."

"Oh, you do not know? Edward said a Lord Dare sought him out, and scolded him quite fiercely for deserting me. I thought perhaps you knew him."

Juliana nodded. "I did say something of your situation to Lord Dare, but I promise you I did not mention either of your names. He must have found out on his own—but why?"

"I do not know, but I am glad he did," said Jenny, patting her stomach. "Yes, I know you are thinking that Edward was very wrong not to come to me sooner. But I cannot love him less for not wanting to grieve his family."

Juliana nodded, though she could not find it in herself to condone Edward's weakness so easily. She hated to think how Jenny's happiness depended on the vagaries of men such as Edward and his father.

The more interesting problem was why Lord Dare had intervened. Was it an act of chivalry? Was it a scheme to earn her gratitude? He had said he was not seeking a mistress, but perhaps he was trying to put her off her guard.

But when she looked back at Jenny, contentedly at her needlework, Juliana could not be anything but grateful.

Juliana pirouetted before a mirror in the Green Room that evening, feigning absorption in her steps after having requested several admirers to leave her be. If they all thought Mademoiselle Juliette was out of temper this evening, so be it. They would never guess that she was avoiding them in part because her scandalous new costume made her self-conscious. But that was not all that troubled her. She could not deny it to herself. She wanted to see Lord Dare once again, unwise as that was.

She paused, staring into the mirror at her reflection. The new costume was composed of enough layers of gauze not to be quite transparent, but it was short, and left her back and shoulders bare. Imitation vines crossed the front of the bodice, and again below her waist, emphasizing her breasts and hips in a quite scandalous fashion. An involuntary warmth arose in her face as she contemplated herself. It only deepened as she detected Dare's reflection behind her own. She was glad of the concealing layers of rouge on her cheeks.

"Milord Dare, I am delighted to see you here again," she said, assuming her French accent and speaking loudly enough for any possible bystanders to hear it.

"Thank you for the kind welcome, Mademoiselle Juliette," he replied softly, trying not to stare at her, but not quite succeeding. Something about his hesitant, polite gallantry touched her. Suddenly he seemed less sophisticated than he had, and more vulnerable.

"What a surprise," she said, striving for an airy, unconcerned tone. "I had quite given up seeing you again."

"I could not stay away."

She looked into his eyes then, and though she knew it was a mistake, allowed herself to be captured by his gaze. She had to think of something to say, and quickly, or she would yield to impulse and beg him to take her in his arms and kiss her again.

"I am so glad you spoke to Mr. Kendal on my friend Miss Church's behalf. It was most kind of you to do so," she said, dropping her French accent and speaking more softly.

"I trust the outcome has been happy?" he said, coming closer to her so they could speak without being overheard. Juliana did her best to try to ignore the intimacy.

"They are to be married. His father has given them his blessing."

"He has? After I spoke to Kendal, I realized that he and Miss Church were truly attached, but I had not expected his father to be willing to do more than provide her some monetary assistance."

"Ah, but by the time he realized that his son *might* have gotten himself entangled with a scheming French hussy, he was positively eager to welcome quiet, modest little Jenny into the bosom of his family," said Juliana, smiling.

"Poor Sir William! You are a wicked woman, Mademoiselle Juliette." Dare laughed, the first time she had heard him laugh. Perhaps he had little opportunity to do so, though she suspected a sense of humor lurked behind his serious demeanor.

"I do my best."

"With excellent results."

"Yes. For Jenny, that is. She truly is a respectable creature at heart. This life was not for her."

"Is it for you?" he asked.

The directness of his question surprised her.

"Of course," she replied quickly, hoping he had not

noticed her hesitation. "I enjoy my independence too much to wish to form *any* sort of entanglement with just one man."

"Not even a man who cared for you?" he asked, leaning over to speak even more softly.

"Are you perhaps referring to yourself again, my lord?" she asked, trying to sound arch, though her pulse began to race again as she felt his breath on her cheek.

He did not answer. Instead he stood very still, his gaze turned inward, as if he searched his soul for an answer.

"Why did you speak to Jenny's lover?" she continued to probe, unable to bear his silence.

"Because he was behaving badly," he replied. "Because I did not want you to think all men would behave so."

"Is that all?"

"That is all," he replied. "If my circumstances were different . . . but they are not. In fact, I shall probably be leaving London very soon."

"That is a relief indeed, for I am not seeking a lover either," she said, to cover her disappointment. Then she realized her words were not in character. "That is, not unless he were *very* wealthy and *very* generous."

His expression became guarded, but she thought she could see a hurt look in his eyes. Impossible! Surely he was wise enough to recognize Mademoiselle Juliette for the abandoned woman she was. Or had he, perhaps, developed a real *tendre* for her?

"Why did you come here tonight? What do you wish from me?" The rash words broke free before she could recall them.

"Nothing," he said almost fiercely. "Only a farewell kiss."

This time he did not await her permission. Her heart pounded wildly as his hands encircled her waist, caressing her through her diaphanous costume, slowly pulling her closer until he held her against his chest once more, so near that she could feel his own quickened breath. She had only to say the word, she knew, and he would release her. But she could not. If this was the last time they would meet, she would not deny him, or herself, this heady delight.

He bent his head down and claimed her lips, more confidently this time than on the first night they had met. She parted her lips readily, welcoming his taste, his mouth, his touch. Time stood still and everything else receded as she gave herself up to pleasure. His kiss intensified, and he pulled her more tightly against him, his strong, deft hands tracing the contours of her form, rubbing flimsy layers of gauze against her tingling flesh.

Her knees trembled as he finally released her, so that she had to fight the urge to cling to him.

"I will leave you now, Mademoiselle Lamant," he said in a louder voice. "I wish you success in all your pursuits."

His formal words sent an abrupt chill through her.

"Farewell, Lord Dare," she said, managing a shaky courtesy. "I have enjoyed our . . . acquaintance."

His face twisted in a rueful half-smile as he turned and left her. She watched him go, regret piercing her at the thought that this was indeed their last meeting. Before he left the room, he turned. Once more their eyes met, and her knees weakened again at the intensity of his gaze.

Then he was gone, leaving her feeling strangely bereft. What was wrong with her? A year ago, she had vowed to live her life independent of the demands of a husband or lover, but now that resolve felt somehow dissatisfying. By wishing to avoid romantic entanglements, was she denying herself some of the sweetest adventures life could offer? What would it be like to travel with a companion like Dare? A man who would not expect her to be a slave to propriety or duty. A man versed in the ways of the world, who kissed with such sublime concentration and attention to her pleasure. . . .

She forced herself to practice her steps again. Dare was not going to return. He had said he was not free to pursue her, and oddly tempting as the thought might be, she could never be his mistress.

Marcus took his place in the pit, not sure he wished to watch Mademoiselle Juliette dance before hundreds of leering bucks, while wearing that wickedly delightful costume. But he could not tear himself away. Despite everything, he found he was himself drawn in to the *ballet* being performed. If only he and Juliette could be like Daphnis and

Chloe, two innocents exploring their passions together for the first time. When the *corps de ballet* entered, he could not take his eyes from Juliette. Tonight, he saw no mistakes, only a repressed passion in all her graceful movements. It was as if she danced for him alone.

After the performance, he returned to Grosvenor Square, only to pace his room, unable to banish Juliette's seductive image from his mind. Or her painfully cynical words. She had a good heart, he reminded himself. She had shown it in the way she had helped her friend Miss Church, even though she had made it clear she wanted no such maudlin sentiment for herself. And, despite what she had said, she had blossomed under his kisses, responding with all the passion of a vibrant, strong-willed young woman.

Did she regret their parting? Would she think of him?

He poured himself a glass of brandy and tossed it off. He resumed his pacing. He had to stop thinking of Juliette, but he could not. The mere act of kissing her had brought him pleasure greater than any he had ever felt, sparking his desire to explore even headier delights that he had only read about. Perhaps he truly was a rake at heart, just like his forebears.

He stopped by the side table that held the brandy decanter and poured himself another glass, even though he knew it would do nothing to dull his feelings. The warmth of the spirit spread through him, but all he could think was that it was no substitute for the glorious feeling of holding Juliette in his arms. Or even for talking with her, enjoying her witty banter, her mischievous smile.

He was a poor excuse for a rake, after all. A true rake might bed an opera dancer. He would not fall in love with her.

He awoke late the next morning, conscious of a dullness of spirit. Determined to shake off this mood and face his future with resolution, if not anticipation, he allowed Pridwell to dress him. He went to his study and penned a brief note to Hutton, inquiring as to the most convenient time to call, and asked Barnes to have it delivered to Russell Square. Before Marcus had finished his breakfast, the footman dispatched on the errand returned with a polite note from Hutton stating that he would be at Lord Amberley's disposal all the day.

Not long after noon, Marcus called for his carriage and set out for Russell Square. There he was again greeted by the obsequious butler, who ushered him once more into Mr. Hutton's study. As Hutton arose from behind his desk and came forward to greet him, Marcus noted that the older man moved more stiffly than before, and his bright blue eyes were shadowed as if he had not been sleeping well. Was his granddaughter causing him so much anxiety?

After they had exchanged conventional greetings and seated themselves in the two comfortable chairs by the fire, Marcus inquired after Miss Hutton's health.

"She is on the mend, my lord. I trust you shall be able to meet her very soon," said Hutton, seeming to pick his words with great deliberation.

"Mr. Hutton, I know this will seem like an impertinence, but I must know. Is Miss Hutton opposed to my suit?"

"How can she be? She has not even met you." There was a trace of annoyance in Hutton's voice, and Marcus was unsure whether it was directed at him or at Miss Hutton.

"I do not know, but perhaps there is something in my reputation or my circumstances that repels her."

"Not at all," Hutton insisted. "Juliana is quite intelligent, for a female. I am certain that once she makes your acquaintance, she will see that you are worth a dozen of the fools that have courted her in the past."

Guilt pricked Marcus. He wondered if Hutton would be so complimentary if he knew Marcus had kissed an opera dancer, not just once but twice, or how much Marcus wished to engage her in even more potent diversions.

"My lord, please be patient with us," said Hutton, clearly misunderstanding his silence. "I know your affairs are urgent, but I am quite certain my granddaughter will be able to receive visitors within the next few days."

"Very well, Mr. Hutton," he said, seeing the look of determination in Hutton's thin, intelligent face. "I shall strive to be patient."

He was just rising from his chair when sounds reached

from the hall. A man's voice, raised in exasperation, and higher-pitched, pleading tones of a girl or a young woman.

Hutton leapt up from his seat with a quickness astonishing for one of his years. He looked back at Marcus for an instant, clearly trying to decide how to handle an awkward situation.

"My apologies, my lord," he said. "Please remain here while I settle this disturbance."

Marcus wondered what was happening, and what Hutton was trying to hide from him.

"You must forgive me, Mr. Hutton," he said firmly. "I have business to which I must attend, and cannot stay here and trespass on your hospitality any longer."

Hutton nodded, though he did not look at all pleased by Marcus's insistence on leaving. Together they went to the entrance hall. First, Marcus saw the butler pushing a confused-looking footman through a different doorway. Turning, he then saw a stout man in a brown coat standing in the middle of the hall, holding tightly to the arm of a girl wearing a shabby cloak. Her blue eyes were wide with fright as she tried to pull away from the man's grasp. Marcus noted neat blond locks peeping out from under her bonnet.

Was this Miss Hutton? What the devil was going on?

He looked back at Hutton, only to see a look of acute disappointment on the old man's face. Meanwhile, the girl had stopped struggling. They all stood for a moment, surveying each other in shocked silence.

Then the burly man spoke. " 'Ere she is. I found 'er."

"Good God! You dolt! That is not my granddaughter," said Hutton, anger replacing the devastation in his face.

"She's not?" replied the man, his forehead creased in puzzlement.

"I told you I am not Miss Hutton," said the girl, still white-faced and holding her cloak tightly around her.

"Do not be afraid," said Mr. Hutton, softening his voice to address the girl. "I am very sorry, child, but there has been a grave mistake. Perhaps we can recompense you for the trouble you have endured?"

"Thank you, but no," she replied, looking relieved. "All I wish for is to return home."

"Order the carriage to be brought round," Hutton said

to the butler. "Let them take this young lady wherever she wishes. In the meantime, she may sit in the drawing room."

The butler nodded, and escorted the young girl off.

Hutton's demeanor was stiff with embarrassment as he glanced back at Marcus.

"I must apologize for this unseemly disturbance, Lord Amberley, but now you must give me leave to speak to this . . . this person in private."

"I beg your pardon, Mr. Hutton," said Marcus. "I think I have some right to understand what has happened here. Who is this man?"

"Benjamin Stockley, milord," the man said, bowing awkwardly.

"I must assume your granddaughter has fled your household, and you have hired this man to find her."

Hutton nodded, scowling. "Why I ever entrusted such an important undertaking to such a bacon-brained bungler I will not know! What were you thinking, to abduct that poor child?"

Stockley shifted his weight from one foot to the other.

"Well, sir, I got word that a young lady answering to your granddaughter's description was seen coming and going from a certain house in 'Alf Moon Street, the day after she had gone missing. I lay in wait for days, sir, but never saw no one like her until this girl came out to walk in Green Park. You *said* Miss Hutton was a yaller-head, with blue eyes. 'Ow was I to know it weren't 'er?"

"If you had half a brain, you would have seen this girl was not tall enough to be my granddaughter. Begone now. I am done with you!"

"What about me time and trouble?"

"Send an exact account of your expenses to my man of business, but do not expect a farthing more! If you're not careful, I shall make a complete report of your mishandling of this case to your superiors in Bow Street."

Cowed, the man slunk out the door, leaving Marcus alone with Hutton. Now that anger no longer drove him, the old man looked tired, bowed and defeated.

"Sir, I believe we need to talk," said Marcus gently, concerned at Hutton's suddenly fragile appearance. "Shall I call your servants to fetch some refreshment for you?"

"No, thank you," said Hutton, straightening and leading the way back to his study. He poured them both glasses of brandy from the decanter on a side table, and drank his own so quickly that he choked.

"My apologies, my lord," he said in a breathless voice. "I keep brandy here for guests, but I myself am not much accustomed to drinking spirits."

"You certainly may bc excused on this occasion."

Marcus sipped his drink, waiting for Hutton to recover before asking the questions burning in his mind.

"When did your granddaughter leave you?"

"Three—no, almost four weeks ago."

"She has been missing for nearly a month?" exclaimed Marcus. No wonder Hutton had a sleepless look. Heaven knew what could have happened to an inexperienced young lady trying to fend for herself for so long.

"It is not quite so bad as that," said Hutton. "I know for a fact that she was safe and well as of yesterday morning."

Marcus cocked an eyebrow.

"She has written me letters several times each week, and sent them through the Penny Post, which makes them almost impossible to trace. She writes that she is in good health, and has found employment, although in what capacity, I cannot imagine. Discreet inquiries have been made at all the registry offices, to no avail."

So Miss Hutton had inherited some of her grandfather's cleverness! Marcus fervently hoped it would keep her safe until she returned to her grandfather. Guilt stung him at the knowledge that Miss Hutton had made her rash escape to avoid his suit. At the same time, he could not help being appalled that Hutton had allowed the situation to proceed to such a crisis.

He drew a breath before saying, "I must assume Miss Hutton ran away to avoid meeting me."

"Do not mistake, my lord! I was not going to coerce her into marrying you, nor does she have any reason to dislike you. The girl has some silly notion that she does not wish to marry. I had thought meeting you would convince her otherwise."

"What is there to do now? You can not pretend she is

ill forever. I promise I shall not reveal what has happened, but how many others know the truth?"

"Only my butler, Mrs. Frisby and Juliana's maid Polly."

"Is there any way I can assist you in finding her?"

"Thank you, but I cannot think of anything you could do that has not already been attempted."

"Did she leave a note? Is there a way you can convince her to return?"

"She has instructed me to insert a particular notice in the *Times* to signify that I have relented. I suppose I shall have to do so now."

"Good God! Why did you not do so from the start?"

Hutton paused, and Marcus wondered why.

"I would have, had I realized matters would come to such a pass."

"I trust you will not hesitate to do so now. Moreover, you must assure your granddaughter that she need not fear that I shall make her any further overtures."

"At least promise me one thing. If my granddaughter is in danger of losing her reputation, will you marry her?"

Marcus's pride prompted him to refuse, but he hesitated. There was a pleading tone in Hutton's voice, and his hand shook as he clutched his empty glass. Marcus knew Hutton was not given to pleading.

"You know I am in no position to refuse. If she is willing, I shall marry her. But only if she is willing."

"Thank you, my lord. You are a true gentleman," said Hutton with a regretful sigh.

Marcus rose to leave. "Do send me word if you find there is any way I can help you."

He allowed Hutton to escort him to the door. Marcus's coachman had been gently walking the horses around the square. On seeing Marcus, he brought the coach back around to the Huttons' doorstep. Marcus climbed in, raising his hand as a final farewell to the bowed figure on the doorstep.

A true gentleman, Hutton had called him. The phrase stung Marcus as he considered the wretched tangle of his life. He had managed to comport himself with dignity during the whole worrisome, embarrassing episode, but it was little comfort now.

In a short while, Hutton would make certain that the appropriate notice was inserted in the very next edition of the *Times*. If all went well, Miss Hutton would return to his fond care, but Marcus had little hope that she would accept his suit.

All his plans were in vain. He had already wracked his brains to no avail. There was no clever investment, no quick scheme that could prevent disaster. Within a month, Sir Barnaby would foreclose, and Marcus would have to swallow his pride and do whatever was necessary to ensure Mama and Lucy's future comfort. The Redwyck lands would fall into further decline under Sir Barnaby's mismanagement. Marcus's efforts, the money spent on clothing and continued maintenance of the town house in Grosvenor Square, even his difficult resolution to cease his pursuit of Mademoiselle Juliette, all were for naught.

But in some cold, fierce way, Marcus was relieved. He had never liked the marriage scheme. Now he was free to go anywhere, do what he wished. Perhaps he'd go to India or America. Somewhere there must be opportunities for an industrious young man with a head for figures. He would have to work hard and live the most frugal of lives, but in time he would earn his fortune, perhaps even be able to buy back the Redwyck lands. If it were not for leaving Mama and Lucy, the prospect of seeing more of the world would be an exciting one.

On his return to Grosvenor Square, Marcus was once again greeted by Barnes, and as before, he was obliged to tell Barnes that he had not yet seen Miss Hutton. It pained Marcus to see that Barnes maintained his foolish faith in his abilities. He went to his study to write some dutiful letters to his man of business and his agent in Gloucestershire. Without quite revealing what had happened, he warned them both to prepare for the worst. This depressing task completed, Marcus ascended the stairs to his bedroom. There, he told Pridwell what he had told Barnes, and like Barnes, Pridwell maintained his optimism.

He had arranged to dine with Jerry and his friends this evening, but when he looked at the clothes Pridwell had laid out, he changed his mind. In his present mood, he would be no fit companion.

"Thank you Pridwell, but I shall not require a change of clothing after all. I will dine at home tonight."

"Very well, my lord. I shall inform Barnes of your change of plans," said Pridwell, only a slight tightness about his lips giving hint that he did not regard this as a good sign.

An hour later, having sent Jerry word of his change of plans, Marcus sat down to his solitary meal. He had no appetite, but in order not to distress the servants, he tried to do justice to the choice meal prepared on short notice by Uncle Harold's expensive French chef. Judging by the béchamel sauce, to which Antoine had added his own subtle blend of herbs, Marcus decided that the chef at least should have no difficulty finding another position.

He took another sip of Burgundy. All the French food and wine only put him in mind of Mademoiselle Juliette. It was pointless to think about her, he reminded himself. Though he now considered himself free of any further commitment to Miss Hutton, he was still in no position to pursue anyone else.

The meal over, Marcus returned to his study, sat down at the desk and prepared to write to his mother and Lucy. Finding his quill needed sharpening, he began pulling open various drawers. He had been through the desk before, but he could not remember where Uncle Harold had kept his penknife. One of the drawers stuck a little, and on impulse, he forced it, pulling it completely out of the desk. Onto the floor fell several small boxes. They must have become wedged in the back, which explained why he had not seen them before.

He picked them up and sat back down by the desk. He lit an additional branch of candles, setting it on the desk so he could better examine the contents of the boxes. The first was made of tin, embossed with designs that put him in mind of pictures he had seen in his rakish forebears' collection. He opened it, and was not completely surprised at its contents. Although he had never seen such things before, he knew their use. Apparently Uncle Harold had been prudent enough to prevent contracting diseases, and perhaps even to avoid siring by-blows on his mistresses.

He set the box aside, and took up the smaller one. When he opened it, a delicate brooch studded with sapphires and diamonds glittered up from the black velvet lining the box. He stared at it in surprise. He remembered having settled his uncle's account with Rundell and Bridge last week, but he had thought Uncle Harold had already given this gift to his latest mistress. Apparently he had died before he'd had the chance.

Marcus stared down at the brooch. He told himself not to be superstitious, but he could not help thinking it was some sort of a sign. He took the brooch out of the box and turned it so the gems glittered in the candlelight. They reminded him of Mademoiselle Juliette's eyes.

I cannot, he thought to himself. *It would be mad.*

He closed his palm on the brooch, hiding its fire. He would sell it, along with everything else of value in this house. To the best of his recollection, Uncle Harold had paid a hundred guineas for it. Though beautifully made, it was a small thing, not as opulent as some of the other jewelry Marcus knew Uncle Harold had given his mistresses in the past. It would probably fetch about eighty guineas.

He opened his palm and turned the brooch again, watching the fiery brilliants and the more subtle, mysterious gleam of the sapphires. What did eighty guineas mean, after all? He needed tens of thousands if he wished to restore the family fortunes, and he was not going to get them.

I should not, he told himself, closing his hand around the brooch, feeling its delicate setting press against his palm, imagining how it might look on the right, perfect breast.

He arose from the seat and paced restlessly about the room, still holding the brooch. Duty and desire dueled within him. Was it wrong to wish for sweet, fleeting pleasure before facing ruin? He stopped by the fire and stared into its gleaming, hot center, as he contemplated the years of toil and self-denial that stretched before him.

I will.

Desire had won.

Chapter Seven

Juliana sat at the small dressing table in her bedchamber, applying the layer of rouge without which she did not dare leave the house. Yesterday, Jenny had helped her restore the reddish tone to her hair, which had just begun to fade. Juliana looked at herself in the mirror, deciding that if the masquerade went much longer, she would forget what she looked like.

She felt listless, and knew the reason. It was foolish to think about Lord Dare; he might already be gone from London. But she could not forget how he had made her feel. He had desired her, for herself, and not for her fortune. Of course that desire was not honorable, and it was unthinkable to yield to it, but for some reason she felt more flattered than offended. She only knew that having been kissed by Dare, she could not even think of marrying the dreadfully respectable suitor Grandpapa had chosen for her.

Still, she was beginning to miss Grandpapa, particularly since Jenny had related the little adventure that had befallen her earlier today when she had gone out for her first walk in a long time. Perhaps Grandpapa would relent, now that he'd dismissed the Bow Street Runner hired to find her. She hoped so.

Later that evening, in the Green Room, Juliana felt unusually vulnerable in her scanty costume. Jeremy Plumbrook and his friends were not in evidence, and neither, of course, was Lord Dare. Conscious of admiring looks from several young bucks who strolled in, she turned to the mirror and pretended to be concentrating on her steps.

She was so absorbed that at first she did not notice a tall gentleman making his way toward her. Then, out of the corner of her eye, she saw the others move aside to let him by, almost as if they were afraid of him. Irrationally, she hoped it was Dare, then she saw that the gentleman coming toward her was a trifle shorter than Dare, his hair and eyes darker.

What beastly luck! It was Lord Verwood, the rake who had eloped with and then abandoned poor Catherine to her fate last summer. As he approached, Juliana prayed he would not recognize her.

"My, my," he murmured in a silky voice, as his gaze roved slowly over her, taking in every detail of her person and her shocking attire.

"*Pardon*, milord? You 'ave the advantage of me," she said, with a coquettish smile.

"I am desolated to think you have forgotten me, *Miss Hutton*," he replied, coming closer to her and speaking softly so no one else could hear.

How could he have guessed so quickly? Despite a sinking feeling in her stomach, Juliana forced herself to stay calm.

"I do not understand, *monsieur*. Perhaps you 'ave mistaken me for someone else?"

"Not at all, my dear. I never forget a face . . . or a figure, particularly when they are as memorable as yours. Surely you do not think a false French accent, some hair dye and the application of some rouge would fool an old friend like me?"

It was no use dissembling any longer.

"You are no friend of mine, Lord Verwood," she replied, as sternly as she could without raising her voice. "Now that you have satisfied your curiosity, please leave me. I have nothing to say to you."

"But I have much to ask of you!" he said, arching his eyebrows. "For instance, what has led you to embark on such a mad escapade? No, let me guess. Your grandfather wishes you to marry some appallingly dull lord, and this is your way of showing your defiance."

"How do you know?" Juliana asked. His knowledge of people and events was almost uncanny.

"I make it my business to know many things," he replied. "Have you no thought of the consequences of such a masquerade?"

"It's none of your affair, my lord. And if I am discovered, perhaps my grandfather would then allow me to go my own way."

"You are bluffing," he accused softly.

She colored. She did not wish her grandfather to undergo the embarrassment of a scandal, and Verwood knew it. How would he use his knowledge?

"Besides," he continued, "there are other, even greater dangers attached to your situation. Not the least of them is being imposed on by unscrupulous members of the opposite sex."

"Such as you?"

"Who better to understand the dangers? However, in this case I assure you I mean you no harm," he said, with a smile that would have tempted her to believe him, had she not known better.

"What do you intend, then?"

"Perhaps I shall restore you to your grandfather."

"Why would you do such a thing?"

"Pure chivalry, my dear Miss Hutton."

"I do not believe you, and in any case, I will not go."

He sighed. "You are so like your friend Catherine. I should have expected you would be stubborn. Perhaps I am mad to offer to help one of you again, but I could assist you in this predicament."

"Whatever do you mean?"

"You could marry me, *ma belle*. I promise I'd not be a restrictive husband, so long as you allow me the same freedom."

"I am not such a fool. You were supposed to marry Cat, but instead you abandoned her to her fate. Pen was right. We should never have trusted you!"

"Miss Talcott is a very perceptive young woman," he

said, a hint of hardness in his dark eyes. "I am sure her assessment of my character is, in general, quite correct. However, in this case she is wrong. As a matter of fact, your friend Catherine is perfectly happy, and much better off than if I had married her."

"Do you expect me to believe that?"

"Believe what you will, but understand this: I shall not leave you here to bc prey to the rogues that prowl here."

"I can take care of myself," she replied. "And if I could not, you are the last man I would turn to for assistance. You need not trouble yourself any further on my account."

She realized she had been unconsciously backing away from him, and stopped. Just then, over Verwood's shoulder, she saw an unexpected but most welcome sight. Her heart leapt as she saw Lord Dare making his way toward them. Why was he here? After such an impassioned parting kiss, why had he returned?

Verwood turned to follow her gaze. This was a ticklish situation indeed. Would he reveal what he knew of her to Dare? If Dare chose to protect her, it could come to a fight. In any case, her masquerade was now in serious jeopardy.

Barely had these thoughts flashed through her mind when Dare joined them.

"Good evening, Mademoiselle Juliette," he said, making her a bow. As he straightened back up, he shot a warning look at Verwood before turning back toward her. "Has this gentleman been annoying you?"

His concern warmed her. Dare was clever and brave enough to be a match for Lord Verwood, and he was obviously willing and even eager to help her. But could she accept, without causing him harm or creating a shocking uproar?

"Lord Verwood and I have met before, milord Dare," she replied. "We were discussing some mutual acquaintances, but I believe we have now said all we have to say to one another."

She hoped Verwood would take the hint and leave, but annoyingly, he stood his ground.

"Lord Dare?" he drawled, bowing. "I believe I've not had the pleasure."

"I have spent the past few years on the Continent," said

Dare, returning the bow. "A pleasure to meet you, Lord Verwood."

"No doubt my own visits to Paris and Vienna were too brief for our paths to have crossed," Verwood replied smoothly.

Juliana watched the interplay between the two men, intrigued by Verwood's hints that Dare was not what he seemed. Looking back at Dare, she noted a tension in his broad shoulders, and a wary look in his intelligent hazel eyes. She could see he was hiding some mystery, and yet she felt sure that whatever it was, it was not to his discredit. Given a choice between the two men, she knew whom she would trust.

"An unfortunate circumstance," said Dare after a pause. His voice remained polite, but held a hint of a challenge as he continued. "Now that we have had the pleasure of becoming acquainted, I must beg you to allow me a word alone with Mademoiselle Juliette."

"I am desolated to disappoint you, Dare, but I was engaged in warning Mademoiselle Juliette of the dangers of encouraging the advances of strange gentlemen. I do not believe she was attending to my wise words."

"I believe Mademoiselle Juliette is capable of deciding for herself whose advances she would like to encourage."

A thrill rushed through Juliana at his protective words, and the desire that radiated from him. Had something changed in his circumstances? Had he come for *her*?

But she could not think about that. It would be unsafe to encourage either of them. Now that Verwood had penetrated her disguise and seemed determined to get her under his control, she would have to think of a way to escape the opera house as soon as she completed her part in the *ballet*.

"You both flatter me! I fear I cannot make such a difficult choice when it is almost time for me to dance. I must beg you both to excuse me now."

"Until later, then, *ma belle*," said Verwood in a low, intimate voice.

Fury coursed through Juliana as she saw a flash of jealousy in Dare's changeable eyes. Did he really think she had arranged an assignation with Verwood, as that scoundrel suggested?

"I am sorry, milord," she said addressing herself to Verwood. "I shall be too tired after the performance to think of anything but my bed."

"I should not wish you to think of anything else," murmured Lord Verwood, bending toward her but speaking just loudly enough for Dare to hear.

She pretended to ignore Verwood, but her heart was heavy. She would not only have to find a way to escape the theatre undetected by either of them, she would also have to think of a new guise and a new haven in which to await Grandpapa's decision. It was time to truly end her association with Lord Dare. Without even the solace of another farewell kiss.

"*Au revoir*, milord Dare," she said softly, trying to express with her eyes all the passion and all the wishes she could not voice in front of Verwood.

"Au revoir, Mademoiselle Juliette," he replied, his voice a caress and a promise, a captivating light in his eyes. Regret assailed her; she should not have encouraged him with that long, passionate look. Perhaps he too would try to seek her out after the performance. For both their sakes, she would have to avoid him, even though her whole being cried out to be held in his strong embrace once more.

Not risking a backward glance, she hurried out of the room.

Marcus tried not to stare at Juliette as she sped away, though desire, hope, jealousy and uncertainty churned inside him. Had he misunderstood her final look at him?

"Well, it has been a pleasure, Verwood," he said, striving to match the other man's easy air. "However, if we do not take our seats soon we shall miss Mademoiselle Juliette's performance."

"That would be a great shame. For you, that is. For myself, I hope to be favored with a more *private* performance, later this evening. You would do well not to interfere."

Verwood's warning only incensed Marcus further, but he bit down on the angry words that arose to his lips. If his instincts were correct, Juliette feared Lord Verwood for some reason. If that was the case, it was better that Lord Verwood did not suspect Marcus would help her.

"I see that I have misunderstood the situation. I beg your pardon, Verwood," he said, forcing out the meek words despite his longing to plant the other man a facer.

"I am delighted that you see reason," replied Verwood, but Marcus could not be sure whether he was convinced. "Now you must hurry, or you shall miss the *ballet.*"

"I've no wish to see it now," he said, assuming the peevish mien of a rival who knew himself beaten. "I bid you goodnight."

He bowed and left, hearing Verwood's tread behind him. They parted ways soon, as Verwood turned to enter the pit. Once Verwood was out of sight, Marcus doubled back. As swiftly as he could despite his bad leg, he ascended the steps, past the level of the balcony boxes, to the high gallery that spanned the upper reaches of the theatre. He looked down, and thought he could make out Verwood's tall, dark-clad form at the end of one of the crimson-padded benches below.

The *ballet* had already begun. Juliette was on the stage with the other dancers, her delightful form ethereal in the distance. Later, he would try to find her in the backstage area and offer her his escort to wherever she wished to go. He had asked Barnes to discreetly prepare for a possible female visitor, and Barnes had been delighted by the request. Uncle Harold must have upon occasion entertained a mistress at home, shocking as it was. Barnes apparently found Marcus's plans proof of his infallible Redwyck blood.

Marcus could only hope his butler was right. The way Juliette had looked at him made Marcus restless with longing, and he paced the gallery, watching her, only half-conscious of curious glances from the servants and idlers who frequented the gallery.

Did she reciprocate his desire? Was she, perhaps, even becoming fond of him, in her cynical way? Why did she fear Lord Verwood? Had he been her lover? She had spoken of lovers who had been too possessive. It was possible that Verwood had frightened her, even used violence. She might even have assumed her new guise in the hope of avoiding Verwood, not as a means of advancing her career on the stage, as she had said earlier.

Marcus's fists clenched involuntarily at the thought of

that scoundrel menacing his Juliette. Jaded and mercenary as she was, she still deserved to have the freedom to make her own decisions.

Especially in the choice of a lover.

Marcus continued to pace, glancing at the stage occasionally to check on the progress of the ballet, and then down into the pit to be sure Verwood was still there. The final scene involved only the two principals. When Marcus saw Juliette dance off the stage, he looked down into the pit and saw that Verwood had arisen from his seat.

Marcus hurried out of the gallery, descended the stairs as quickly as he could and hastened toward the backstage area. Hearing a number of voices issuing from one of the doors, he decided that must be the common dressing room shared by the members of the *corps de ballet.* He took a deep breath, and entered the room. He was greeted by stares, giggles and coy shrieks from dancers in various stages of undress. Repressing his embarrassment, he scanned the dimly lit, crowded room, but could not find Juliette. The elderly little Frenchwoman he remembered from his first night at the opera came forward, bristling, her dark eyes shining menacingly up at him.

"You are wasting your time if you seek Mademoiselle Lamant, milord," said the woman. "She has already gone."

"Madame, you misunderstand," he replied in French, hoping this would inspire her to trust him. "I am not the villain from whom Mademoiselle Juliette flees. It is Lord Verwood. Please tell me which way she has gone, so I may help her."

The woman's brows came together in a frown. "Lord Verwood! He has a bad reputation, that one." She stared up at Marcus for an instant, then motioned with her hand. "Juliette went that way, toward the second stage entrance. Hurry!"

Marcus did not tarry, but sped through the backstage area toward the indicated entrance, praying he was not too late. Out under the colonnade in front of the theatre, he peered up then down the street. The street was full of carriages awaiting their owners, but there were not very many pedestrians about. The performance must not have ended yet.

Then Marcus saw Juliette further down the street, wearing her dark green pelisse, Verwood beside her. They appeared to be heading toward one of the carriages. For an instant, Marcus's heart plummeted. Perhaps Juliette had merely been pretending to resist Verwood, all the while plotting an assignation with him. Verwood did have the appearance of a very wealthy man.

Then Marcus saw her try to break free from Verwood's hold. Instantly, he ran up behind them, and shouted for Verwood to release her. Verwood turned, still holding Juliette's arm. She glanced over her shoulder at Marcus, looking relieved to see him.

"Juliette, tell him this is no concern of his," said Verwood. "I've no desire to harm him."

"I have no wish for either of you to fight," she said, her voice defiant. "I only wish to go home quietly. *Alone*."

"You heard Mademoiselle Lamant. Let her go or it will be the worse for you," said Marcus, stepping in front of them and fingering his walking stick as if it concealed a sword. Which, unfortunately, it did not.

"Are you presuming to threaten me, *Lord Dare*?" Verwood looked contemptuous and amused.

"I do not believe in threats, Lord Verwood. Only in action."

His fist hit Verwood's nose with a satisfying crunch that sent the other man staggering backwards, to land on his backside on the dirty pavement.

"Good God, not again," Verwood muttered, struggling to sit up, then lifting a hand to his bleeding nose.

Marcus did not pause to try to understand these words. A few passersby were already staring at them. Soon the audience from the theatre would fill the street.

"Come with me," he commanded Juliette. He took her hand and together they sped down the pavement. Luckily, his own coach was not far down the line. He lost no time in opening the door. Juliette jumped nimbly in and he followed her, shouting to the startled coachman to drive on, and quickly.

Penelope ran out into the street, heart racing madly from the exertion, but even more so from worry. She peered about, but at first all she could see was servants and carriages awaiting the crowd soon to pour out of the theatre.

Where was Juliana? And where was Lord Verwood?

Somehow, her eye had alighted on him as she had looked down at the pit from the box in the balcony that her aunt had hired for the evening. Had she only imagined that his gaze was riveted on Juliana's figure? Had he somehow recognized her friend, or was his interest the same as that of the majority of the male audience? In any case, it was suspicious that his hasty departure from the pit coincided with the end of Juliana's part in the *ballet*. She didn't know what she could do, but she could not sit idly by while Jule might be in danger. She'd ignored her aunt's scandalized shrieks and run headlong from their box, hoping she was not too late to help.

She looked up and down the street again. This time, she caught sight of a man's figure, half-sitting, half-lying on the cold pavement, facing up the street toward Pall Mall. She ran toward the figure, and saw that it was indeed Verwood, holding a handkerchief up to a bloody nose. As he looked up at her, she thought he looked a trifle dazed.

Juliana was not in sight.

"Ah, thank goodness!" she exclaimed, relief flooding through her. Her intrepid friend must have escaped Verwood, and in the process dealt him a much-deserved blow.

"My dear Miss Talcott," murmured Verwood, pulling himself up a little straighter and seeming to come back to himself. "What a thing to say to a gentleman wounded on an errand of chivalry!"

Doubt replaced her sudden sense of relief.

"What do you mean?"

"I mean your friend Juliana has just departed with a scoundrel of no common order. One with an unexpectedly punishing left," he said, somehow regaining his urbane manner even while pressing a blood-soaked handkerchief to his nose.

She pulled her own handkerchief out of her reticule and handed it down to him.

"Tell me what happened. My aunt will be coming after me soon, so make it quick," she said tartly.

"A ministering angel, in truth," he said, with the glimmer

of a smile, half-amused, half-cynical. Slowly, he got to his feet and leaned against the side of the building.

"This is no time for your nonsense. What has happened to Juliana?"

"To escape me, she has flown with a gentleman who calls himself Lord Dare. Whether that is his real name I take leave to doubt. As to his intentions, I am quite certain they are most dishonorable."

"And yours were not?"

He straightened up, and she was startled by a sudden flash of anger in his dark eyes.

"No." Then, in a blink, he smiled. "Miss Talcott, you have the most extraordinary tendency to arouse my ire. While your assumptions are quite understandable, I assure you my only intention was to prevent your friend from landing herself in the devil's own mess. However, I should know better by now than to yield to good intentions."

She studied his face for a moment.

"I do not know why, but I believe you," she said. "Do you know where this Lord Dare might have taken Juliana?"

"I might be able to find out. I collect you are asking me to rescue your friend from the consequences of her folly?"

"Yes. *Please*."

She watched various emotions—exasperation, reluctance and others she could not name—steal across his face, then heard Aunt Mary's voice from the direction of the theatre entrance.

"*Penelope!* You foolish girl, what are you doing?"

She turned to see Aunt Mary hurrying down upon them, then turned back to Verwood.

"Please help Juliana," she entreated him once more.

"Very well. I will try." He strode off with surprising energy, considering his recent injury.

Penelope turned to face her aunt, bracing herself for the inevitable scolding, and praying once again that she had not misplaced her trust in Lord Verwood.

As Marcus's coach rattled off, he settled into the seat beside Juliette. Lights from the streetlamps intermittently pierced the darkness of the carriage, and he saw that her eyes were wide with fear or excitement.

"Juliette, you have nothing to fear now," he said softly, taking one of her hands in his. It was a trifle cold. He began to chafe it between his own, relieved that she did not avoid his clasp.

"I must thank you for rescuing me from Lord Verwood," she said, sounding breathless.

"It was my pleasure," he replied. "I trust he did not frighten you too much."

"No," she replied, but there was a shaky quality to her voice that belied her brave words.

He caressed her hand, exploring it's delicate bones and the velvet texture of her skin as it warmed to his touch. She had always seemed so bold, so independent. What had Verwood done to frighten her so? Had he threatened her with exposure, or perhaps physical violence? Marcus damned his own circumstances, that he could not do more to protect Juliette. But then, she had said she wished for no man's protection.

"Where are you taking me?"

"To my house," he said, and felt her hand tense within his grasp. Heart sinking, he continued, "Or to your lodging, if you think you will be safe there. Do you think Verwood will continue to pursue you?"

"I am quite sure he will," she replied, an unusual hint of despondency in her voice. He'd never seen her at a loss before.

"Have you thought what you will do? Is there any way I can help? Perhaps if you tell me how Verwood threatens you, I can try to put a stop to it."

"I cannot tell you," she replied. "I am grateful for your kindness, but there is nothing you can do."

Marcus felt torn. He wished she would confide in him, but most likely Verwood was a past lover of hers. He did not wish to think about that.

"What will you do, then?"

"I shall have to leave the opera, and London," she replied. "I have a friend in the country who will offer me a safe haven."

A hard rain began to fall, pattering on the roof of the carriage. Marcus knew he should have felt relief in hearing Juliette's plan. He certainly had nothing better or more permanent to offer her. Still, it was a wrench to think their paths would part so soon.

But there was still tonight.

"Then I beg you at least to consider accepting my protection and the shelter of my home for tonight."

"Does Verwood know where you live?"

"He does not," Marcus replied with a glimmer of a smile. Perhaps Verwood had guessed he was not Lord Dare, but there was no reason to think he had discovered his true identity.

The carriage jolted over an uneven patch of cobblestones, flinging Juliette against Marcus. Her hip bumped against his, and he put an arm around her protectively, steadying her even as the carriage righted itself. He heard her let out a little gasp, of fear or excitement, he did not know. An instant later, she slid out of his arms, once again keeping her distance from him.

The surge of excitement he had felt at holding her in his arms ebbed. It was selfish to think of such things when she had just been through such a frightening experience. Still, he longed to make love to her, to see if he could arouse her passions without betraying his own vast inexperience. To pierce her world-weary facade and spark at least a flicker of true feeling in her cynical heart.

Could he reassure her somehow, let her know she was safe in his arms, without destroying the last shreds of hope he held for the evening?

"Come with me, Juliette. I assure you nothing will happen that you do not *desire*."

He knew she was looking at him, but in the fitful light he could not gauge her expression. Finally she answered.

"Very well, my lord. I accept your kind offer."

Chapter Eight

Juliana's pulse raced from the unexpected intimacy of having been thrown against Lord Dare, and at her own boldness in accepting his offer of shelter for the night. Try as she would, she could think of no other choice. She had meant to return to Half Moon Street to gather her belongings before setting out to visit Catherine, but now she knew it would be unsafe. Verwood had made it quite clear he would stop at nothing to get her back under his control, and it would be far too easy for him to discover where she lived.

She risked another glance at Dare, but could not see his face clearly in the dim light. Although she would have preferred to escape from Verwood on her own, she was grateful to Dare for coming to her rescue. She sensed she could trust him not to exact a payment she was not willing to give.

If only she could trust herself as much. Although she could not see him clearly, she felt the warmth of his body beside her, smelled the cologne he wore. She had only to slide closer, press herself against him, and he would take her into his arms and kiss her until she forgot all else. . . .

Desperately, she reminded herself of all the good reasons she had for maintaining her virtue and her independence, why she could not afford to become entangled with any man, even this one. It would take all her resolution to resist him, and she didn't even know how she could do it without jeopardizing her disguise. If she told him even part of the truth, if he guessed that she was a young lady from a respectable household, his chivalrous instincts would prompt him to restore her to her home and family. Unlike the hapless Bow Street Runner Grandpapa had hired, Dare had the intelligence to discover her identify.

The carriage made another turn, once more bringing her in contact with Dare, sending another jolt of unruly excitement through her even as she moved back to her corner of the carriage. Soon they came to a stop. Outside, all was obscured by the driving rain. Juliana realized she had no idea where they were.

"I wish I had brought an umbrella," said Dare, removing his voluminous greatcoat. He climbed out of the carriage, and held the greatcoat out over her with one arm as he held out his other to help her descend.

Quickly, she climbed out. Together, they sped up the steps, Dare's limp exaggerated a little as he hurried to keep her dry. His greatcoat provided some protection, but still one side of her pelisse was drenched by the time they reached the entrance hall.

"Good evening, my lord," said the elderly butler who held the door for them.

"Good evening, Barnes," replied Dare.

Juliana looked about the marble entrance hall, gaining a brief impression of elegance. She looked back at the butler, feeling some embarrassment at arriving at a nobleman's establishment in such a scandalous manner. The butler's expression registered only a polite welcome, but Juliana thought she detected a gleam of pride in his eyes as they rested on Dare. It was confusing. She was glad there were no other servants about to witness her entrance.

"My lord, perhaps you and the lady would prefer to repair to the drawing room. There is a good fire there where you may warm yourselves."

She followed Dare through a door to the left. She saw an elegant room, decorated in shades of blue and dull gold. A gilded *chaise longue* upholstered in blue velvet had been drawn up to face the hearth, with a low Pembroke table in front of it. Vases of hothouse flowers and slender branches of candles adorned several mahogany side tables, filling the room with a soft, flickering light and beguiling fragrance. Now she knew for certain that Dare had been expecting her to return with him.

She shivered, unsure whether she felt hot or cold.

"I hope you've not taken a chill," said Dare, looking over at her as Barnes helped him out of his dark coat, folding it over the greatcoat he had already taken from his master.

Then Barnes cleared his throat. "If you remove your pelisse, Madame, I can make sure it is dry by the morning. Or would you prefer a maid be summoned to assist you?"

"Thank you, but that will not be necessary," she said. She fumbled a little as she undid the buttons of her wet pelisse, then handed it to Barnes. She went to stand in front of the fire. Dare and the butler exchanged a few words she did not catch, then the butler left them alone.

Dare came to join her in front of the fire, his snowy white shirt and gray satin waistcoat gleaming in the candlelight and somehow enhancing the breadth of his shoulders. Odd how merely the removal of his coat made their situation seem even more intimate. There was a disturbing warmth in his eyes, making her acutely conscious of the costume she had not taken time to remove before leaving the theatre. Although the rain had not soaked through to the filmy layers of gauze, her dress was still revealing enough to make the heat mount in her cheeks. Somehow, it seemed more wicked to wear it in the privacy of Dare's home than it had to let hundreds see her in it on the stage. There, she had been playing a role. This was *real*. She would have to keep her wits about her or she would find herself yielding to the seduction Dare evidently planned for her.

She started as he cleared his throat.

"I have asked Barnes to bring us some food and wine," he said, an unexpected hesitancy in his voice. "I thought perhaps you might enjoy a small supper."

"Thank you, my lord," she replied. "I dine lightly before performances, so I am usually ravenous once the *ballet* is over."

She hoped her voice did not reveal how breathless she felt. She'd spoken the truth, except that tonight she could not even think about eating. She forced herself to think about her plans. After supping with Dare, she would ask to be conducted to her bedchamber. He might be disappointed, but she felt sure he would comply. On the morrow, she would pack the few possessions she had at Half Moon Street and begin the journey to Cumberland.

She would probably never see Dare again.

The butler reentered the room, bearing a tray containing several covered dishes, two crystal flutes and a silver bucket containing a bottle of champagne. Deftly, he set the tray down on the table in front of the *chaise longue*, whisked the covers off the dishes and poured champagne into the flutes. After he had gone, Juliana sat down, and Dare joined her. She took a cautious sip of the sparkling wine, knowing it must be a drink Mademoiselle Juliette enjoyed. The effervescence tickled her mouth, and a tingling warmth spread through her as she carefully set her glass down. In doing so, she shifted slightly, and came into contact with Dare's muscular thigh. Trying to appear unaffected, she took a bite of one of the lobster patties. It was delicious, but she did not know how she would do justice to it, or the rest of the meal, while sitting so intimately with Dare.

"Do you not care for the champagne?" he asked, raising an eyebrow at her glass.

"It is delightful," she replied, and resolutely sipped some more.

He refilled her glass. After finishing the lobster patty, she sampled some of the other carefully prepared delicacies on the tray, and recklessly emptied her glass. The champagne was delicious, and even Grandpapa's chef was not capable of such culinary delights. Was this how gentlemen treated their mistresses? Had Dare entertained other ladies here in such a manner? She did not care for the thought.

"Would you care for a bite of the raspberry tart?" Dare asked. "My chef takes great pride in his pastries."

Before she could help herself, he lifted a bit of the tart to her mouth. She accepted it, finding the berries and cream made somehow even sweeter and richer by Dare's feeding them to her. Knowing she should not, she allowed him to serve her the rest of the tart. A flush rose in her cheeks as he wiped crumbs from her lips. His hazel eyes seemed darker, almost green, full of a different sort of hunger.

When he finished, she slid over on the *chaise longue*, away from the small round table, and stood up.

"Thank you for the delightful meal, my lord. Now I should like to retire."

"If you wish, although I had hoped you would stay and keep me company for a while longer," he said as he stood up. "Please trust me, Juliette. You will come to no harm here. I will do nothing you do not *desire*."

Once again that word hung temptingly in the air between them. She hesitated, poised to leave but unwilling to go.

"Stay," he repeated quietly. "I wish to talk to you."

Desire curled warmly in her stomach at his softened voice.

"What is it you wish to discuss with me?" she asked, desperately striving for a dispassionate tone.

"A number of things," he replied steadily, though doubt clouded his eyes at her manner. Stiffly, he walked over to a bellpull and pulled it.

Almost instantaneously, the elderly butler reappeared. With quick, deft movements, he cleared the trays and glasses from the Pembroke table, folded it and set it to one side of the hearth. Having ascertained that Dare had no further orders, he bowed himself out, leaving them alone once again. There was a resigned note in Dare's voice as he broke the silence, but she sensed a deep underlying regret in his manner.

"I will be leaving London myself within a few days. Before then, I should like to know that you are out of Verwood's reach. Are you certain your friend in the country can provide you with a safe refuge?"

"Yes," she replied, pretending a confidence she did not feel. She knew Catherine would welcome her, but would Catherine's respectable husband extend his protection as well? If he did not, she might have to return to Grandpapa.

She felt chilled, now that half the room separated her from Dare. Suddenly the thought of a future without him held little appeal.

"If you wish, I will escort you back to your lodgings tomorrow so that you can prepare for your journey."

"Thank you," she said, grateful for his unspoken promise of protection.

"It is nothing," he replied, going over to the mantel. From it, he picked up a small, dark box that had escaped her notice earlier. "Please sit down. I have something for you."

She sat back down on the *chaise longue*. He sat down beside her and handed her the box, which she now saw was a small jewelry case.

"I cannot accept this," she said on impulse, holding it toward him. He recoiled, and she wondered if she had given herself away. Surely Mademoiselle Juliette always accepted such gifts from her gentlemen friends.

"I expect nothing from you in exchange," he said, almost roughly.

She relaxed slightly. Still, it would not be right to take it from him.

"It is a mere trifle," he insisted. "Take it, and remember me when you wear it."

His words reminded her that he would be leaving England soon. That she might never see him again.

The firelight clearly illuminated his profile. She thought the faint lines around his eyes and mouth that pain had etched onto his young, aristocratic features had deepened. She remembered what his foolish friends had said about his mysterious occupation. Was he planning to leave for the Continent on some mission of secret diplomacy? Could his life be in peril?

He was still waiting for her to open the jewelry case, so she obliged him. Sapphires and diamonds in a delicate brooch shaped like a spray of flowers shone up at her from the dark velvet case. He could not have chosen anything more beautiful, or that suited her better.

"It is lovely," she said, "but I would think of you even if I did not have it."

"I am glad."

"Where are you going? What will you do there?" She could not help but ask the questions.

"I cannot say."

"When will you return to London?"

"I cannot say. Perhaps never."

So it was true. He was leaving on some dangerous errand, from which he might not return. Instinctively, she moved closer to him. He put an arm around her, lightly brushing her bare arm.

"Oh, Juliette," he whispered, leaning his face against her hair. "I wish I knew your real name."

"I wish I could tell you," she said, moving her head, making the mistake of looking in his eyes, darkened with suppressed passion.

Then he pressed her close, kissing her with an ardor even greater than their earlier kisses at the theatre. Overcome with warmth and champagne and the bitter feeling that they were soon to part, she returned his caresses. Greedily, desperately she twined her tongue with his, but glorious as their kiss was, still she hungered for more. Tears pricked her eyes as he finally released her lips.

"Be my love tonight, Juliette," he whispered.

She could not even speak, but summoned up the last shreds of her self-control and shook her head.

"I cannot."

"If you are concerned, I have the means to prevent . . . consequences."

A few weeks ago, she might not have understood what he meant, but she had learned much from her fellow dancers. To make love without consequences. . . . No, it was impossible. Once she had thought they could kiss without consequences, but she had been wrong. Now she knew that every intimacy would only strengthen her attachment to him, and deepen the pain of their parting.

She did not want to care so much.

"Please. All I ask is one evening of beauty and passion and pleasure. I may not have such an opportunity again."

The longing in his voice pierced her to the core. Perhaps it was love, heightened by the sort of desperation a soldier felt on the eve of battle. How could she deny him? And yet, how could she comply, inexperienced as she was?

"What do you wish from me?" she asked, her voice shaky.

"Let us pretend we are young lovers, that we have not known any others. Let us explore each other as if it were our first time."

Our first time. Was this some sort of game he enjoyed? But no, there was a desperate urgency in his voice, and she found herself melting. How could she walk away now, when he offered her the greatest adventure of her life? How could she part from him, tomorrow, knowing that she had denied him what might be a final glimpse of joy before he faced his fate, whatever it was?

She leaned forward and gave him his answer in a kiss. He encircled her in his arms for a moment, then gently pushed her down until she arched back against the large, soft bolster on her end of the *chaise longue*. Realizing she still held the jewelry box, she set it carefully down on the carpet under the sofa. Dare lifted her legs up, then lay down beside her and kissed her again. As they lay, touching from head to foot, she knew there was no turning back. She only hoped he would not stop when he discovered her innocence.

He kissed her ear, her neck, the hollow at the base of her throat. She gasped as his long fingers caressed her shoulders, parting the sides of her bodice, pushing down the twining leaves and pale gauze of her costume until he had bared her almost to the waist. He raised up on one elbow to gaze at her. Instinctively, she raised a hand to cover herself.

"Let me look at you, love."

Feeling as if her entire body blushed, she lowered her hand. Dare watched her longingly, almost as if he had never seen a lady's body before. But it must be part of his fantasy. He probably thought her own modest gesture part of the game as well.

To cover her confusion, she raised a hand to loosen his cravat. He stopped her, holding her hand in his.

"Wait, my darling," he murmured. "I wish to please you first."

He captured her lips again, then released them to press his own hotly against the base of her throat. Then, with a slowness that was at once a torture and a delight, he trailed kisses down her chest, touching and tasting all the tender, sensitive flesh he had exposed earlier. She gasped with pleasure, first at the heat of his mouth, then at the cooler air that wafted over her as he lifted his head away from her.

"That did not hurt, did it?" he asked.

She shook her head, amused. He was pretending again. Surely he knew the pleasure he gave her.

He kissed her again. Now his hand roved over her, gliding down her stomach, down her legs. Then back up, sliding the flimsy fabric of her skirt up between her legs. Blushing, she closed her legs, but he soothed her with sweet, soft whispered endearments. Slowly, she opened herself to him, every muscle taut with anticipation of what might come next.

After an agonizing moment, he moved his hand, slowly pushing her dress aside, then beginning a slow, feather-light exploration that stoked her hunger for even more intimate caresses. She moaned. He paused, and she pushed herself against his hand, shocked at her own boldness. He continued to stroke and tickle and tease until the pleasure became almost unbearable. She twisted, turning away from him, caught between his firm body and the low back of the *chaise longue*, but as quickly turned back, ravenous for more. She put up a hand to stifle a sudden cry, and once again he soothed her in a soft whisper.

"Cry out if you wish, love. I want to know if I please you."

He caressed her again, using his fingers to wicked effect. As he touched and searched, each spot seemed more sensitive than the last. A frantic hunger possessed her, causing her to twist and push against him, seeking ever greater heights of pleasure. She closed her eyes and threw an arm around him, desperate to hold onto something. A sudden ecstasy shook her to the core, and she could no longer hold back her cries.

She came back to herself, slowly, awed by the power of what she had just experienced. She opened her eyes and looked at Dare. He was smiling, looking absurdly delighted at having brought her to such a peak. The joy in his eyes deepened as he continued to gaze at her.

"Take me with you," she said.

He stared at her in astonishment, and she wondered what madness had prompted her.

"What do you mean?"

"Take me with you, away from London," she repeated, with growing confidence. Surely this was meant to be. She could not go back to the opera; she had no wish to go back to her previous life. Why not share in the adventures that awaited Dare? Perhaps she could even help him somehow.

He shook his head, but his voice was hoarse as he replied. "I wish I could, but I cannot. All we have is this night."

He laid his head against her breast and held her against him, running a hand gently along her back. Then he began to kiss her again. She put her arm back around him, and his touch became less gentle, more insistent as he traced her contours, pressing her against him so closely that she heard his quickened breath, sensed his growing excitement. She shivered a little, wanting him to take *his* pleasure, too. Dare lowered her onto her back, and began to caress her intimately again. A renewed hunger took hold of her. He was so skilled. She relaxed, knowing all would be well.

Suddenly, Dare lifted his head.

Juliana noticed muffled sounds. The butler's voice, raised in protest, mingled with the deeper tones of another man and the higher notes of several ladies. They were all coming closer.

Dare got up, looking angrily toward the door. Juliana sat up, bereft of Dare's warmth, her passion draining away at the thought of being observed by strangers. With trembling fingers, she rearranged her dress to cover herself as much as possible.

The door opened.

"Why shouldn't he receive us? What is it? Is he drunk?" a voice bellowed, and Juliana realized at least one of Dare's visitors was no stranger. Why would Lord Plumbrook come here of all places?

She dove down behind the back of the *chaise longue*. Perhaps she could hide while Dare diverted his visitors elsewhere. Holding her breath, she listened to the butler make one final attempt to repel the visitors. She peeked up at Dare, in time to see the stunned expression on his face as one word fell from his lips.

"Mama!"

Chapter Nine

Juliana huddled quietly behind the low, curved back of the *chaise longue*, horrified at the prospect of being discovered in such a position, not only by Lord and Lady Plumbrook, but by Dare's mother as well.

"Yes, dear Marcus, it is I," answered the sweet, cultured voice she had heard earlier.

There was a rustle of skirts, and Juliana realized Dare's mother must be coming forward to embrace her son. Swiftly, Dare moved away from the *chaise longue*.

"What is going on here?" his mother asked. "The roses . . . the champagne . . . ah! You have a ladylove here with you! How wonderful for you, my darling! But so dreadful of us to interrupt you. My friends, we must leave them alone at once!"

Juliana's mind reeled at this speech. The lady sounded positively delighted.

"*You* may think this is wonderful, ma'am," said Lord Plumbrook. "Have you thought of the consequences if the wrong parties get wind of this?"

"My dear Margaret, Plummy is right," added a voice Juliana recognized as Lady Plumbrook's. "If word were to get round, all our plans could come to naught."

What plans? Juliana wondered. How could Lord and Lady Plumbrook possibly be involved in any scheme involving Dare?

"I am afraid the plan you so kindly proposed has failed

already," replied Dare, a grim note in his voice. "Now, perhaps, we could retreat to my study to discuss the matter?"

Juliana breathed a prayer that they would all fall in with Dare's suggestion and she could leave the house without being discovered. She had no idea where to go now, but she would think of something, anything to escape this insane situation.

Before anyone could reply, more voices were heard from the hall. The butler's voice again raised in protest. And then, Grandpapa's. Dear heaven! He must have traced her here somehow. She tensed, hearing more footsteps come over the threshold.

"Good evening, my lords, my ladies," said Grandpapa, in a hurried greeting. The anxiety in his voice tugged at Juliana. "I would not disturb you all at such an hour were it not that I have received some frightening news."

"It is not something to do with . . . with the letter you wrote us about dear Juliana, is it?" asked Lady Plumbrook nervously.

"I am afraid it is. Today, Lord Amberley discovered the truth, that she has run away. Now I have just received a missive from a Lord Verwood informing me that she has been masquerading as a dancer at the King's Theatre, and has now been foolish enough to run off with a gentleman of dubious reputation."

"Verwood!" exclaimed the Plumbrooks in unison.

"An opera dancer?" asked Dare, in an odd, strangled voice.

Juliana cringed. She could no longer see his face, but there was no doubt that he now suspected her identity.

A short pause ensued, broken by Lady Plumbrook.

"Mr. Hutton, Lord Verwood is one of the most notorious rakes in London," said Lady Plumbrook, sounding puzzled. "I am surprised he did not run off with her himself."

"It is said," replied her husband, "that Verwood maintains his style of living by blackmailing persons of wealth who have secrets they wish to hide."

"Good God!" said Grandpapa. "But scandal is not the worst I have to fear. If what Verwood says is true, Juliana may be in the clutches of an even more dangerous rake.

Verwood wrote that the gentleman calls himself Lord Dare, but Verwood doubts that is his true name."

"Is this why you have come here tonight?" asked Dare, his voice still sounding taut and strange.

"I've come because that dolt from Bow Street claims he saw the tall dancer who pretends to be French ride away in a carriage with the Amberley crest. But I doubt—"

"Amberley!" The name escaped Juliana's lips before she could stop herself.

Another brief silence ensued.

"Who is that? Show yourself," Grandpapa demanded hoarsely.

She heard muffled footsteps on the carpet coming closer, and knew it was useless to hide any longer. She got up and turned to face Grandpapa, steeling herself for his ire. A collective gasp echoed faintly through the room, and Juliana blushed, realizing what a shocking appearance she must present.

For a moment everyone stared at her. She met Dare's gaze. His eyes were wide with shock and consternation.

No, not Dare's eyes. *Amberley's.*

As she struggled to make sense of what had just happened, he moved his hand as if to remove his coat, perhaps to give it to her, and then stopped, apparently realizing he no longer wore it. Then the tall, graceful lady beside him rushed over to Juliana and draped a shawl around her shoulders.

"My dear Miss Hutton, I am so delighted to meet you. I am Mrs. Redwyck, Marcus's mother," she said, a comforting smile on her face.

Juliana pulled the shawl around her, a sense of disaster conquering her ability to think. She looked to Grandpapa. His expression was grim.

"Good God, look at you, child!" he said. "What have you done with your face? Your hair? You look like a veritable trollop! How could you do such a thing?"

She lifted her chin and met his gaze. Defiant words came to her lips, but then she saw the tears leaking from the corners of his eyes, eyes she'd never seen shed tears before.

"Oh, Grandpapa," she cried, and ran into his arms. He pulled her into an awkward but warm embrace.

"My little Juliana," he murmured. "Thank Heaven you are safe. Why did you run away?"

She lifted her face, her resolve returning. "I did not mean to worry you so, but I had to prove to you that I could fend for myself. I *could* not marry Lord Amberley—"

She disengaged herself, and turned to stare at Dare. *Amberley.*

"You!" she exploded. "You knew, did you not? It was all a scheme, a plot to get me here and compromise me so I would have no choice but to marry you!"

"I did not know," he insisted, but she knew better than to trust his air of candor.

"You must have, but how did you find out? How did I give myself away?"

"I tell you I did not know who you were!"

"If you did not, why did you call yourself Lord Dare?"

"Yes, why?" asked Grandpapa. "Perhaps you will tell me how it comes that you and my granddaughter are here, alone, at such an hour?"

Juliana relaxed slightly as she watched Amberley pause, struggling to think of a satisfactory answer. Perhaps now Grandpapa would support her resolution not to marry the rogue.

Then Lord Plumbrook cleared his throat, drawing attention away from Amberley.

"He rescued her from Lord Verwood, of course," he said, once they were all looking at him.

Grandpapa looked sharply at Lord Plumbrook, then at Amberley.

"Is that the truth?"

"Lord Verwood certainly tried to take Miss Hutton with him after the opera," said Amberley slowly. "As she was clearly unwilling, I could not help but intervene."

"Why did you call yourself Lord Dare?"

Amberley paused before replying. "Friends invited me to accompany them to the theatre, and to the Green Room where the dancers practice. I did not wish to cause you or Miss Hutton embarrassment by letting it be known that I visited such a place while I am thought to be courting her."

She looked over at Grandpapa. There was a thoughtful expression on his face. Heavens! Was he wavering?

"You do not believe him, do you?" she demanded. "I still think he planned the entire thing."

Grandpapa looked back at Amberley. "Can you honestly say you did not know her identity? What were your intentions, my lord?"

Surely Grandpapa had Amberley at a disadvantage now. He would have to admit either to being a fortune hunter, or a libertine. Looking over, she saw Amberley look back at her, his eyes full of unspoken meaning, as if entreating her to go along with what he was about to say.

He squared his shoulders and turned toward Grandpapa. "I told you the truth when I said I did not know who she was. I must admit, however, that my intentions in bringing her to my house were . . . amorous."

Juliana studied the faces of everyone else in the room. Neither Amberley's mother nor the Plumbrooks looked particularly shocked. Even Grandpapa's expression was less disapproving than she had hoped.

"Well, it seems you *are* a Redwyck, but at least you're honest," he said, somewhat grudgingly, then looked back at Juliana. She knew he was wondering how far Amberley's plan had progressed. If her folly was exposed. . . .

"I must tell you, sir, that your granddaughter resisted all my advances," said Amberley. "Being a gentleman, I did not force myself upon her. We were just discussing how she could most safely hide from Lord Verwood when the Plumbrooks and my mother arrived."

Grandpapa looked relieved, but Juliana did not know what to make of Amberley's lies. Was he protecting her reputation? Or was he just trying to win Grandpapa's approval?

"Yes, and we have not yet been properly introduced," said Amberley's mother, smiling at Grandpapa.

Amberley performed the introductions, and Grandpapa bowed courteously toward Mrs. Redwyck.

"I am delighted to meet you, Mr. Hutton," she said.

"The pleasure is mine, Mrs. Redwyck, but I must apologize for my granddaughter's wild behavior. I don't doubt you find all of this terribly shocking."

"Not at all," she replied. "I must admit, I was not pleased with this scheme for my son to court your granddaughter. However, now that I have met her, I see she is just the bride for dear Marcus."

Juliana stared at her, wondering if the lady had escaped from Bedlam. But there was no sign of insanity in Mrs. Redwyck's liquid brown eyes, only a friendliness Juliana could not fathom. What sort of mother would welcome a daughter-in-law who had graced the stage?

One who coveted that daughter-in-law's dowry as much as her son did. Juliana's resolution hardened at the thought of the trap she had nearly fallen into. Perhaps now she could turn Amberley's lies to her own advantage.

"I am not going to marry Amberley," she announced. "He has not compromised me, so there is no need for us to marry."

"Of course you must marry him," objected Lady Plumbrook.

"Why?"

"If you do not, Verwood will bleed your grandfather dry to keep silent about this whole business," said Lord Plumbrook sternly.

Juliana shivered, and looked at Grandpapa.

"Lord Plumbrook is right. You must marry Amberley," he said, his resolve evident in the set of his jaw.

"Is that all that matters to you? Money? Do not let it worry you. I should rather lose my reputation than be wed to a two-faced fortune hunter!"

Amberley winced. Everyone else looked shocked.

"Of course it is not the money!" said Grandpapa.

Looking into his ravaged face, she saw how anxious he was over the possible loss of her reputation. But she could not give herself to Amberley just to avoid a scandal.

"I spoke in anger, Grandpapa," she said in a milder tone, "but you must believe I am in earnest when I say I will not marry Amberley."

Mrs. Redwyck stepped forward and laid a gentle hand on her shoulder. Juliana backed away defiantly.

"My dear Miss Hutton, please reconsider," said Mrs. Redwyck. "Please allow my son to explain himself. Perhaps in private?"

"No," said Juliana, resolving never to allow Amberley to explain anything to her. Particularly not in private.

"Enough of this nonsense, child," said Grandpapa, impatiently. "There is nothing to discuss. You are coming home now, and we will insert the notice of your engagement into the newspapers tomorrow."

"You may insert all the notices you wish, but I will not marry him!"

It seemed to Juliana that each person in the room, except for Amberley himself, began to harangue, scold or cajole her. She stood stock-still, letting their words rain over her, determined not to give in.

"May I make a suggestion?"

Juliana glanced over at Lord Amberley, but it seemed that the others had not heard his soft-voiced question. He repeated himself, more loudly, and the others fell silent.

"I am afraid Miss Hutton's reluctance to marry me is quite understandable," he said, his voice disarmingly rueful.

Both Grandpapa and Lady Plumbrook began to speak, but Amberley raised a hand to stop them.

"No, please do not interrupt me. Miss Hutton has not had the opportunity to become acquainted with me or my character. Although I am willing to marry her in any case, I cannot think our marriage will be happy if she is forced into it."

He paused to let his words sink in. Juliana winced to see how the others were nodding their understanding. She could not tell them she *had* become acquainted with Amberley, not without exposing her own folly.

"However, I do see that Miss Hutton's reputation is now at risk, for which I am partially to blame," Amberley continued. He looked over at her, his expression entreating her understanding.

She looked back coldly. His calm, reasonable manner was infuriating, along with the way he had assumed command of the situation.

"What I should like to suggest is that we make public our engagement, but allow Miss Hutton some time, perhaps a month, in which to become better acquainted with me. If she decides that she still does not wish to marry me, she may end our engagement."

"Do you think that will stop Verwood from spreading his vile tales?" asked Grandpapa.

"Of course it would," said Lady Plumbrook. "Once it is known that dear Juliana is to marry an earl, and one of such ancient lineage, Verwood will find it hard to convince people she ever made an appearance on the stage."

"Would it not cause a great deal of talk if my granddaughter breaks off the engagement?"

"People would gossip," replied Lady Plumbrook, "but it would be nothing compared to the scandal that threatens us now. Besides, once Juliana comes to know dear Amberley better, she will not wish to cry off."

Lady Plumbrook looked at her fondly. Once again, Juliana was thrown into indecision. Lord Amberley's suggestion presented a compromise, one that offered her a chance of escape while sparing Grandpapa the grief of a scandal. Could she refuse?

"Of course she will not wish to cry off," said Mrs. Redwyck, echoing Lady Plumbrook. "May I make a suggestion now? I think Miss Hutton should come to visit us at Redwyck Hall. We can say she wishes to begin making some changes there before the marriage, which will give her some time to become better acquainted with all of us before she makes up her mind."

"A capital idea!" said Grandpapa.

"Yes, and it will allow time for the dye to fade from her hair before she must appear in public again," added Lady Plumbrook, ever practical.

Juliana could not deny that the plan was sensible, but she felt as if a soft net was slowly twining itself around her.

"Please, Miss Hutton, consider our suggestion," said Amberley. "For the sake of your own reputation, and for your grandfather's sake, if nothing else."

She looked back at him. He stood still, his face tense and expectant. Their eyes met, and for an instant, he was Lord Dare once more, his expression full of yearning. She could almost believe that he did long to know her better, to discover who she was now that he knew her name. But it was all very likely a ruse to win her trust. Could she trust him to keep the line when she was at his home?

She looked back at Grandpapa. A muscle twitched in his cheek. Clearly, he was taking pains to keep quiet, desperately trying not to antagonize her while at the same time hoping the others' arguments would win her over. It hurt to see him so troubled.

"Very well, my lord," she said, addressing herself to Amberley. "I will consent to be engaged to you, and to be a visitor in your home."

An almost audible sigh of relief arose from the older members of the group. Even though she did not look at him, she knew Amberley watched her closely as she finished her speech.

"But know this: I agree to your plan only to spare my grandfather concern. In one month's time I *shall* cry off from our engagement, and nothing you say or do will dissuade me."

Marcus endured Miss Hutton's cold looks as he bade her and her grandfather farewell, and saw them and the Plumbrooks to their carriages. He would not place even the smallest of wagers on the chance of her anger cooling by morning, when he was pledged to visit the Huttons again.

As the coaches drove off, he came back to the entrance hall, to find Mama smiling at him tenderly.

"Well, my darling, I suspect it will take a few more minutes for your servants to get a bedchamber ready for me, and for Dora to unpack my things. Let us go back to the drawing room and sit down, so you can tell me the whole story."

The whole story flashed through his mind, which boggled at the thought of relating it to his mother.

"Come, you know I am not easily shocked, dear. Can you not see I am positively dying to hear about your lovely Miss Hutton?"

"Yes, Mama, I can see that," he said, taking her arm to lead her back to the drawing room. "I would rather know why you have arrived here at such an hour."

As he had hoped, the question diverted her. She smiled coyly as she replied.

"The Plumbrooks were coming down for the Season, and were kind enough to offer me a seat in their coach. Then we were delayed by the rain."

"Yes, but you know that is not what I asked, Mama. Why have you come to London?"

"Mr. Wilson at the Minerva Press has expressed an interest in *The Perils of Francesca*!"

"That is excellent!" he said. "But I am not at all surprised. I knew all you had to do to engage their interest was to complete the story."

"So sweet of you to have such faith in me, my darling son. However, the terms Mr. Wilson offered were so paltry that I thought it would be better to come in person to negotiate with him rather than to do so through correspondence."

They entered the drawing room, and his mother sat down. Marcus stood by the fire, shaken by the thought of what had transpired in this room, how the warm, passionate Juliette had suddenly transformed herself into the cold, contemptuous Miss Hutton. He still found it difficult to reconcile the two; he felt as if he had tried to seduce a stranger.

"Did you hear what I said, Marcus?"

He wrenched his thoughts away from Juliette—*Miss Hutton*—and back to his mother.

"I am sorry, Mama. What did you say?"

"I was telling you how I planned to manage things with Mr. Wilson. But I see your mind is more interestingly occupied. I cannot blame you, darling. She is delightful!"

"She is furious with me."

"She has spirit as well as beauty—just the sort of girl I would have chosen for you. By the way, I think you handled the situation beautifully."

"I could not allow them all to coerce her into marriage with me. You do believe me when I say I had no plan to compromise her?" He flushed as he asked the question. One did not discuss such matters with one's mother, no matter how liberal-minded she was.

"I know you are always truthful," his mother replied, nodding. "I am only delighted to see you finally allowed your Redwyck tendencies a little free rein."

"And you can see where it has led."

"Do not browbeat yourself! Of course, things are in

rather a muddle now, but I have every confidence in a happy outcome."

Marcus remained silent, thinking of the fury he had seen blazing from Miss Hutton's brilliant blue eyes as she had accused him of intentionally compromising her. Would he ever convince her that he had acted out of a *grande passion* for Mademoiselle Juliette? And would it help if he did?

Which was worse—to be thought a rake or a fortune hunter?

"You are in love with her, are you not, dearest?" Mama asked with a knowing look.

"Can I be in love with someone whom I hardly know? Perhaps I was only letting myself get caught up in a fleeting fantasy. But there was . . . is . . . something about her. I can't explain. In any case, I've ruined everything."

"Don't be so gloomy! She may be angry now, but she will come around. Now, I think you should drink a little of your uncle's excellent brandy, and go to bed. Things will seem better in the morning, I assure you."

She yawned and got up from the *chaise longue*. "Dora must be ready for me by now. Good night, Marcus."

She kissed him, and left.

He remained in the room. Now that Mama was gone, the smell of the flowers he had ordered, the candles flickering low in their sconces, were all a potent reminder of Juliette. Of her vivid blue eyes, darkened with passion, of her soft skin, of her sweet cries as she had responded so delightfully to his first attempt at seduction. They had come so close . . . and *that* would have been an even greater disaster.

He paced, knowing he should be thinking of his lands, of his mother and Lucy, and how he could salvage this situation to their advantage. It was useless; all he could think about was the mysterious creature who had so enthralled him, and who was now so fiercely determined to spurn his suit. He still ached with desire for her, but could he ever hope to recapture the passion they had shared this night?

Chapter Ten

The carriage ride back to Russell Square was a quiet one. Juliana was thankful that Grandpapa did not seem inclined to question her further over what had happened. Mrs. Frisby greeted them, apparently having stayed up to watch out for their return. Her thin face, already lined beyond her years, lit up with relief at the sight of Juliana.

"My dear! Thank goodness you are safe," she said, giving Juliana a shaky embrace. "What have you done with your hair? You must tell me everything that has happened. What—"

"You had better get her upstairs first, before any of the servants see that hair," interrupted Grandpapa, sending Mrs. Frisby nervously spurting towards the stairs.

"Good night, Grandpapa," said Juliana as she turned to follow Mrs. Frisby.

"Good night, child," he added in a softer voice.

Once in the safety of Juliana's room, Mrs. Frisby rang for Polly to come and attend her mistress. Polly hurried in, looking overjoyed at Juliana's return. As Polly helped Juliana prepare for bed, both women pelted her with questions and fussed over her as if it were a miracle that she had survived over a month away from their care. Juliana kept her explanations brief, bearing their shock and subsequent excitement at her engagement to Lord Amberley as best she could.

When they left, she sat down at her writing table to compose short notes to Madame Bouchard and to Penelope, reassuring them that she was safe and well, at her grandfather's house. She would make sure they were delivered next morning.

She got into bed, feeling restless despite the late hour. She tried to think through everything that had happened, and plan how best to escape her engagement to Lord Amberley. However, her mind stubbornly refused to concentrate, instead recalling the way he had looked, how he had touched her, the pleasure he had given her, the like of which she had never even imagined. . . .

She turned over, reminding herself that Amberley had seduced her in order to win Grandpapa's fortune. Like a perfect ninny, she had woven a fantasy about him that had nothing to do with the reality, believing him when he had all but told her he was departing on a dangerous mission for his country. She had even offered to go with him, thinking he offered her a chance for freedom and adventures she'd only imagined. Fool that she was!

He was probably laughing at her right now, and congratulating himself for having maneuvered her into a pretense of an engagement. No doubt he hoped that once at Redwyck Hall, he would be able to charm her back into his arms.

She was not going to allow it. She would cry off, even if it meant more years spent in suffocating dullness in this very house, with Grandpapa and Mrs. Frisby. How to avoid that fate was a far more difficult matter, and she finally drifted off, still struggling for an answer.

She slept late into the next morning, and awoke feeling disoriented by the sight of the blue and gold bed curtains and painted furniture with which Grandpapa had furnished her room just prior to her return from Miss Stratton's school. It was almost as if her masquerade, the time she had spent living at Madame Bouchard's house, and her association with Lord Dare had all been an outlandish dream. Sitting up, she caught a flash of reddish-gold hair reflected in the mirror across the room. No, it had not been a dream. Once again images and sensations from the previous night assailed her as her traitorous body tingled with remembered delight.

Then she recalled what Lord Amberley had done, and why, and she burned again, this time with fury at the trap that he had laid for her. Resolutely, she got out of bed and rang for Polly to help her dress.

"Good morning, Miss," said Polly, smiling far too cheerfully as she brought in a cup of steaming chocolate a few minutes later.

Juliana resisted the impulse to ask Polly what was good about it, and instead returned her maid's greeting. As she accepted the cup of chocolate, she asked Polly the time.

"It's just past eleven o'clock, Miss. Mrs. Frisby and your grandfather are at church. Seeing as you were so tired last night and we have been telling everyone you've been sick, they decided to let you sleep. Breakfast is still laid out in the parlor, if you fancy some."

"Of course." Juliana set down her cup, and arose from the bed. She remembered that Grandpapa had bade Lord Amberley to visit them today, and decided she wished to speak to Grandpapa before that happened.

She chose one of her most modest morning dresses. After Polly had helped her into it, and tied a cap onto her head, Juliana eyed herself in the mirror. She could not help chuckling at her demure, Quakerish appearance. Nothing could be a greater contrast with the dashing Mademoiselle Juliette. If only it were bad enough to make Lord Amberley regret their engagement!

She sobered, knowing it was no use hoping she could disgust him into withdrawing his offer. No doubt he was just like Charles Bentwood. The only difference between them was that Bentwood had been a clumsy villain, and Amberley had been anything but clumsy. . . .

"That will be all, Polly," she said more sharply than she intended. "Thank you," she added in a softened tone before leaving the room.

She had barely sat down when Grandpapa and Mrs. Frisby entered the morning parlor, where it was their custom to breakfast after services. They both smiled at her broadly, and she wished she could be as delighted to have returned as everyone was to see her.

As she poured some coffee for Grandpapa, Juliana once

again had to endure her companion's felicitations on her engagement.

"Thank you, Mrs. Frisby," she replied. "But I must tell you that I have every intention of crying off from this engagement after a suitable period has elapsed."

Mrs. Frisby threw a nervous, questioning look at Juliana's grandfather.

Juliana watched Grandpapa for signs of anger. Though there was a worried crease in his forehead, he remained calm as he replied. "Juliana has not had a proper opportunity to become acquainted with Lord Amberley. She may change her mind after a month at Redwyck Hall."

"She may indeed. I imagine it is a lovely place, and from what I hear, Lord Amberley is the handsomest of gentlemen. To think we shall see you a countess!"

There was a wistful note in Mrs. Frisby's voice, and a trace of anxiety in her smile, but her good wishes were sincere. Mrs. Frisby had shared Grandpapa's hopes that Juliana would make a good marriage, but at the same time there was no doubt she wondered what would become of her once that happened.

Juliana smiled at her reassuringly. "Dear Mrs. Frisby, I assure you Lord Amberley's rank means nothing to me, and no matter how beautiful a place Redwyck Hall is, it cannot tempt me into matrimony. But even if I do marry someday, you will always have a place with me."

Mrs. Frisby's eyes filled with tears of gratitude.

"In fact, I fully expect you will accompany me to Redwyck Hall," said Juliana, realizing that would be no bad thing. Much as Mrs. Frisby had supported Grandpapa's wishes for Juliana to marry, she had always been a careful chaperone.

"Surely Mrs. Redwyck's chaperonage will suffice," objected Grandpapa, scowling.

Juliana bit her lip to hold back a rash reply, and forced herself to maintain a cool demeanor.

"Grandpapa, have you thought that perhaps Mrs. Redwyck is in league with her son to draw me into this marriage?"

"Do you have reason to think so?"

She relaxed slightly. At least he was listening to her.

"I cannot imagine why else such a lady would willing to accept as her daughter a girl who—" Juliana lowered her voice, "who has been masquerading as an opera dancer."

"There's no doubt the Redwycks need money," said Grandpapa. "That may be why Mrs. Redwyck is willing to overlook your indiscretions. But I cannot think that she, or a gentleman such as Lord Amberley for that matter, would stoop so low as to wish to entrap you into marriage."

"You think not? Amberley is not the first *gentleman* to have tried to compromise me so that I would marry him."

"What? Who did such a thing? Why was I not told?" Grandpapa looked accusingly at Mrs. Frisby.

"It happened while I was staying with Lady Plumbrook in Brighton last summer," Juliana hastened to reply. "I did not tell you, for I did not wish to worry you."

"Do you think Lord Amberley capable of the same villainy? He seems every inch the gentleman!"

"He is a charming scoundrel," she replied bitterly.

"So you believe he knew who you were when he brought you to Amberley House?"

"I do. And even if he did not know who I was, what does it say about his character?"

Grandpapa looked perplexed. It was an unusual expression for him, but Juliana was heartened to see him taking her opinion seriously.

"Do you think such a man would prove a faithful husband?" she continued, hoping to drive her point home.

"I do not know," he said, and paused, his white brows drawn together.

"There is nothing unusual in it, my dear," said Mrs. Frisby, breaking the silence. "Few men are above such vices, but it is still better to marry than become an old maid. And of course, you will have his children to comfort you."

Juliana was not surprised to hear the resigned tone in Mrs. Frisby's voice. She had always suspected Captain Frisby had not been the most reliable of husbands. She only knew *she* had no need, or desire, for a marriage with a husband who would neglect her as soon as his need for heirs was satisfied.

"There is no reason for Juliana to have to settle for a

philandering husband," said Grandpapa. "I have already told Amberley as much."

"So you will allow Mrs. Frisby to come along with me?"

"You really do not trust Lord Amberley to keep the line while you are at Redwyck Hall?"

"I do not."

"Very well, then. I still do not think Lord Amberley capable of such base schemes as you suggest, but if it will make you more comfortable, Mrs. Frisby and I will *both* come with you." He smiled indulgently, then added, "I'd like to see Redwyck Hall for myself, and see if it's all it's cracked up to be."

"Thank you, Grandpapa," she said. She went around the table and kissed his brow, feeling more hopeful that all would end well. Grandpapa had not amassed and maintained his huge fortune without learning to beware of the greedy and unscrupulous. Soon he would realize that Lord Amberley fell into that category.

After they had all breakfasted, Grandpapa retreated to his study, and Juliana accompanied Mrs. Frisby upstairs to begin selecting clothes to pack for their upcoming journey. Polly chattered excitedly as she sorted through Juliana's clothes, exclaiming over the prospect of going to a grand country house. Juliana smiled at Polly's enthusiasm, though of course she did not share it.

Polly glanced out the window and exclaimed, "There's a carriage with a crest just arrived, Miss. Oh, is that Lord Amberley? He's ever so handsome, isn't he, Miss?"

Despite herself, Juliana went to join Polly and caught a brief glimpse of the earl's elegant, dark-coated figure as he climbed the stairs up the entrance. She noticed that he still walked with a slight limp. So that at least was real, and not just a ruse to arouse her interest and sympathy. She remembered all her romantic conjectures on how he had acquired the limp, and once more cursed herself for having been such a fool.

She found she could no longer concentrate on the packing, and wondered when she would be asked to go downstairs to meet Lord Amberley. When ten minutes had dragged by, she realized he must be alone with Grandpapa.

"I must ask Mrs. Frisby something," she told Polly, and left the room.

She went downstairs. Seeing that the door to Grandpapa's study was closed, she tiptoed softly toward it, glad he had had the hall covered in a thick carpet so that servants' footsteps would not disturb him at his work. Looking about to make sure no one observed her, she put her ear by the door. Perhaps it was wrong to eavesdrop, but how else could she know what lies Amberley told Grandpapa?

She caught her grandfather's voice, and was relieved to hear his disapproving tone.

"—not best pleased with what I saw last night. Forgive the question, Amberley, but how do I know you're not some sort of rake? That you won't indulge yourself with opera dancers after you've married my granddaughter?"

"I assure you, Mr. Hutton, that was the first time I have ever done anything of the sort."

Juliana suppressed a snort of indignation.

"It was wrong of me," Amberley continued in that same disarmingly honest voice, "but I had already given up hope of Miss Hutton ever accepting my offer. I promise you that if she does decide to marry me, I will treat your granddaughter with all the respect and consideration she deserves."

A pause ensued, and Juliana could imagine the piercing look Grandpapa was giving Amberley. She knew it was a look that made even the innocent cringe with guilt over imagined crimes.

"Well," Grandpapa said slowly. "I consider myself a fair judge of character. You're telling the truth, or I'm a pigeon."

Juliana tensed. How could Grandpapa allow Amberley to draw the wool over his eyes?

"However," Grandpapa continued, "Juliana has her doubts of you, and I have to admit you've given her some reason. That's why I would like to accompany her to Redwyck Hall, along with Mrs. Frisby, who's been her companion this past year. If it is agreeable to you and your mother, of course."

"Of course. Mama and I shall be delighted to welcome you all to our home," said Amberley.

"Very kind of you, my lord. I've heard Redwyck Hall is a lovely place."

Juliana could almost see Grandpapa's smile through the softening of his voice. Horribly, unbelievably, he had succumbed to Amberley's wiles. What was she to do now?

"I trust you will not be disappointed, sir," said Amberley. "The Hall is a beautiful old place, but I will admit, it is in need of serious repairs."

"I've heard as much from Lord Plumbrook," said Grandpapa, not sounding surprised. "And there's that matter of the mortgage, too. What would you say if I said I'd pay the next installment for you right now?"

There was a pause, and Juliana could imagine Amberley restraining himself from jumping too eagerly at the offer.

"I would say thank you, sir," he said. "I know I have not done anything yet to merit such kindness, but I cannot afford to be too proud."

"Good. I would've been suspicious if you had pretended to refuse," said Grandpapa. "Damn it, I like you, Amberley! Come to think of it, you handled the situation last night very well. Maybe I've been too heavy-handed with Juliana. Maybe you'll manage her better."

Amberley lowered his voice. Juliana could not hear his reply, but rage at his duplicity boiled up inside her. It was all she could do not to burst through the door and scream at them both.

"It goes without saying," Grandpapa continued, "that I will pay off the entire amount once you convince her to marry you."

"I shall do my best, sir."

Again, Juliana resisted the impulse to enter the room and tell Amberley exactly how unlikely he was to succeed. As the men's conversation passed on to details of their trip to Gloucestershire, she realized she should leave if she did not wish to be caught. Softly, she walked down the hall, still furious with Amberley, and shocked at how easily he had managed to worm his way back into Grandpapa's good graces. She forced herself to breath deeply. She had to stay calm, think of a way to expose Amberley for the rascal he was. But how?

She was at the bottom of the stairs when she heard Mrs. Frisby's voice calling toward her.

"Oh, there you are, Juliana, dear. Your friend Miss Talcott has come to visit. She is in the drawing room, waiting for you."

When they reached the drawing room, Juliana saw Pen quickly get up from her seat.

"Good morning, Juliana. I am so happy to see that you are feeling more the thing," said Pen, her smile radiating a mixture of relief, concern and curiosity.

"Yes, I am perfectly recovered from my . . . indisposition," she replied, continuing the pretense. Now that her masquerade was at an end, there was no point in letting Mrs. Frisby know Pen had been in on the secret.

"Yes, and we have such exciting news," said Mrs. Frisby. "Dear Juliana has accepted an offer from the Earl of Amberley himself!" Her eyes pleaded with Juliana not to contradict her.

"I wish you every happiness," said Pen, her eyes widening as she looked from Mrs. Frisby back to Juliana.

"Thank you," she replied. "Now, dear Mrs. Frisby, perhaps you will allow us some time alone so I may tell Pen all about our plans, and say our good-byes."

"Our good-byes?" Penelope asked.

"We are all going to visit Lord Amberley and his mother at Redwyck Hall," said Mrs. Frisby with a nervous smile as she looked at Juliana. Perhaps she did not wish to leave them alone, for fear Juliana would confide in Pen. Which was exactly what she hoped to do.

"Yes," said Juliana. "I am sure there are still a thousand details to arrange before we go."

Mrs. Frisby looked uncomfortable, clearly unsure whether she should leave them alone, but also fearful of giving offense. Juliana knew she would bow to a stronger will, but hated to play the imperious employer to her nervous companion.

At that moment, Grandpapa entered the room, Lord Amberley following behind. Instantly, she felt an unexpected, treacherous response to the sight of his tall, elegantly clad figure, which made her stupidly conscious of her dowdy, unbecoming garb. Then her anger reasserted itself, and she greeted him with a cold, challenging look. She had the satisfaction of seeing doubt and anxiety in his eyes as they briefly met hers, before he turned back to listen to her grandfather, who introduced him to Mrs. Frisby and Penelope.

"I am delighted to make the acquaintance of one of Miss Hutton's friends," said Amberley, smiling at her friend as she looked up at him curiously.

Penelope actually smiled back at him. Shy little Pen, who shrank from strangers, was actually smiling at that snake Amberley, innocently responding to his charm. Juliana reminded herself that Pen did not know what had happened, or how Amberley had plotted to seduce her into marriage.

"I trust you are in good health this morning, Miss Hutton," he said, turning back toward her. He said the words smoothly, but she sensed nervousness in his voice. Did he doubt his ability to fool her again? Well he might!

"I am perfectly well, thank you," she replied in a tone that did not encourage further discussion.

The gentlemen sat down, and a brief, uncomfortable silence ensued. Mrs. Frisby broke it with exclamations of delight at having been invited to Redwyck Hall. Then Penelope talked of the Cotswolds, saying she had read of the beauty of the region. Amberley responded politely, and a moment later, they had somehow passed on to a discussion of country life, and the hardships that the country people were enduring. Juliana sat quietly, disgusted at the seeming sincerity of his replies to Pen's knowledgeable questions about his tenants and laborers, and appalled to see her friend growing every minute more comfortable chatting with the duplicitous scoundrel.

"I know little of farming," admitted Grandpapa during a brief pause. "I have heard Redwyck Hall is a fine old place. Juliana and I are quite looking forward to seeing it." He looked fiercely over to Juliana, wordlessly exhorting her to join in the conversation.

"Yes. Quite," she replied, determined to give no further encouragement.

"Perhaps, my dear, you would wish Lord Amberley to tell you more about it in private."

She looked to Mrs. Frisby, hoping she would disapprove of the plan, but her chaperone disappointed her by saying, "Of course, my dear. A certain degree of license is permitted to engaged couples, you know."

"I think I must take my leave now," said Penelope, looking uncertain as to what Juliana would wish her to do.

"We can send you home in your carriage, Miss Talcott," said Grandpapa. "I do not know what your aunt is about, allowing you and your maid to trudge so far by yourselves."

"Oh, we are both country girls, and prefer to walk on a fine day such as this one," said Pen, as she rose from her chair.

Lord Amberley got up and bowed as Grandpapa escorted the two ladies out, leaving Juliana nothing to do but fume. Not only had she missed her opportunity to confide in Pen, now she was left alone with the author of her predicament. It was tempting to plead an indisposition and leave the room, but Amberley might take that as a sign of cowardice. No, it was better that she throw down the gauntlet right now, and let him see exactly how impossible a task he faced.

Accompanied by her maid, Pen descended the steps into Russell Square, wishing she had had an opportunity to talk to Juliana in private, but on the whole, satisfied with her visit. It was a relief to know that Juliana was once more safely under her grandfather's roof, although her sudden engagement still presented a mystery. Perhaps Lord Amberley had rescued her from the rakish lord that Verwood had spoken of, and offered the protection of his name to prevent any resultant scandal.

As they began to walk along one side of the square, Pen reflected that Juliana had not looked pleased with her engagement. Perhaps it was just her friend's usual rebellion against her grandfather's plans. She herself liked Lord Amberley very much. In her experience, few handsome young lords were kind enough to speak so cordially to plain young ladies of no particular consequence. It was a sign of Amberley's good nature. Moreover, few lords demonstrated Amberley's awareness of their obligations to their dependents.

Perhaps, in time, Juliana would come to love him. From the way he looked at Juliana, it seemed that he was already at least half in love with *her*. But how could that be?

She was startled out of her musings by the entrance of a smart curricle drawn by a pair of dark bays into the Square. Holding the reins was none other than Lord Verwood. Noticing her, he drew up his horses and jumped down. He handed the reins to his groom, who began walking the horses around the square.

"Good morning, Miss Talcott," he said, arching his eyebrows over those dark, clever eyes. "I suppose you have been visiting your friend, Miss Hutton. I trust she is in good health."

Conscious of Susan beside her, Pen answered, "Yes. Miss Hutton has quite recovered from her earlier indisposition."

"Ah, I am glad to hear it," he replied, with a rather secretive smile. "I was hoping to find out how she was, having received such uncertain reports of her health yesterday."

Apparently he had not succeeded in finding Juliana. Had he even tried? She had spent the night wondering whether she had been right to put her faith in him. The sight of his wicked smile by the light of day sent her doubts soaring even higher.

"You may rest assured that Juliana is going on very well," she replied. "She is going to marry the Earl of Amberley."

"Is she?" he asked, looking thoughtful. Did he think to take advantage of a potential scandal? Did he pose some threat to Juliana's future with that nice Lord Amberley?

"Yes, so you see she has no further need of your . . . solicitude," she said, hoping to convey a sense of warning through her words.

He paused before replying. Usually she was quite adept at reading expressions, but his was annoyingly unfathomable.

"Very well, Miss Talcott," he said, in the manner of a gentleman accepting a rebuff. "Unless of course, I may assist *you* some time in the future?"

She supposed he was laughing at her.

"That will not be at all necessary, my lord," she said as coolly as she could. "Unlike my friends, I prefer to have nothing to do with rakes."

"I am relieved. When dealing with you and your friends, I find my best intentions often bring some rather unfortunate, er, consequences."

He rolled his eyes in a droll gesture, and Pen saw that the noble contour of his nose was still somewhat marred by the punishment it had received the previous night.

"I am sorry. That must pain you greatly," she said more softly.

"Not at all," he said. Briefly, his smile warmed her, then, like the sun disappearing behind a cloud, it departed. He gestured for his groom to bring the curricle and horses back towards them.

"I bid you farewell then, Miss Talcott. Or should I say *au revoir*?"

"Good-bye, my lord," she said firmly, and watched him jump gracefully back up into the high carriage and drive away.

After the others had left, Marcus remained standing. Miss Hutton had returned to her seat across the room from him, and was now watching him coldly, as if daring him to speak. He gazed at the prim maiden sitting before him, in a concealing cap, a gown that came up to her throat, and sleeves that buttoned tightly at her wrists. Somehow, neither her apparel nor her forbidding expression could erase the memory of the charms she had revealed the night before.

"Lord Amberley? You wished to say something to me?"

His face heated as he realized that he had stared at her far longer than was polite.

"My apologies, Miss Hutton. I did not mean to stare at you so rudely." He sat back down.

"I am sorry if my altered appearance disappoints you," she said, with thinly disguised sarcasm.

"Not at all. You are even lovelier without the rouge you wore as Mademoiselle Juliette."

She colored at his words, and he had the pleasure of seeing how much better a natural blush became her.

"Of course, I do look forward to seeing your true hair color," he added with a smile, hoping for further signs of thaw.

"You have a quick tongue, my lord," she said, recovering her complexion. "However, in this instance it will avail you nothing."

"Miss Hutton, you must allow me a chance to explain everything that has happened."

"Very well. Speak on."

"First I have to assure you again that I did not know who you were until last night."

"Do not play games with me, Amberley!" she said impatiently. "How did I give myself away? Was it my faulty French grammar, or did you suspect even before that?"

"I tell you I did not know. How could I have guessed?"

"Any number of ways, I imagine. Perhaps you saw that picture." She gestured behind him, and he turned to see a very fine full-length portrait of her between the room's two windows. Ah, she was lovely. He stared at the picture for a moment, realizing her hair would be golden blond in a month or so. Then he turned back to her and shook his head.

"No, I have never been in this room before. You have merely to ask your grandfather to learn that that is true."

"Then perhaps you received the same information that they had at Bow Street, that I had been seen in the vicinity of Half Moon Street. It would not have been difficult for someone with your address and rank to discover that Mademoiselle Lamant came to lodge at Madame Bouchard's house soon after I disappeared."

"I had no idea you had run away," he insisted. "They told me you were ill. I suspected that you did not wish to see me, as you were known to have spurned a number of suitors."

She was silent for a moment, and he could only hope she was considering the truth of what he had said. It was impossible to read her expression.

"So your motives in bringing me to your home were purely chivalrous?" she asked, skeptically.

"No," he answered, determined to be perfectly candid. "Not purely, that is. I did not wish Lord Verwood to continue to harass you, but I hoped my own attentions would be more welcome."

"How odious!"

"You did not find it so odious last night," he retorted, stung by the palpable disgust in her voice. Then he wished he had not reminded her.

She colored angrily, and fury flashed from her eyes for a moment. Then, with a visible effort, she contained her ire.

"I thought you were going to die," she said, a trace of bitterness in her voice.

"What?"

"You lied to me. You told me your life was in danger."

"I never said such a thing!" he replied, staring at her. What could have put such a notion in her head?

"You said you were leaving London, that you might never return again. That you might never again have such an opportunity. What was I to think but that you were going into some sort of danger?"

"I never meant you to think *that*," he said, still puzzled.

"What did you mean, then?"

"When I learned that you had run away, I thought I had lost my last prospect for saving my estate. I planned to go to India, or America, to try to seek my fortune. What did *you* think I was going to do?"

"I thought you were going to the Continent. They—they said you were a spy."

"Who did? Oh—Jerry and his friends! Good Lord!" He nearly laughed at the insane irony of the situation, but he knew she would not find it amusing.

"Don't laugh at me!" she said. "I did *not* believe them. Not at first. But you talked so mysteriously. You would not say where you were going, or what you were doing. And your command of French is so good. . . ."

Agitatedly, she jumped up from her chair. In a few quick but graceful strides she reached the window and looked out. Marcus said nothing. It was clear she needed some time to recover from her mortification at the mistake she had made, but his own heart felt lighter than it had since the past evening. She had cared for him. Had even been distressed at the thought that he faced untold dangers. *She had cared for him.*

She turned around, looking more composed, but her expression effectively chilled his budding hopes.

"Well, my lord, you have duped me quite finely," she said. "Do not expect to do so again."

"Can you not believe I did not mean to deceive you?"

"If you did not mean to deceive me, why did you have your friends tell me what they did?"

"It was all just a silly notion George and Oswald took into their heads. I could not convince them otherwise."

"I can believe that," she admitted, searching his face. She took a few steps toward him, and he struggled not to be distracted by her graceful movements, or the subtle scent of roses that clung to her.

"Why all the mystery, then?" she asked. "Why did you assume a false name?"

"I did not wish to embarrass you or your grandfather. Think how it would have looked, if people heard I had come to London to fix my interest with you, and then found out I had been consorting with the most sought after opera dancer in London."

Stopping a few feet away from him, she looked up, a challenge in her eyes.

"Grandpapa would have turned you away from our door if he had gotten wind of it. That was your real reason, was it not?"

He winced. There was too much truth in what she said for him to deny it.

"You did not want Grandpapa to discover what a rake you really are," she continued.

"I'm not a rake," he protested. "That was the first time I ever—"

He broke off, overcome by a flush of embarrassment and longing at the memory of their interrupted lovemaking. Suddenly the room felt far too warm.

"Really?" she retorted, startling him with her vehemence. "How could it have been the first time? You knew just what to . . . just how. . . ."

This time it was Miss Hutton who could not continue. Her cheeks flamed, her eyes blazed and the lace at her bosom rose and fell with her quickened breath. He knew she was angry, but he couldn't help being flattered that he had pleased her so well. Perhaps he had inherited his share of the Redwyck charm, after all.

"Don't look at me like that!" she said, drawing back. "Oh, you are a scoundrel! But don't think I'm idiot enough to believe you." She put a hand up to her cheek, as if hoping to cool it, then reassumed her haughty manner.

"I think I have heard enough fairy tales for one day," she announced. "Good day, my lord. You will forgive me for not seeing you out."

She made him a mocking courtesy, turned and strode out of the room, leaving him feeling chilled. He sat back down in the chair he had just vacated. He should probably seek out Hutton and take his leave, but he badly needed a few minutes to recover from his stormy encounter with Miss Hutton.

He had tried his best to convince her of his integrity, but he had failed. He wondered why she was so stubbornly cynical, and realized she had always been so, even as Mademoiselle Juliette. It was not difficult to understand, after all. As an heiress, she must have been subjected to the advances of any number of fortune hunters, and of course, in her role as Juliette, gentlemen sought to impose on her in other ways. And he was no better than any of them.

Except, perhaps, for the fact that he had fallen in love with her as Juliette, and was now falling even more deeply in love with her as Miss Hutton.

He stood and took another turn around the room, still feeling unable to face anyone, still unsure of how to proceed. She had come to care for him as Dare. Was there a way he could rekindle such feelings? She would never believe him if he told her he loved her. No, words alone would never convince her, and she would regard any attempt at lovemaking with suspicion.

He continued to pace, trying to think of a way through the coil. He stopped suddenly, struck by the absurdity of the situation. His fiancée had thought him a spy, then a scoundrel, then a rake!

Perhaps all that was needed was time. Time for her to become better acquainted with him, with his home, his people, his hopes and plans. She was an intelligent woman; she would soon realize there was nothing sinister or mysterious about him.

But would she find Marcus Redwyck, seventh Earl of Amberley, a sad comedown after her association with the fascinating Lord Dare?

Chapter Eleven

Five days later, the Huttons' carriage finally turned through a set of iron gates and onto the drive that led up to Redwyck Hall. Grandpapa, though somewhat tired from the journey, straightened up and peered eagerly through the carriage window. Juliana did her best to appear uninterested, but she couldn't help noticing the increased swaying and bounding of the carriage. She glanced out of the window, and saw many ruts, and places where stones added to the roughness of the ride. The outcroppings were of the same golden-colored stone used to wall in all the pastures they had recently passed.

"I see there is some work to be done here," said Grandpapa, looking about speculatively.

The carriage wound on, past many fine old trees and enormous rhododendrons.

"This drive will be quite lovely in a month or so, when the rhododendrons come into bloom," ventured Mrs. Frisby.

Juliana did not respond. It was no use telling either of them that she did not care in the least about this place, and would be delighted to leave it as soon as possible.

A moment later, they rounded a bend and came out into the open. From her side of the carriage, Juliana could see little of the house, only a lawn.

"Not particularly large, is it?" said Grandpapa, sounding

anxious. Did he find Redwyck Hall a disappointment? She was glad of it, Juliana thought fiercely.

"I expect we are seeing just one wing," said Mrs. Frisby, in a consolatory tone. "Come, sit on this side, dear Juliana, so you may see better."

The coach was moving so slowly that there was no excuse not to fall in with Mrs. Frisby's suggestion. Reluctantly, Juliana exchanged seats with her companion and took her first glance at Redwyck Hall.

Lit by the sun to a golden shade, the honey-colored stone seemed alive, as if it would be warm to the touch. With tendrils of ivy caressing its walls in places, the house looked as if it had been there forever. The unkempt lawn, the overgrown shrubbery behind it, only added to its aura of age and mystery. No doubt Grandpapa had expected something more grand and formal. She had shared his expectations, and had fully expected to dislike the place.

"What d'you think, child?"

She pulled herself out of her daze. "It is well enough," she replied, trying to sound indifferent.

"You like it," he said, shrewd eyes alight with satisfaction. "Well, it's not what I expected, but if you care for it, that's all that matters."

As they approached the entrance, more of the house came into view. Larger than it had first appeared, it was clearly in need of repairs. Chimneys crumbled and, in places, carved stones were missing. She wished Grandpapa could be daunted by these signs of decay, but he was smiling.

Moments later, the carriage had pulled up at the front entrance. Lord Amberley and his mother had already descended from their coach. He came forward quickly to help Juliana out.

"Welcome to Redwyck Hall, Miss Hutton," he said with a hesitant smile as he held his hand out to her.

Reluctantly, she laid her hand in his. She made the mistake of meeting his eyes. For a moment, she forgot her surroundings, caught in their hazel depths. The warmth of his clasp penetrated her gloved hand, an unexpected, potent reminder of what they had shared as Lord Dare and Mademoiselle Juliette.

Abruptly, she alighted and withdrew her hand, giving him a cool thank-you before proceeding toward the steps where his mother awaited.

"Welcome, my dear Miss Hutton. Mr. Hutton, Mrs. Frisby," said Mrs. Redwyck, with a welcoming smile.

Behind her, a massive oak door stood open. Just inside stood an elderly man in the garb of a butler, and a neat, plump gray-haired woman. They passed into the entrance hall, and Mrs. Redwyck introduced the pair as Critchley, the butler and his wife, the housekeeper. Both bowed, looking nervously at Juliana. Knowing they were probably anxious at the prospect of a new mistress, she smiled at them reassuringly. She was glad they had not chosen to assemble the entire staff for her inspection; this was embarrassing enough.

"You must all be very tired from the journey," said Mrs. Redwyck, looking fresh as a daisy herself. "Mrs. Critchley tells me your rooms are ready, and your servants and baggage arrived several hours ago. Perhaps you would all like to go up and rest a bit before dinner?"

Juliana had only a brief impression of the house, as she was shown through the hall and up the carved oak staircase. There were few furnishings and decorations, in strong contrast with Amberley's London town house, which had shown no signs of the family's straitened circumstances.

"I trust you will be quite comfortable here," said Mrs. Redwyck, who undertook to personally escort Juliana to the bedchamber where Polly awaited her.

"I am certain I shall," she replied politely.

Looking about, she saw that she had been conducted to a corner room, decorated in a more modern style than she had expected. The wallpaper was faded, and the curtains a trifle threadbare, but it was spacious and sunny. The tall windows offered enchanting glimpses of the surrounding lawns and gardens.

"This is not a guest bedchamber, is it?" she asked, struck by a sudden suspicion.

"No. This room has always been the countess's bedchamber."

"I cannot stay here," she blurted, noticing a door that

connected this room with the corresponding one at the other corner of the wing.

"Do not fret, dear," said Mrs. Redwyck. "My son still occupies his old bedchamber. I thought you would enjoy the views from this room."

"Thank you," she replied, still blushing.

"Now I shall leave you to rest. We will dine at six. If there is anything either of you need," she said, smiling at Polly, "just tell Mrs. Critchley."

When Mrs. Redwyck had left, Juliana walked about the room, gazing out of the long windows at the untidy but somehow romantic gardens below. The hedges were overgrown and ragged, but in the flower beds daffodils and tulips added splashes of color. She stifled the urge to go out and explore the gardens further, and turned to allow her maid to remove her pelisse and hat.

"Have they made you comfortable here, Polly?"

"Oh yes. Mrs. Critchley and the rest of them have been more than kind." Polly paused a little, and said thoughtfully. "I think they're all afraid to offend us, Miss Juliana, for fear you might change your mind about marrying his lordship."

Juliana remembered the nervous expressions on the faces of the butler and housekeeper. She hadn't thought how many lives would be affected by her decisions. She hated the thought that these innocent persons were likely to lose not only their positions but their home if she did not marry their master. But it wasn't her fault that the Redwycks had brought their estate to such a pass!

An hour later, after Polly had helped her into an evening gown and tucked her hair into yet another lace cap, Juliana followed her maid toward the drawing room where the party assembled before dinner. She saw that Mrs. Redwyck and the servants had been busy. In the brief time since her arrival, the bleak, empty rooms had undergone almost a magical transformation. Branches of candles adorned the few, ancient pieces of furniture, and each surface held simple earthenware bowls of varied heights and sizes filled with a artful mix of both garden and wildflowers: narcissus, tulips and bluebells, pale yellow primroses. It was as if an ancient castle had been abandoned by its human dwellers and taken over by fairies for their revels.

Juliana mentally shook herself. Goodness! She was becoming fanciful. This was all just part of the Redwycks' scheme to beguile her into becoming one of them.

As they came to the threshold of the drawing room, she thanked Polly for her guidance, then entered. Grandpapa and Mrs. Frisby had not yet come down, but Lord Amberley, his mother and a young lady who must be his sister all looked up as she entered. Amberley, in an elegant black coat, and his mother, in violet satin, both arose as she entered, but the other young lady remained seated, opening a book in front of her with an air of total absorption.

"Good evening, Miss Hutton," said Amberley, coming forward to meet her.

"What a delightful gown, my dear," said Mrs. Redwyck. "Blue becomes you."

Juliana thanked her, uncomfortably aware of Amberley's warm gaze upon her. If only she owned at least one dress suitable for evening wear that was cut as modestly as her morning dresses! Unfortunately, the one that Polly had laid out for this evening had a fashionably low, square neckline. It only reminded her of how Amberley had seen her much more scandalously attired.

"May I introduce my sister to you," he murmured, then frowned as he realized his sister hid behind her book. "Lucy, come and meet Miss Hutton."

The tall, dark-haired girl set down her book and got up to survey Juliana with a sullen expression.

"May I present my sister, Lucinda," said Amberley, with a look of brotherly warning in his eyes.

"How do you do," said the girl, in a voice that would have been pleasant had it not been laced with hostility. Apparently, she did not consider Juliana worthy of her brother, but Juliana was more amused than hurt. What did it matter if Amberley's sister liked her or not?

"Very well, thank you," she replied. "I am delighted to meet you. I see you are quite an accomplished lady."

"Oh?" said the girl, looking blank.

"Well, I see that you are adept at reading upside down, which is truly an amazing feat," she said with a smile.

Miss Redwyck's face darkened, but after a moment, she recovered. "No doubt *you* are highly trained in all of the feminine accomplishments, Miss Hutton. I suppose you embroider beautifully, speak sixteen languages and can perform any number of airs on the pianoforte."

"In truth, I embroider abominably, I speak a little French and Italian, and I have no particular aptitude for music."

"Do you ride?"

She shook her head. "I have never had the pleasure of learning."

The girl raised her eyebrows contemptuously, then returned to her seat and her book. Both Amberley and his mother looked embarrassed and apologetic. At that moment both Grandpapa and Mrs. Frisby arrived, and so the awkward moment passed in the following exchange of pleasantries.

Soon after, they all went into dinner. Polly had told Juliana that Amberley had brought his French chef from London, and that there was currently a state of warfare in the kitchens between that individual and the old-fashioned cook that had been employed at the Hall for decades. However, the meal was delicious and showed no sign of the strife below stairs.

She was seated beside Lord Amberley, but took little part in the conversation. Her grandfather took the lead, asking many questions about Redwyck Hall, the surrounding neighborhood and local society. Juliana ached with embarrassment at his questions, which were clearly designed to discover just what sort of position awaited her as the next Countess of Amberley. Mrs. Redwyck gamely answered her grandfather's probing questions, and Mrs. Frisby struggled to help maintain a flow of polite small talk, to help cover for the fact that neither Juliana nor Miss Redwyck had much to say. Lord Amberley seemed rather subdued as well.

Presently, Juliana went with the other ladies back to the drawing room, leaving Grandpapa to continue to discuss the Redwyck estate with Lord Amberley over port. Miss Redwyck announced she had an headache, and excused herself from remaining with them. Soon after, Juliana saw Mrs. Frisby press a hand to her temple, and knew her companion's pain was not feigned. Mrs. Frisby was not a good traveler, and no doubt the journey had taxed her limited energies. It took only a little coaxing to convince Mrs. Frisby to retire to her room, and Juliana found herself alone with Amberley's mother.

"I trust your companion will soon recover," said Mrs. Redwyck, taking a seat beside Juliana. "But I cannot regret that we have this opportunity to chat. I have been wishing to speak with you, Miss Hutton. May I call you Juliana?"

Reluctantly, Juliana nodded. It was no part of her plan to become close to the Redwycks. She did not desire Mrs. Redwyck's kindness, and distrusted the motherly warmth in the woman's voice. But it would be rude to refuse.

"I know this all seems very sudden to you, and it is quite natural you should question my son's motives in courting you. We can make no secret of the matter that your grandfather's assistance is greatly needed here. But you must believe that my son's feelings have nothing to do with that. Marcus has conceived a very real and lasting passion for you, my dear."

Juliana said nothing, merely looking back at Mrs. Redwyck skeptically.

Mrs. Redwyck sighed. "I suppose it is too early to expect you to believe it. I just hope you will try to listen to what he has to say to you. There are many advantages to marriage with a Redwyck, you know."

Her words seemed to refer to the privileges of marrying into an ancient and honored family, but the tone of her voice and the expression in her eyes were soft and dreamy, and even a trifle melancholy.

"You look puzzled, dear," said Mrs. Redwyck. "What I meant to say was that the Redwyck men are famous for being the most charming lovers and husbands."

She concluded her speech with a knowing smile that brought the blush back to Juliana's cheeks. She reminded herself that Mrs. Redwyck was only trying to assist her son in his scheme to win her over.

Moments later, Grandpapa and Lord Amberley joined them. Juliana wondered what they had been discussing. Grandpapa looked to be in excellent spirits, which was disquieting in itself.

"Marcus, you must show Juliana the portrait gallery," said Mrs. Redwyck.

Juliana swiftly looked back at Amberley, to see how he would react to this obvious attempt to throw them together.

"Only if she wishes it. Perhaps you would like to see it as well?" he said, directing his question to Grandpapa.

"No, I find I am a trifle fatigued, and would rather sit here by the fire for a bit," said Grandpapa. "But you should certainly go, child."

Juliana bit her lip. She should have known that her chaperones would abandon their posts at the first opportunity! Tempted as she was to imitate Miss Redwyck, she decided against pleading a headache. If she did, Grandpapa would say she had not given his lordship a fair opportunity to prove himself to her.

"Very well, my lord. I will accept your kind offer," she said formally, and arose to leave the room with him.

To Juliana's surprise, Amberley made no attempt to take her arm. Instead, he picked up a branch of candles, and quietly led her back toward the entrance hall. There he stopped, set the candles down on a carved Jacobean table, then turned to look at her.

"A bit awkward, is it not, how everyone is trying to throw us together?" he asked. "If you would prefer to retire to your room, I will make your excuses to your grandfather."

"No, I do not wish to retire," she said, and wondered at the impulse that led her to go with him.

"I am glad," he replied. "I had hoped we would have an opportunity to speak alone."

He led her down a dark hallway leading down the opposite wing of the house. It was very quiet, and she realized how far they were from Grandpapa. Even the servants were two floors above them. Yet somehow she did not feel afraid. Much as she suspected Amberley of being a rogue, she also felt certain his methods involved seduction, not coercion. She had merely to show him how indifferent she was to his charms, and that would be an end of it.

They entered a long, narrow room which appeared to span half the length of the house. Tall, pointed windows along one long side streaked paths of pale moonlight across the stone floor. Amberley led her toward the far end of the room, and she wondered when he would try to take her in his arms.

"This is the earliest surviving portrait of my ancestors," said Amberley, lifting the branch of candles to illuminate the portrait of a gentleman in Elizabethan garb. "It depicts Harold, first Baron Redwyck."

She turned her gaze from him to the portrait, and found herself fascinated by the uncanny resemblance between the subject of the painting and her companion. Both had the same high forehead, the aquiline nose, the determined set of chin and jaw. The eyes even held the same look she had seen in Amberley's eyes the night he had tried to seduce her.

"Harold was one of Queen Elizabeth's privateers, and won his title and fortune by plundering any number of Spanish galleons. Or so the story goes," said Amberley. "By all accounts, my ancestor was something of a rogue."

"There is quite a resemblance between you," she said tartly.

"I shall take that as a compliment."

She stifled an unexpected chuckle at Amberley's dry tone.

They continued down the gallery, and Amberley pointed out various ancestors and provided her with interesting tidbits of their history. Although he did not boast, it was clear he cared about his family heritage, and wished to preserve it. Even knowing herself to be the instrument of that preservation, Juliana still could not help being fascinated by the Redwycks. After meeting the first Baron, she was better prepared to see that all the subsequent lords shared the same aristocratic cast of countenance, and the same bold expression. Although it might have been the artists' flattery, the women were lovely as well, attired in rich fabrics and adorned with costly jewelry.

"And this is the first earl, and his countess, both painted by Sir Peter Lely," said Amberley, pointing to a sumptuously attired gentleman with the long, luxuriant curls popular during the reign of Charles II. Beside the first earl hung a portrait of a beautiful lady with dark ringlets, lavish lace draped about her elbows, and a blue silk gown that flowed about her body and fell off her curving white shoulders. She smiled a secret smile, and Juliana was grateful for the darkness that hid her blushes from Amberley. She had seen such portraits before, but now she understood just what could bring such a glow to a lady's face.

As Amberley introduced more rakish gentlemen and smiling ladies, she felt as if she were being offered a seductive glimpse of the life being prepared for her. She lifted her chin defiantly. Perhaps the Redwycks' brides had been happy with their lot, but she had no desire to submit to a husband's will, no matter how pleasurable her servitude. Besides, who knew if those husbands had remained attentive after being presented with the requisite heirs?

Amberley lifted the candles to illuminate a small, more modern portrait.

"And this is my uncle Harold," he said.

She studied the portrait curiously. Amberley's uncle had the typical Redwyck looks, but his expression was more languid, less bold, than any of his relations. She had no difficulty imagining him carelessly dissipating a fortune.

They had reached the end of the portraits, and Amberley turned to face her. The branch of candles he held clearly illuminated his face. She could see desire shining from his eyes, and reminded herself it was one of his tricks. Her heart began to pound painfully in her breast as she realized the moment she had been waiting for was at hand.

"Miss Hutton," he said, surprising her with his formality. "I know you were very angry—and rightfully so—on being thrust into this awkward situation. But I hope you've spent some time thinking over what I said to you when we talked at your grandfather's house."

She nodded, feeling somehow deflated. Was he going to try to make love to her, or not?

"Do you believe me now when I say I had no idea of your identity?" he continued. "That I am not the sort of villain who would try to seduce an innocent, for money or any other reason?"

His words were delivered forcefully, earnestly, and she found herself almost wanting to believe him.

"I do not know, my lord. I *do* know that you came to London with the cold-blooded intention to win the hand of an heiress. Can you deny it?"

"I cannot deny it, but I did not make such a plan on my own account. There are many who depend on me. Perhaps you do not understand. You have lived in the lap of luxury all your life; you've no notion what it is to be without proper shelter, or sustenance."

"I can see for myself that your family is not living in luxury, but I do not think you are starving."

"I am not speaking of my family," he said curtly, "although I do wish I could provide better for them. I am speaking of the people that live and work on my estates—my tenants, the shepherds, the farm laborers, and their families. They are not precisely starving—yet—but times have been hard. When Bonaparte was defeated I rejoiced like any good Englishman, but since the war prices have fallen, and so have wages. My uncle has dissipated what funds I might have used to institute more efficient farming practices, and foreclosure is imminent. What choice do I have but to try to improve matters by any means available to me?"

She looked down, not wanting to hear about any more souls who would suffer if she did not marry Amberley.

"I am sorry," he said unexpectedly. "My problems are none of your making, and I have no right to expect you to solve them. I only wished to explain myself. I never had any desire but to be perfectly honest with you, and to promise that I would do everything in my power to make you happy. That offer still stands."

He took a step forward, and his voice softened and warmed as he concluded his little speech.

"Oh, do not pretend you are in love with me," she said, stiffening.

"Very well," he said, stopping. "I will not pretend."

His words were meek, and yet he hinted at something quite different.

"Your words are noble indeed," she said, "but while in London you were every inch the fashionable buck. How can I know that you are not seeking a fortune so that you may follow in your uncle's footsteps?"

"A fashionable buck? *I?*" He looked torn between anger and amusement. "Hasn't your grandfather told you that I've spent the last eight years acting as my uncle's land steward, riding about the estates, collecting rents, studying crop rotation and sheep breeding? I've had no time to be *fashionable*, as you say."

She raised her eyebrows while taking in his impeccably tailored evening attire.

"You speak of these clothes?" he asked, lifting his arms slightly. "This was all Pridwell's—my uncle Harold's valet's—doing."

She did not know how to reply, acutely aware of the breadth of his chest, of his well-muscled limbs encased in tight pantaloons. Even more acutely embarrassed to have made him aware of her interest. Before she could think of a reply, he laughed.

"I should not be so angry," he said. "After all, you do not know me very well. Perhaps instead of telling you about myself, I could show you around the estate, so you can judge for yourself. What do you think?"

She pulled herself together and considered his suggestion. If she did not go along with it, Grandpapa would say she had not given Amberley the chance he deserved. Moreover, she wanted to know the truth, for her own peace of mind.

"It sounds like a sensible plan," she replied.

"Good," he said, smiling. "We can start tomorrow morning. Your grandfather has asked to go over my affairs with me, but we can very well do that later in the day. You are welcome to join us for that discussion as well."

She blinked, not having expected such an invitation. Grandpapa had always tried to keep her in ignorance of matters of business.

"Thank you," was all she could say.

He gave a slight sigh of relief, then asked her if she wished to return to the drawing room. She agreed, and followed him back out of the gallery.

"By the way, I must apologize for the rude reception Lucy has given you," he said. "She is too young to realize that one should not judge a person's worth solely by whether or not he or she loves horses."

"I have not had the opportunity to discover whether or not I would like horses," she said, a bit defensively. "Grandpapa thought it too dangerous for me to learn to ride."

"Would you like me to teach you?"

Surprise rendered her temporarily speechless.

"You would do that?" she asked.

"Yes, if your grandfather does not object."

Grandpapa would allow anything that would further Amberley's suit. She had always wished to learn to ride, and if she ever gained her independence, it would be a useful skill. But how could she allow herself to be so beholden to a man she was determined not to trust?

"I have long since sold the hunters, and all the carriage horses except for a cob that draws our gig, but we still have a few riding horses," he continued. "Mama's mare is gentle and should be an excellent first mount."

"I do not wish to inconvenience your mother."

"Mama will be more than happy to lend you her mare. Sonnet gets little enough exercise as it is."

"But I have no riding habit," she said.

"Mrs. Smith, a widow in the village, makes most of Mama's and Lucy's clothes. I am sure she would be happy to make you a riding habit. Or if you wish for something more modish, we could convey you to Gloucester where there are no doubt some more fashionable dressmakers."

"I would be happy to deal with Mrs. Smith, but—"

"Don't worry so much, Miss Hutton. You need not feel yourself under an obligation for a few riding lessons. You are a guest in my house, and it is my duty to see you are properly entertained. Will you allow me to do that much, at least?"

She nodded, realizing that further objections would only make her look foolish.

"Good. I look forward to teaching you," he said, his eyes alight with anticipation. She looked away, so he would not see the devastating affect his smile had upon her.

They had nearly reached the drawing room, and she realized that the attempted seduction she had looked for had not occurred. Was this Amberley's way of lulling her suspicions? Or was he indeed a man of honor?

Surely the upcoming days and weeks would reveal the truth.

If nothing else, she would learn to ride!

Chapter Twelve

Grandpapa stood at the top of the steps, beaming, as Juliana descended to meet Lord Amberley, who waited beside the placid dun cob harnessed to his gig. Amberley smiled, and helped her up into the carriage. As he climbed in and took up the reins, she waved back to Grandpapa. Then they were off.

Despite its lazy appearance, the cob trotted on smartly, and the gig bounded over the rutted drive. Juliana was not accustomed to riding in open carriages, but liked the feeling of the wind on her face. It served to cool her blushes as she discovered that a light gig such as this one had barely room for two persons. With each bump in the road, she was jolted against Amberley and made keenly aware of his hard, muscular thigh and hip brushing against her own. She looked up, and saw that his face had reddened slightly as well. Perhaps it was merely the brisk spring wind.

"I shall not overturn us, I promise you," he said.

"I did not think you would," she replied, looking down. She noticed he was now attired in serviceable buckskins and a loose-fitting dark green coat, its elbows positively threadbare.

"I see you have put off your town clothes," she said, wondering if he did so in response to what she had said the previous night.

"Yes. They are not at all suitable for driving down dirty lanes and calling upon tenant farmers," he replied.

Abashed, she fell silent. Perhaps there were good reasons why ladies should not mention a gentleman's clothing!

Despite his rough, provincial clothing, Amberley looked dangerously, ruggedly attractive. The color of his coat emphasized the green lights in his eyes, and there was something very fresh and manly in his demeanor as he dexterously turned the gig onto the lane leading to the village of Redwyck.

To divert her mind from his proximity, she began to question him about all she saw. As they drove past fields and pastures, Amberley described to her the crops and breeds of sheep being raised in each. She had no means of judging his expertise and could only pose the most elementary questions, but he did seem extremely knowledgeable and answered her questions respectfully. After about half an hour spent in this fashion, he drew up before a rambling farmhouse.

"We are going to visit my tenants, the Coles. I sent word for them to expect us," he said, descending from the gig and helping her down before securing the cob.

Before she had even alighted, a middle-aged couple with honest, kind faces hurried out from the house. They welcomed them politely, but Juliana could see they could barely contain their curiosity as they looked at her. Like the staff at Redwyck Hall, they were eager to see the heiress Lord Amberley had chosen for his bride, and discover how she would affect their lot.

Mrs. Cole invited them in, shyly offering them tea and scones. Juliana accepted politely, and sat down with Amberley and the Coles in their small parlor. The men began to discuss lambing, and Mrs. Cole, relaxing in response to Juliana's friendly manner and praise of her scones, took the opportunity to offer her good wishes on her approaching nuptials.

Their visit was short, Amberley telling the Coles that he wished to show her the village before returning to Redwyck Hall. The Coles saw them out, rendering Juliana uncomfortable with all their congratulations and good wishes on the upcoming marriage.

"I hope you enjoyed your visit," said Amberley as they drove off once more.

"The Coles seem to be excellent people," she replied.

"Sam Cole is the best of my tenants. Would that they were all so. The tenancy agreements drawn up by my uncle's steward leave much to be desired."

"In what way?"

"To keep land in good heart, one must rotate crops, raising a different crop each year for every three or four years, and occasionally leaving fields fallow for a season. Some landlords often include a provision that the tenant farmer must follow such practices. Longer leases also help, since that discourages the tenant from exhausting the land for a quick profit. My uncle's steward was not so astute. If I could, I would buy back some of the leases."

"What would you do then?"

"I'd offer those farms to Sam Cole's sons. He has two. Both served on the Peninsula, and since then they've been helping him. I would be happy to help them to farms of their own. In the long term, it would be to my advantage to have such trustworthy tenants."

She sat silently thinking over all he had said. It began to seem possible that all he had said about himself was true.

"My apologies, Miss Hutton. I see I have bored you."

"No, I find it quite interesting. Do you think I am not capable of understanding the business of farming?"

"Not at all. I suspect you have inherited your share of your grandfather's acuity."

She wondered if he mocked her, or found her interest in business demeaning, but there was no trace of it in his voice.

After they negotiated a bend through a small grove of trees, the village of Redwyck came into sight. It seemed to consist mainly of several curving rows of cottages, all built of the same honey-colored stone as Redwyck Hall. Like the Hall, some of the stonework seemed in need of repair, but overall the image was quite charming. Most of the cottages boasted a narrow line of spring flowers in front, and appeared to have more extensive gardens behind.

"Those are allotment gardens," Amberley explained, noticing her gaze. "I own most of this land, and have allocated these plots for the cottagers' use. When times are hard, a few cabbages and turnips can make a great difference."

Her gaze then turned to some children running about the green. Their clothes were ragged, and several were barefoot, but they played with all the abandon of healthy young animals.

"Those are some of the farm-laborers' children. I've tried to discourage too great a use of children in the fields. Much as I like seeing them play, I wish I could institute a village school. I don't expect that farmwork will provide enough occupation in coming years for all the children born here. A rudimentary education might prepare them for other positions."

A ball suddenly flew out from the group of children, landing in Juliana's lap. The children turned as one to stare up at the carriage, wide-eyed, perhaps fearing punishment. She tossed the ball back to them, and smiled, but the burden of responsibility weighed on her. Even though she had never penetrated into the poorer areas of London, she had seen too many ragged and hungry children on its streets. She had urged Grandpapa to contribute to a number of worthy charities, but had always felt overwhelmed by the magnitude of the problem. This was different. Here, she could make a real difference, if only she did what was expected of her, and married Amberley. Was she terribly selfish to feel that her independence was a huge price to pay?

Marcus drove back toward Amberley, trying not to steal glances at Miss Hutton. She sat silently, evidently deep in thought over all she had seen, all he had told her. Her delightful form beside his had nearly driven him to distraction, but by droning on about farming, he had managed to control the urge to pull her close. Now he wondered what she really thought, whether her interest in his concerns was real or feigned. She was not unaffected by the poverty she had seen, of that much he was certain.

A pang of guilt shot through him. It was unfair to burden her with his troubles, but he could not help doing so. If only she would learn to trust him, so he could tell her how he loved her. How he longed to make her as happy as she could make him.

* * *

The next morning, Juliana accompanied Mrs. Redwyck into the village to be fitted for a riding habit. Although she enjoyed Mrs. Redwyck's conversation, she tried to hold the lady at arm's length, determined not to raise any false expectations by becoming too familiar. The party reconvened for a cold nuncheon, and as on the previous day, Amberley's sister was nowhere to be found. The earl looked annoyed, but Juliana told herself it was just as well; the last thing she wanted was to be drawn into the Redwyck family circle.

Afterward, Lord Amberley took her for another drive about the estate. Try as she would, she still could not sit in such close proximity to him and be unaffected, but she did her best to maintain her composure. Now he showed her lands farmed by some of his less favorite tenants, and she felt more troubled than she had the day before at seeing the hovels in which those laborers dwelt.

Finally, they turned down a lane, following a signpost to Upper Tilden. Before they had gone far, however, she felt Amberley stiffen beside her. Then she saw a smart phaeton coming their way, bearing two persons. As they came closer, she saw it was a man of early middle age, with pale hair and a handsome face marred by lines of dissipation, and a pretty younger woman with brown curls who was obviously in the family way.

"Good day, Amberley," said the gentleman as the carriages drew abreast of each other in the narrow lane. His polite words were belied by his expression. Instinctively, Juliana did not trust him, and when Amberley replied, she knew why.

"Good day, Bentwood, Lady Bentwood," he said in a carefully modulated voice.

So it was Sir Barnaby Bentwood, Charles Bentwood's older brother. No wonder she had detected a resemblance.

"We hear we must congratulate you. Will you introduce us to your lovely bride-to-be?"

The couple stared at her curiously as Amberley introduced her. Lady Bentwood's critical gaze reminded Juliana of the unflattering combination of cap and bonnet she was obliged to wear. She lifted her chin and coolly answered their polite nothings, sensing that the couple were displeased to see her. She wondered why.

"Have you decided on a date for the happy event?" asked Sir Bentwood, his hard-eyed gaze on them both.

"Not yet," said Amberley, in a light tone, though she felt the muscles in his thigh bunch with tension.

A glance flickered between the other couple. Clearly the Bentwoods hoped to discover just how happy she and Amberley were in their engagement. She decided that she did not want them to guess any more than he did.

"I am shocked, my lord," said Lady Bentwood. "I should have thought you would rush to secure such a *treasure*."

"I have no desire to rush Miss Hutton into anything," said Amberley.

"Of course, you must be taking the opportunity to completely redecorate the Hall, and purchase your trousseau," said Lady Bentwood.

"In truth, I think Redwyck Hall has a lovely antique air," said Juliana. "I would hesitate to change it too much."

Lady Bentwood pouted for a moment, before changing the subject. "Do you not find it a dreadful bore to be in the country at this time? We only left London because dear Sir Barnaby thinks rural air is better for my health." She patted her stomach suggestively and gave her husband a coy smile. He did not look amused.

She looked back toward Juliana and said, "Of course we all know how dear Lord Amberley loves the country. I am sure you will learn to feel the same."

"I have lived all my life in London," she replied. "I find being in the country a refreshing change."

Amberley relaxed a trifle.

"Now we must be on our way," he said, "or I will not have time to finish showing Juliana around my lands."

They made their farewells, Lady Bentwood promising to call upon her soon. As the other couple drove off, Juliana stole a glance at Amberley and saw that his expression was sober.

"They did not seem pleased to see me," she ventured.

"Sir Barnaby holds the mortgage on my lands. He stands to make a greater profit if I default. So you see, you are all that stands between him and the land he wishes to acquire."

"It explains a great deal," she said, though she sensed that Amberley was not telling her everything.

"I must thank you for not making your feelings toward me apparent."

"Oh, I had not the slightest desire to satisfy their curiosity. A delightful couple, all in all."

He chuckled in response to her sarcasm, then said, "I am surprised you had not met them before. They usually spend the entire Season in London."

"No, I have not met them. I *have* had the pleasure of meeting Sir Barnaby's brother Charles, in Brighton."

"Oh?"

Conscious of his gaze intent upon her, she replied, "Yes. Charles Bentwood was the first to show me the lengths a *gentleman* might go to to secure an heiress."

"I assume you mean he tried to compromise you into marriage," he replied, in a tight voice. "I've told you before, I am not such a blackguard. I acted out of pure passion for you, nothing more. And nothing less."

Suddenly she felt breathless. He had treated her with such restraint for the past several days that she had just begun to forget all he had done the night she had run away from the Opera House.

"Yes, that is exactly what Charles Bentwood said when my maid Polly came to my rescue," she said, to hide her confusion.

The glow she thought she'd seen in his eyes faded. Perhaps she'd imagined it. Perhaps his attraction to her had withered, after all. Some men were like that, she'd heard, fascinated by women of easy morals but indifferent to ladies of character.

She looked away, studying the village they were just entering. The contrast between it and Redwyck was shocking. Here the buildings were in an even greater state of disrepair, there were no allotment gardens, and the few children she saw were not only ragged, but thin and dirty as well.

"Sir Barnaby owns most of this village," said Amberley in response to her distressed look.

"Is that why you brought me here? So I could see what will befall Redwyck if I do not marry you?"

His jaw tightened briefly before he replied.

"No, that was not my intent. I only wished to show you the border of my lands. But," he continued, looking down at her, "you are here to learn about me. You must understand it is my duty to care for my dependents, and that I must use any fair means at my disposal to do so."

His words were ruthless, but his tone pleaded for her understanding. Suddenly, she no longer believed him guilty of trying to trap her into marriage. Only a man of honor would care so for his tenants, and a man of honor would not stoop to so vile a scheme. She sensed he would go to almost any lengths to prevent the Bentwoods from seizing his estates. She could not blame him. She even wished she could help.

A new, bold idea began to form in her mind.

She arose early the following morning, restless, knowing she was on the verge of a momentous decision. She got out of bed and crossed to the window. It was very early; a morning mist still shrouded the gardens below her window. A movement below caught her eye; looking down, she saw Lord Amberley walking briskly toward a grove of trees that grew just beyond the garden. The sight reminded her of how he had spent part of each day of their journey walking to take the stiffness out of his bad leg. Once again, she wondered how the injury had occurred, and whether it pained him much. She would ask him later today.

As he disappeared into the woods, she realized just how her image of him had changed in the past few days. He now seemed less like a cold-hearted fortune hunter, and more like an intelligent, honorable man determined to do his duty despite formidable challenges.

Of course, that still did not mean she loved him, or wished to be bound to him in marriage.

After breakfast, Mrs. Redwyck and her daughter departed on an errand to visit a sick pensioner, and Juliana once again joined Grandpapa and Lord Amberley in his lordship's study, to continue studying his accounts. After yesterday's perusal of the estate books, she was not surprised that neither she nor Grandpapa could find any error in his calculations, or the slightest evidence of waste or extravagance.

Late in the morning, they were interrupted by Critchley, the butler, who brought word that Lady Bentwood had come to call on Miss Hutton.

"She awaits you in the drawing room, Miss," he said, a hint of disapproval in his voice.

"Thank you, I will go to her," she replied, smiling at Critchley, who permitted himself to smile back.

Before she left, she saw a worried look cross over Lord Amberley's face as well. No doubt he, like Critchley, feared that Lady Bentwood had some scheme to prevent their marriage.

"Good morning, Lady Bentwood," she said, as she entered the large though sparsely furnished room where her visitor waited. "I had not expected you to visit so soon."

"Oh, I could not keep away," said Lady Bentwood. "There is so much we have in common, after all."

Juliana seated herself in a hard chair across from the sofa her visitor had chosen, and raised her eyebrows. "We do?"

"I must confess to you that there was a time when I, too, cherished a . . . a particular fondness for Lord Amberley."

"Indeed."

Lady Bentwood sighed wistfully. "Of course, it was but a youthful romance, doomed to failure. My dowry was not sufficient to satisfy his lordship's needs, you see. I am so relieved he has found a more *suitable* bride."

Juliana pondered Lady Bentwood's words for a moment, and concluded they were uttered in a spirit of mischief. Did Lady Bentwood think she could influence her into breaking off her engagement to Lord Amberley?

"I trust it does not cause you pain," she said, in a tone of spurious sympathy.

"No—well, only a trifle. He is such a handsome man, of course, and quite charming as well," said Lady Bentwood, with a coy smile. "A bit of a rake, just like all the Redwyck men, of course, but what woman does not have a soft spot for a rake?"

"What woman indeed?"

"Well, I have long lost count of the silly country girls who have lost their hearts to him," said Lady Bentwood, then tittered. "As to anything *else* they may have lost, well, I would be loath to speak of such a thing to an innocent miss like you."

"I cannot imagine what you mean," she replied, assuming a wide-eyed expression, as if she did not understand Lady Bentwood's attempts to blacken Amberley's character. In fact, she had it on good authority—Polly's—that Lord Amberley was nothing like the sort of scoundrel who pinched housemaids' bottoms. Though he could not be as inexperienced as he claimed, he was no despoiler of innocents.

Juliana noted the disappointed pout on Lady Bentwood's lips with satisfaction. More than ever, she was convinced this was a scheme to gain control of Amberley's estate. She had no intention of letting the Bentwoods think they might succeed.

"I *do* think Lord Amberley quite the handsomest man I have ever seen," she said, with a sigh. "Of course, Lady Bentwood, you must be so happy in your own marriage that you are no longer conscious of his charm."

"I am, indeed," said Lady Bentwood, but her words sounded forced.

Juliana was pleased to see she had rendered Lady Bentwood speechless. A moment later, Mrs. Redwyck entered the room.

"Good morning, Lady Bentwood. Perhaps you would care to join us for a cold collation in the small dining parlor," she said. Her words were polite, yet there was something intimidating in her manner. Clearly, Mrs. Redwyck disliked and distrusted Lady Bentwood.

Juliana was not surprised to see Lady Bentwood heave herself awkwardly off of the sofa and make her excuses. She and Mrs. Redwyck saw her to the door. As Lady Bentwood's carriage drove off, Mrs. Redwyck turned to Juliana. Her expression, which had been almost angry, softened.

"I trust Lady Bentwood has not ruined your morning, dear," she said, watching her closely.

"Not at all. Her visit was no more than an annoyance." Juliana decided not to tell Mrs. Redwyck that Lady Bentwood's visit had had the opposite effect of what she had intended.

"Well, thank goodness for that. Shall we join the others? I hope your grandfather and dear Marcus have decided to shut their dusty books by now."

As they entered the parlor, Amberley looked up. Across the room, her eyes met his. He looked worried, but there was nothing she could say to reassure him now. Instead, she busied herself with helping Grandpapa and herself to cold meats, and trying to decide how to broach her new plan to Amberley.

As they finished their meal, he offered to drive her about the estate again, to show her the lands that bordered Lord Plumbrook's. She thought about making her proposal in that narrow-seated little gig, and decided it would not do.

"Perhaps another day," she said, conscious that everyone was listening eagerly to their plans. "Today I should really like to take a stroll about the gardens. If you are not too busy to show them to me, that is."

She blushed, hating how very forward she sounded.

"I should be delighted," said Amberley.

Fifteen minutes later, having donned a bonnet and apple green spencer, she joined Lord Amberley at the entrance to the gardens. He offered her his arm, and she accepted it, conscious of Grandpapa's gaze from the French doors behind them. A little tingle crept up her arm as Amberley tucked it in his own, and she tried to ignore it.

"I am afraid we have not been able to afford a gardener in recent years," he said, smiling down at her. "Mama does what she can to tend the roses, but I am afraid the rest of the garden is quite untidy."

She looked about, seeing that the garden was laid out in a series of "rooms," surrounded with high, overgrown hedges, some of them with formal flower beds which at present sported spring blooms and wildflowers. Canes of rosebushes sported new leaves and buds that promised glorious color and scent in a few months. In a number of places, garden seats had been tucked into secluded nooks, often sheltered by trellises bearing climbing roses and other plants, and nowhere was there a clear view from one room to another. It was a place made for lovers' trysts. Had any of the rakish lords and beautiful ladies she'd seen in the gallery made love in the seclusion of these arbors? Did their ghosts continue to sport together out here in the moonlight?

The warm tingle Amberley's touch had stirred in her spread. She drew slightly apart from him. It was time to ask him some questions.

"Lady Bentwood had some very interesting things to say to me," she began.

Amberley's arm stiffened. His expression became guarded, but he said nothing.

"She said that you once paid court to her," she continued, not wishing to say too much, hoping he would volunteer his side of the story.

"I did at one time try to fix my interest with her, but I've since been glad that it came to naught."

"What happened?"

He paused, a hint of pain in his eyes. "This," he said, gesturing down toward his leg. "After the accident, Arabella—Lady Bentwood—told me she had a natural revulsion against deformity, and could not bear to see my limp. She asked me not to call upon her any more."

"What a stupid, unfeeling chit!"

"No, not stupid, actually. I believe her revulsion was actually against the circumstances that led to the accident."

"How did it happen?" she asked. "I see talking about it pains you, but I do truly wish to know. When we first met, I wondered if you had been wounded in a duel."

"Nothing so romantic, I'm afraid," he said. His mouth twisted. "The servants' wages were in arrears, so I went up into the attic to see if there was anything stored there which might be sold. The floorboards were rotten, and I fell through, dislocating a hip and breaking a leg."

"It must have been dreadfully painful," she said softly.

"Yes."

No doubt it had been even more painful to discover that his young love was so appalled by his circumstances that she broke off their courtship. Juliana's resolution to thwart the Bentwoods' scheme grew.

"Well, my lord, I am not shocked by your circumstances. Perhaps I can help."

Amberley turned to stare at her, cautious hope in his eyes.

"You will marry me?" he breathed.

She detached herself from his arm and stepped back a few paces.

"Yes, I will marry you. Upon certain conditions."

The glow in his eyes faded. "What are they?"

She clasped her hands together, so they would not shake.

"My lord, in the past few days I have concluded that you are a man of honor. I know that the law gives a husband many rights over his wife, and I will have only your word that you will abide by the terms of our agreement. I trust it will be good enough."

"If we make an agreement, I will not break it," he said. "What are your conditions?"

"That I stay with you here for a reasonable period, so that I can see that the improvements you spoke of are set in motion. During that time, we will be husband and wife in name only. Afterwards, you will allow me my freedom to go where I wish."

Marcus stood still as he tried to grasp what Miss Hutton was saying. For an instant, he'd known a pure, unreasoning joy that she would marry him. Then her talk of conditions had chilled him like a March rain. How could he agree to such terms? The past few days with her had only increased his longing for her. He wanted her in his bed, but also by his side, working with him, laughing with him. . . . But it was hopeless. He had won her trust, apparently, but not her heart. Perhaps she found the real Marcus a sad bore.

He gazed across an expanse of rough grass at Miss Hutton, who stared back at him watchfully. He sensed the risk she felt she was taking in trusting him, and his own disappointment was tempered by concern for her.

"Miss Hutton, you need have no fear that I will be a domineering husband, and I would not expect you to live always at the Hall, as Lady Bentwood implied. In fact, once my affairs are in better order, I have every intention of taking an active role in Parliament. Although I must attend to my duties here, we could live in London much of the year."

"That is not what concerns me," she said. "I wish to be free to go as I please, and set up my own establishment."

The hard resolution in her voice cut him, but he could

not give in without at least an attempt to persuade her otherwise.

"I know we have been thrown together in awkward circumstances, Miss Hutton. But I had hoped that we would, in time, form a real marriage."

Bland words for what he really wished, but how could he tell her he loved her? She would never believe him. The moment was not right, and it might never be, with his needs and her money between them.

"I don't wish for a real marriage."

"Can you not at least give it some thought?" he asked, trying to keep the frustration from his voice. "As your husband, I would always respect your rights and wishes. The past few days have proven that we could go on well together. And we know we *are* compatible in . . . in other ways. . . ."

He trailed off, wondering if he had said too much.

"If we marry, you must promise not to kiss me, or . . . or touch me. Those are my conditions," she replied, her eyes huge and dark. A flutter of lace at her throat testified to her quickened breathing. His blood stirred at the sight. So she was *not* as indifferent to him as she pretended. Perhaps there was hope for them, after all.

"Very well," he said, roughly. "I have no choice but to agree to your conditions. All I ask is that you agree to one of my own."

"And that is?"

"That I have the right to try to change your mind. At any time."

She swallowed, and he watched the subtle ripple down her neck, wishing he could trace it with his lips. Her prohibition only made him think of exactly how he wished to touch her.

"Very well. You may try anything you like, as long as you do not touch me," she said, a suspicious huskiness in her voice.

"I shall have to think of other ways to convince you."

She raised her brows skeptically, but a delicate blush tinted her cheeks. His spirits rose.

"Do we have an agreement?" he asked.

"Yes, my lord. We have an agreement."

Chapter Thirteen

Juliana breathed a sigh of relief at Amberley's capitulation. She had not expected him to agree readily. It would cause a considerable scandal when she left him, and like most men, he probably hoped for an heir of his own body. But bearing his child would mean an end to all her plans. He would have to content himself with knowing that some obscure cousin—no doubt he had one—would carry on the line.

"Shall we return to the house now?" she asked. Now that they had decided everything, it was time to let the others know.

"If you wish," he replied. "May I offer you my arm, or is that against your rules?"

"I meant—oh, you know what I meant!" She broke off as she saw the hint of a wicked grin on his face. "Of course you may offer me your arm. People would remark on it if you did not show me such ordinary courtesies."

"Thank you. I am glad you will allow me at least such small pleasures," he said, holding out his arm for her to take.

Again, a tingle crept along her arm at the slight contact. He made no attempt to bring her closer, but he radiated possessiveness. Glancing up and seeing his smile, she made a shocking discovery. He clearly thought he could change her mind. No wonder he had given in!

There was nothing to be done about it now, but prove

to him that this time he would not be able to seduce her so easily. She cast about her mind for an impersonal topic of conversation.

"Grandpapa is very interested in your plans for improving the estate. We both look forward to hearing more about them, my lord."

"I am glad, but please, call me Marcus. It will look odd if we don't drop this cold formality."

"Very well . . . Marcus."

"It sounds lovely from your lips . . . Juliana," he said, caressing her name with his voice.

"Don't try your flummery on me, my—Marcus," she scolded. "Perhaps I should have made it a rule that you not speak to me."

"People would certainly wonder about that," he replied. "I *do* quite like being addressed as *your* Marcus."

She decided to keep her gaze firmly ahead, and remain silent for the rest of the walk. Perhaps once she had become more used to their arrangement, Lord Amberley . . . *Marcus* would not be able to cast her into such a flutter.

As Juliana expected, Grandpapa was delighted with their news. If he wondered at her sudden change of heart, at least he did not ask any awkward questions. Both he and Mrs. Redwyck threw themselves eagerly into planning the wedding, and before Juliana knew it, she found herself swept along in their plans.

Having decided on this course of action, Juliana would have preferred to proceed quickly, but she was overruled. A hasty wedding by license would give rise to too much gossip, she was told. Instead, she and Marcus would be married at the Redwyck church, in a month, which would give ample time for her hair to return to its original color, and for Grandpapa to make all the lavish arrangements he wished for the long-awaited event. It pained her to think of his future disappointment when he learned that her marriage was a sham, but there was nothing she could do about that. She could only go ahead, and look forward to a time when she would finally be her own mistress.

A few days after Juliana accepted the earl's proposal, her new riding habit was ready, and Marcus gave her her first lesson. They met in the stable yard, where he waited beside a dark bay mare.

"Juliana, this is Sonnet," he said. "She will teach you as much as I will. Come and meet her."

Suddenly shy, she approached the mare. She'd never actually stood so close to a horse before. Sonnet was *big*.

"Try stroking her nose, and her neck."

Tentatively, she lifted a hand. Immediately, Sonnet's head came up and her ears flicked around alarmingly. Juliana hastily retracted her hand, then Marcus murmured some inaudible endearment to the mare and patted her neck. Sonnet lowered her head once more.

"Try again, and don't be afraid. Sonnet is perfectly gentle, I assure you."

Burning with embarrassment, Juliana took a deep breath and raised her hand back to the mare's neck, stroking it as she had seen Marcus do. Sonnet's dark coat was amazingly soft, and her eyes were large and a dark brown, with purplish lights in their depths. She did *look* gentle, now that she stood perfectly still except for the occasional swish of her tail.

"Very good," said Marcus. "Now you'll learn how to lead her about."

He showed her how to hold the reins, but the first time Juliana tried to lead Sonnet, the mare stayed in place as if rooted to the ground.

"Don't look back at her. Just walk ahead as if you've no doubt that she'll go along."

Juliana gritted her teeth and did as he bade her. To her relief, Sonnet went along obediently, and Marcus did not laugh.

After a few turns about the yard, he took the reins and directed Juliana to watch as he explained the parts of the sidesaddle, and how she was to arrange her legs. Then he brought Sonnet over to the mounting block and held the mare while Juliana climbed aboard for the first time. She put her right leg over the pommel, as he'd shown her, then tried to locate the stirrup, hampered by the voluminous skirt of her habit.

"Let me help," he said, turning the mare slightly and coming alongside. He arranged Juliana's skirt, adjusted the stirrup length and helped her foot into it. Although his movements were deft, and he made no untoward comments, Juliana tingled with awareness of his touch.

"Shall I hold the reins now?" she asked, to cover her confusion.

"Not yet," he replied, his own voice slightly unsteady. He cleared his voice before continuing. "First, you must learn balance. If you snatch at the reins, you could hurt Sonnet's mouth. It is a very sensitive part of a horse. If it is abused, the horse can become ill-tempered and unresponsive."

"I had no idea," she said, looking nervously down at Sonnet, whose ears wiggled around as Juliana and Marcus spoke. She certainly didn't want to do anything to put this huge creature out of temper.

"Just hold your arms quietly at your sides. If you feel you must grasp something, let it be the mane," said Marcus. "Are you ready to walk on?"

She nodded, and he led the mare off at a placid walk. A sudden, humiliating rush of panic swept through Juliana. She had not realized quite how high she would be sitting on a horse's back, or how strange it would feel to have such a great, living, breathing beast moving beneath her.

"Are you quite comfortable?" Marcus asked, smiling as he looked up at her.

"Quite comfortable, thank you," she replied, determined not to reveal her craven feelings. She took a few deep breaths, and forced herself to relax. By the time they had reached the grassy paddock where the lesson was to take place, she began to feel more accustomed to the motion.

Marcus attached a long rein to Sonnet's bridle and began the lesson, letting the mare circle him at a walk as he instructed Juliana.

"Sit very tall and straight, and look forward, between your horse's ears," he said.

It was rather like being with Monsieur Léon again, Juliana reflected, then concentrated on following Marcus's instructions. Apparently there was more to this riding business than she'd thought.

"Keep your shoulders back."

She did her best to comply, uncomfortably conscious that

he closely watched her every movement. He was only instructing her in horsemanship, she reminded herself.

"We shall trot now. It may feel a little jarring at first," he warned.

He had understated the case, Juliana thought. She felt wretchedly awkward as the mare's motion bounced her around on the saddle. No doubt she looked ridiculous.

"Relax," he reminded her. "Just sit tall, and let your weight sink into the saddle. Don't try to lean forward."

She straightened herself, and took a few more deep breaths. Marcus was right. Sonnet's movements seemed far less jolting now that she did not try to fight them.

"Good," said Marcus, and Juliana felt a glow spread through her at the approval in his voice.

After a few more circles, he stopped and turned Sonnet. They trotted in the other direction. Juliana's confidence rose, and her nerves gave way to a sense of heady excitement. She was disappointed when Marcus stopped the mare once more.

"You really are doing very well," he said. "Would you like to try to canter?"

"Yes, please," she said eagerly.

"A slow canter is actually the most comfortable pace for a lady," he said. "Remember to sit up straight, and keep your head up. Always remember that if you look down, your body may follow."

Obediently, she kept her head high. Marcus commanded Sonnet to canter, and the mare launched into a gentle rocking pace that nevertheless covered the ground faster than before.

"How is it?" asked Marcus.

"It's delightful," she replied, enjoying the motion, and the rhythmic sighing of air against her face with each stride. "Why, it's just like a waltz!"

Out of the corner of her eye she caught an amused expression on her instructor's face.

"The rhythm is the same," she explained. "One-two-three, one-two-three . . ."

"I should have known you would show great aptitude as a student," he said, a hint of laughter in his voice.

After a few more turns, he stopped Sonnet and then

commanded the mare to canter in the other direction. Juliana gave in to enjoyment, and could only feel sorry when he halted the mare.

"I think that is quite enough for today," he said. "You can give Sonnet a pat to tell her she has done well."

"Can we not go on a little longer? That is, if Sonnet is not too tired?" she asked, patting the mare's velvet neck.

He grinned. "Tomorrow morning, you will thank me for stopping now."

She was not sure what he meant, but followed his instructions and dismounted. Unaccountably, her legs shook as she reached the ground, and continued to do so as Marcus put an arm around her to steady her. It was just the riding, she told herself.

"You may let go now. I am perfectly steady," she said, somewhat breathlessly.

"Very well," he said, releasing her.

"Thank you . . . for the lesson."

"It was my pleasure," he replied, putting just the slightest emphasis on the last word.

"Shall I lead Sonnet back to the stables?"

He gave her the reins, and all the way back, she concentrated on leading the mare, and not looking back at Marcus. She'd become comfortable with him; she'd nearly forgotten that he'd vowed to change her mind about their marriage. Until he'd said the word *pleasure*. . . .

Suddenly he was Lord Dare all over again. Was she wise to allow him to teach her, to spend so much time together with him? But she had enjoyed herself so much, all she could do was eagerly await her next lesson.

The next morning, she discovered aches where she had not even known she had muscles, and realized Marcus had been wise to keep her first lesson short. With each succeeding lesson, though, she gained strength and skill, under his patient and gentle instruction. After about a week, Marcus's sister came to watch. Conscious of Miss Redwyck's critical scrutiny, Juliana took her first tumble. She was unhurt, having fallen on soft turf, and the fact that she treated the mishap with indifference somehow seemed to establish her worth in Miss Redwyck's eyes.

From then on, it was Lucy and Juliana between them. Lucy even offered Juliana her own spirited mare to ride as soon as she had mastered all she could learn on Sonnet. Marcus was clearly pleased at sister's change of heart, but Juliana was troubled. It would be so much simpler to leave Marcus if his family did not take such a liking to her.

She toyed with the notion of ceasing their lessons, but found herself enjoying them too much. Once Marcus was satisfied with her seat, he taught her the use of the reins, and began to take her for gentle rides down nearby lanes and pastures, and ultimately, for a glorious gallop up on the wolds.

Meanwhile, Grandpapa had set forth on a positive orgy of spending. Not only for Juliana's trousseau, which entailed several visits to Gloucester's finest dressmaker, but also on carriages and horses, the hiring of additional servants and the purchase of furnishings for her new home. When Juliana protested at his plans to completely redecorate Redwyck Hall in the latest and most expensive mode, Grandpapa seemed to defer to her opinion. It was only later, when cartloads of furniture and paintings began to arrive, that she learned he had wheedled from the housekeeper a list of the antiques that had once adorned the Hall, and sent his agents dashing about the country to buy them back from their new owners, or find appropriate substitutes.

When she asked Marcus if Grandpapa's high-handed behavior offended him, he replied that he could only be grateful. She sensed that his pride was wounded, that he sometimes felt he had done little to merit what Grandpapa was doing for him.

Her own feelings were becoming increasingly tangled. She truly enjoyed being with Marcus, felt a growing bond of friendship with him, even found a guilty enjoyment in his looks and teasing comments. She suspected he did truly desire her, just as he had Mademoiselle Juliette. But it was lust, not love, she told herself. It would be a poor foundation for marriage. They might share a fleeting, grand passion, but then she would have a lifetime in which to regret the loss of her independence.

* * *

The morning of Juliana's wedding, Polly helped her into her new gown of white silk with delicate blue embroidery about the low bodice, sleeves and hem. For the first time, she would wear her hair uncovered, and it was surprisingly pleasant to see the yellow curls around her face once more. Polly set a dashing little bonnet decorated with more blue flowers on her head, and declared her to be a vision. She thanked Polly, who went into the adjacent dressing room to fetch her shawl.

Juliana took another glance in the mirror, then back at the little writing desk in the corner. There sat two letters: one from Pen, the other from Cat, both in response to those she had sent to them announcing her engagement. On the wall hung Pen's gift: a watercolor sketch she had made of the three of them sitting together on a hillside.

I wish I could be there with you, Pen had written, *but Aunt Mary says she cannot spare me now, at the height of the Season.* Juliana could imagine Pen's disappointment. Of course, it was impossible for Cat to come, although she and her husband had sent a fine oil painting of Ullswater, which now hung in the library, along with an invitation for her and Marcus to visit them after their honeymoon.

Longing for her friends washed over Juliana as she looked back at Pen's portrait. But perhaps it was best they could not come. She had not written to either of them about her true plans, not knowing into whose hands the letters might fall. Pen would disapprove, and Cat would worry. Her own mouth felt dry, and her stomach unsettled, as she contemplated her future. Soon Marcus would have full legal rights over her fortune, and her very person. Would he honor their agreement?

Polly came back to drape a narrow blue shawl around her shoulders, and Juliana reminded herself that Marcus was not one to go back on his word. Over the past weeks, he had behaved with gentlemanly restraint. Once they were married, however, he would surely redouble his efforts to change her mind.

The truly frightening thing was that she was not sure she would be able to resist him.

Well-wishers of every station in life crowded the little church in Redwyck. Juliana was glad to see that her decision had brought so much joy. Then she saw Marcus, looking disastrously handsome in a smartly tailored dark blue coat and snowy white pantaloons. She wondered what he would think of her changed looks, and an instant later had her answer in the spellbound expression in his eyes.

His reaction, and the solemnity of the occasion almost overpowered her, but she managed to play her part calmly until the point where Marcus accepted the ring from the vicar. Repeating the vicar's words, he said, "With this ring I thee wed, with my body I thee worship. . . ."

She blushed at the warmth in his voice, and had to force herself to concentrate on the rest of the ceremony. Finally, they exited the church, amid much cheering, and Marcus tossed coins amongst the cheering children assembled outside.

A wedding breakfast followed, attended by the vicar and his wife, the Plumbrooks, and a few other local landowners who had not removed to London for the Season. Despite feeling dazed by the impending changes in her life, Juliana smiled and did her best to speak to all present.

Grandpapa smiled fondly throughout, and Mrs. Frisby shed tears of joy over Juliana's marriage, and sorrow over their separation. Juliana had been relieved to learn that Grandpapa had provided her companion with a very generous pension, which would enable her to live very comfortably in Bath, where she had a few friends.

Grandpapa and Mrs. Frisby were all going to leave soon after the breakfast. Mrs. Redwyck and Lucy were also departing, having accepted an invitation from Lady Plumbrook to join her in London for a month. It was as if everyone had conspired to allow Juliana and Marcus a honeymoon.

Her stomach fluttered again at the thought that she and her husband would soon be alone. Glancing over at him, she felt the full heat of his gaze. It would take all of her resolution to resist him tonight.

Chapter Fourteen

It was late in the day when everyone had finally departed, and Juliana joined Marcus in the dining room for their first meal alone as man and wife.

"Good evening, my lady," he said, as he helped her to her chair, waving one of the newly hired footmen away.

"Good evening, Marcus," she replied, trying to sound matter-of-fact.

"It has been a long day. I trust you are not too tired."

She searched his face, wondering what he implied, but all she could see now was polite concern.

The meal was small, but choice, reminding her of the supper they had shared back in his London town house. She wondered if Marcus or Mrs. Redwyck had ordered it, for it consisted of many of her favorite dishes. Mercifully, throughout the soup and the duckling, Marcus kept the conversation to commonplace subjects.

Almost too soon, she finished her meal. Looking up, she saw Marcus gazing at her, eyes darkened with desire. An answering warmth spread through her, and she realized she'd been foolish to let him lull her suspicions. Clearly, he thought the time for gentlemanly restraint had passed.

"Must you look at me that way?" she asked.

"There is nothing in our agreement that says I cannot look at you, my darling. Did you know that you took my breath away when you entered the church this morning?"

"I don't care. And don't call me darling!"

"You made no rule about that, either," he said, with a smile. "So I shall say and look as I please."

He looked into her eyes first. Then his gaze traveled to her lips, her throat, then slowly down to the deep neck of her gown, making her feel just as she had over a month ago, when he had pulled open the bodice of her costume.

The terrible thing was that she enjoyed the sensation.

"I shall leave you to your wine now," she said, and got up from her chair. He might claim the right to look at her, but that did not mean she had to sit there and allow him to seduce her with his eyes.

"I don't wish to sit alone and drink port, my dear," he said, rising from his chair. "I have a much better idea for how we might spend the evening."

She stiffened and raised her eyebrows, but before she could say anything, he continued.

"I thought we could go sit in the library for a while. Perhaps you will indulge me with a game of chess. Your grandfather says you are a fine player."

She let out an involuntary sigh.

"I would be happy to play chess with you, though I warn you Grandpapa dotes on me so much that he quite exaggerates my skill."

A cheerful fire burned in the library, warming the room on the cool May evening. Like most of the Hall, the library had undergone a transformation in the past few weeks, its worn rug replaced by a thick, richly colored Oriental carpet, and its chairs re-covered in the same warm hues.

She joined Marcus at a small oak table where a chess set had already been laid out. It was difficult at first to concentrate on her moves, and she made some mistakes, but soon found that concentrating on the game steadied her. She began to play better, challenging Marcus's considerable skills, though she could not quite recover from her earlier mistakes.

"Do you wish to play again?" she asked, having congratulated him on winning their first game.

"If it would please you. I had hoped I could interest you in another sort of . . . diversion."

Though his words were spoken in a cajoling manner, there was a hint of sincere disappointment in his voice that pierced her somehow. She tried to ignore the feeling, and arose from her seat.

"I am not interested in such . . . diversions, my lord. I think I shall retire now."

"Please stay," he said, pleading now rather than teasing. "I truly do wish to talk to you."

She paused for a moment, then sat down.

"There is something I have been wanting to say to you, for ages, it seems. I could not say it before, for I knew you did not trust me. But now that your grandfather has redeemed the mortgages on my lands for me, and I have nothing more to gain, perhaps you will believe me when I say this. I love you, Juliana."

The constriction in her heart tightened. She had expected flattery and seduction, but not this.

"Do you believe me?"

"I . . . I don't know. No. You are infatuated. You still think of me as Mademoiselle Juliette, some sort of *femme fatale*. But I am not."

"No, you are just as lovely, and even more desirable. But in other ways you are one and the same. I see the same kindness you showed for your friend Miss Church now lavished on my dependents. I see the same intelligence, the same independent spirit. . . ."

She clasped her hands in her lap, trying to hide the tumult his words raised in her head and her heart.

"Juliana, I want you. I want you as my wife, my friend, my helpmate. And my lover. Please, give me back my promise and let me come to you tonight."

Part of her cried out to yield to his wishes, warring with the other part that screamed caution. The huskiness of his voice brought back vivid memories of the pleasure he had given her that night on his *chaise longue*. Impossible to think clearly while he spoke to her so!

"No," she said, forcing the word out past the tightness in her throat.

She got up, and instantly he arose.

"Do you not trust me? Have you not come to care for me, at least a little?"

"I do . . . like you, Marcus. But I told you, I do not wish for a true marriage. I must go. Good night."

"Good night, Juliana."

She left quickly, before she could change her mind. Polly awaited her in her room, wide-eyed with excitement at preparing her mistress for her wedding night. She helped Juliana out of her bridal raiment, and into a lace-trimmed nightgown. After brushing out her hair, she bade Juliana goodnight, telling her with an encouraging smile that she was only to ring for her the next morning when absolutely ready. It was a delicate hint that none of the servants would disturb her or his lordship. Once Polly was gone, Juliana slid under the new, luxurious coverlet of her four-poster bed. Alone, just as she wished.

She glanced over to the door that joined her rooms with the earl's. To maintain appearances, he had had his things moved to that room. No one would know whether he visited her tonight or not. Although Polly might guess, she was too loyal to gossip.

She heard Marcus moving about in the other room, speaking with his valet. She curled up, wondering if what he had told her was the truth. Did he love her, or was he deluding himself and her in order to get what he desired?

What did it matter if he loved her or not? She turned restlessly in her bed. If she were to become his wife in truth, he would expect her to obey him, just as she had promised during the ceremony. She would lose her independence before she'd even had a chance to enjoy it.

Then she remembered what Pen had said about her parents, how they had loved each other and worked together as equals. Could she and Marcus have such a union? The possibility challenged everything that she had previously thought about life and marriage, all the plans she had made so carefully. Did he love her? And did she love him?

How could she be sure of anything, when a wanton longing for his touch turned her mind to jelly?

Marcus was disappointed, but not surprised that Juliana had resisted his advances on the night of their wedding. Knowing how strong willed she was, he did not despair. He sensed that she cared for him more than she admitted, and that she longed to repeat the pleasures they'd shared over a month ago, as Lord Dare and Mademoiselle Juliette. Perhaps with a little patience, he would learn just why she so dreaded the prospect of a true marriage, and find a way to soothe her fears.

Over the next few days, they continued much as they had before, riding every day, and working together on such humdrum tasks as drafting new tenancy agreements, and making plans for a parish school. Yet somehow it all felt different now that they were alone. Marcus took advantage of their intimacy and began to woo his wife in earnest, using every art he could think of to please, attract and seduce his love, without breaking the rule she had imposed on him.

Doggedly, he resisted the impulse to pull her into his arms and cover her with kisses. To force her affections would destroy the fragile trust that had grown between them, so he continually reminded himself that patience had its rewards. Still, it was a sweet torture, watching her try to hide her blushes and her agitated breathing while he called her his darling, and told her how desperately he desired her.

On the third day after the wedding, he was obliged to go out early to resolve a dispute between his tenants. He left a note for Juliana, apologizing for not breakfasting with her. On his return, he sought throughout the house for her, and finally found her in the library, curled up with a book in a window seat, her hair lit by the sun shining behind her. Two slippers sat on the floor before her. When she saw him, she quickly set her book aside and tucked her feet back into them, but not before he caught a brief, tantalizing glimpse of her shapely limbs.

"Good morning, Marcus," she said, straightening up and smoothing her skirt down over her ankles.

"Good morning, love," he said, smiling at her. "Do you know you have the loveliest legs in Christendom? I thought so the first time I saw them. So cruel of you to hide them from me!"

She said nothing, but colored delightfully, just as he had hoped.

"What are you reading?" he asked. "Anything of interest?"

"No," she said, looking self-conscious as he picked up her book.

Glancing down, he was surprised to see, not a lurid novel, as he had half-expected, but a guidebook on France.

"Juliana, is this what you have been longing to do? Travel? Is that why you ran away from your grandfather?"

She nodded, looking wary.

"My darling, I never wished to stand in the way of anything that would make you happy. You should have told me. Did you think I would not understand?"

"Do you?" she asked, doubt and hope reflected in her eyes, and he sensed how important his answer would be.

"As a boy, I read my grandfather's accounts of his Grand Tour," he said. "I've always wished to make one myself. I just never thought that circumstances would allow me to do so. I'll always have a responsibility to my people here, and to take my place in Parliament, but once the improvements I plan for the estate are in train, and I have hired a proper steward, there's no reason we cannot take an occasional trip to the Continent. What do you think?"

She looked dazed, almost as if she could not quite believe what he offered. Much as he longed to press his point, he knew it might ruin everything.

"You don't need to answer me just now. We have plenty of time to discuss such things. Meanwhile I must apologize for leaving you alone this morning. I thought that perhaps, since it is a fine day, I could wheedle a basket from Cook, and we could enjoy a picnic."

After she had agreed to meet him in an hour's time, he left her, feeling well-satisfied with their interchange. He'd gained an important insight into her character today, though it might still be weeks, or even months, before she learned to trust him completely. Still, as he strode down the hall to make preparations for their picnic, he found himself whistling.

Juliana sat for a few minutes in the sunny nook, her initial surprise at Marcus's words giving way to a sense of new possibilities. She remembered how she'd dreamt of traveling with Lord Dare, had imagined what it would be like to explore the world's wonders with such a charming and attentive companion. Now, Marcus offered to make that dream real for her, and with every indication that he wished for it as well.

A deeper joy stirred within her, as she remembered what he'd said about not wanting to stand in the way of her happiness. Was this the proof she had been seeking, that they might have a marriage of equals, such as Pen had talked of?

Perhaps she had been wrong to wish for complete independence. Perhaps it would be an even greater joy to share decisions with a kindred spirit. Marcus loved her. She believed him now. Was there any reason to resist the happiness he offered?

She jumped up from the seat, feeling light, eager, restless. In an hour's time she would be alone with him again. How should she tell him of her change of heart? How would he look? He would be surprised, at first, but then, perhaps, that slow, roguish smile would spread over his face. He would kiss her. . . .

She hurried out of the library and ran lightly up the stairs. It took far too little time to button a deep blue spencer over her sprigged gown, and tie a matching bonnet over her locks. A mere half hour had passed when she took a seat at the meeting spot he suggested, a bench overlooking the stream that flowed through the grounds.

Finally, Marcus arrived, a basket in one hand, a carriage blanket draped over the other shoulder, looking so handsome that her heart nearly stopped at the sight of him.

"I hope Cook has packed what you like," he said as they set off across the lawn.

"I am sure it will be lovely," she said, feeling suddenly shy. A few minutes ago it had seemed so easy to declare her feelings. Now she wondered what he would think of her.

She looked up at her husband, and realized that he too seemed ill at ease.

"Is something the matter, Marcus?" she ventured.

"No, not at all," he replied, but his voice sounded strained. He turned left, taking her along the stream. She had walked this way before, but he led her farther than she had previously ventured. They stopped in a small glade next to the stream, surrounded on all sides by willows and other trees she did not yet recognize.

"A pleasant spot, is it not?" he asked, spreading the blanket down on the turf.

She looked about. It was not just pleasant. It was beautiful, all of it: the willows, shimmering silver and green as a light breeze ruffled their long leaves, the rippling pools where trout could be seen rising, a plump duck with a brood of ducklings paddling along behind her. And her handsome husband, the sun bringing out burnished hues in his rich brown hair, mysterious lights in his hazel eyes. . . .

Embarrassed, she sat down on the blanket to unpack the basket. She unfolded several parcels wrapped with napkins, revealing wineglasses, several joints of herbed, roasted chicken, a bunch of hothouse grapes and several small cheesecakes. Marcus retrieved a bottle of wine from the bottom of the basket. It was a fine hock, a white wine from Germany that was one of her favorites. Had he noticed how much she liked it?

It was a delightful meal, but she couldn't help being distracted, with Marcus sitting just a tantalizing few inches away. She took a few sips of her wine, and tried to eat some chicken. She began to relax after Marcus asked her how she had become interested in travel, and she told him all about Grandpapa's sea captains and their stories, and all she had heard and read about Lady Hester Stanhope.

"Do you hope to follow in her footsteps, and see Palmyra?"

She leaned back a little, feeling more relaxed now, and replied, "It would be exciting, would it not, to see some of the things she has? But in truth, I do not wish for the life she leads now."

He chuckled. "So you do not wish to embroil yourself in Eastern politics?"

"Not at all. It sounds dangerous, and futile."

Seeing that he had finished eating as well, she began to gather everything up to put it back into the basket.

"Well, I am glad," he said. "I think Paris would be a much more pleasant destination, at least for our first trip. What do you think?"

She swallowed nervously, realizing the moment for truth had arrived.

"Yes, I think Paris would be lovely," she replied.

He gazed at her, unblinking, for a long moment, then shifted, moving as close as he could without quite touching her.

"Juliana, tell me what you want. It doesn't really matter to me whether we go to Paris, or Rome, or the Antipodes. So long as we are together, as man and wife."

Her heart began to pound furiously.

"Darling, will you release me from the promise I gave you?" His breath caressed her cheek as he whispered the words he had said so many times these past few days.

"Yes," she replied, too overcome to say more.

"What did you say?" He looked stunned, as if he had all but given up hope that she would give in to him.

A sudden gurgle of laughter caught in her throat, and her embarrassment vanished.

"My dear husband, if you cannot do me the courtesy of listening to my words, I certainly shall not repeat myself," she replied, giving in to a wicked impulse. He was not the only one who could tease.

He looked at her hungrily, then leaned over to kiss her cheek. She shivered at the feather-light touch.

"Please, Juliana, I want to hear you say it. Tell me you will give me back my promise," he repeated, even more softly.

He put one arm around her and drew her closer, turning her to face him. For a moment she looked up at him, her chest pressed against his, his powerful thigh against her leg, her heart beating a mad rhythm. He untied the ribbon under her chin and removed her bonnet, then kissed her, slowly and deeply. Eagerly, she kissed him back, nearly sobbing as she gave way to the passion that she'd been resisting all these weeks. She drew a shaky breath as he leaned back and looked down at her, her own joy echoed in his expression.

"Give me back my promise," he begged, his voice husky with desire.

She pursed her lips, finding an impish pleasure in making

him plead. But he had his revenge. He raised a hand to caress her through the layers of her morning gown and spencer, and a little moan escaped from her lips as the fabric rubbed against her skin. He kissed her again, under her ear, then down her neck, his lips soft and teasing.

"Say yes, Juliana. I long to hear it again," he said. Still she remained silent, half-afraid to break the spell. Soon they would have to return to the Hall. Would he wait until the evening, or take her to a bedchamber immediately? She did not know how she could bear the anticipation.

To distract him, she put one arm around him, and raised her other hand to his face, cupping his chin. She kissed him, savoring the warmth, the wine-laced taste of his lips, the powerful ebb and flow of his breathing. Then, somehow, she found herself lying beside him on the blanket, clasped in his arms. He relaxed his hold, so that she lay on her back, then raised himself up on one elbow.

She gasped as he unbuttoned the top button of her spencer.

"Marcus—"

"Hush, darling. No one will disturb us."

She knew it was true. She'd realized several days ago that the servants were under orders to leave them alone. But this was scandalous!

Thoughts of the servants fled as Marcus continued to unfasten her tiny jacket, his fingers tickling her as he struggled with the small buttons. When he had undone the last one, he raised her slightly and pushed the spencer down off her shoulders. He trailed kisses around the opening of her low, square neckline, pushed down first one sleeve, then the other, then inched her bodice down with his fingers, following with his lips. Then he sat up, to look at her, and she blushed and tingled with the coolness of the air and the heat of his gaze.

"Say you will release me from my promise, Juliana," he murmured, lowering himself down beside her again, warming her with his hands and his mouth.

She wondered how he could keep playing this game, and if one really could die of desire, as the poets said. She licked her lips, not sure she could stand much more, but daring herself to try. He gave her another full-mouthed kiss, harder this time, his hands roving up and down her back, tracing the curve of her waist and hip, until she moved restlessly beneath him, almost delirious with longing. He reached down to the hem of her skirt, and began to draw it up, stroking the inside of her leg through her stocking as he did so.

"Say yes, my darling," he commanded, cruelly stilling his hand just as she willed him to touch her more intimately.

"Yes," she breathed, unable to play this game any longer.

"Oh, Juliana," he said hoarsely. "How I've longed for this."

Then he took mercy on her, plying those clever, wicked hands just as she remembered, except that it was even more wonderful. Soon she was lost in pleasure, twisting and rolling on the blanket, letting her cries ring out to mingle with the sounds of birds and the sighing of the wind.

In a daze, she realized that Marcus had shifted his position, saw anticipation and a hint of anxiety in his eyes. She put her arms around him and opened herself to him, so he would see she was unafraid. Slowly, he began to enter her, and after a moment, she felt a slight pang.

Though brief, the pain brought her back to a sense of what she had just done. She closed her eyes, trying to adjust to the feeling of her husband inside her, while a disturbing inner voice reminded her that she had taken an irrevocable step.

"Did I hurt you?"

She opened her eyes and saw her husband, looking adorably distressed. With a rush of warmth, she remembered that he loved her. No, this could not be a mistake.

She shook her head in response to his question, and pulled him down to kiss him. For a moment, they lay still, bodies intimately joined, then he began to move slowly inside her. Shyly, she tried to match his movements, and her doubts receded as she followed him to new and different heights of pleasure.

Chapter Fifteen

That night, Marcus came to Juliana's bedchamber and made ardent love to her once more. The next morning he awoke to find her sleeping peacefully beside him. He lay very still, fearing she would be startled to see him when she awoke. Instead, she turned, stretched like a cat, and smiled at him in a way that clearly showed that she did not regret anything that had passed between them the previous day.

Her smile led to a kiss, which led to another, which led to their coming down to breakfast at a scandalously late hour. Juliana blushed delightfully in response to Critchley's indulgent smile. After the butler left them to their meal, she hungrily devoured eggs and toast while Marcus talked to her of his plans for the coming months.

"We will not be able to go to the Continent for a few months, darling," he said, hoping she would not be disappointed. "There are still too many things that need doing regarding the estate. I hope you won't find it too slow here during the summer months."

"Well then, you must make certain I am well entertained, my lord," she said demurely.

"You are insatiable, my lady," he said, grinning across the table at her. "But seriously, the Plumbrooks will return by the end of June, and they often host parties throughout the summer. Just informal dinners, with some cards and conversation afterwards, and sometimes a little dancing. I think you will enjoy them. I'm also thinking about Lucy. Though there are still a few years before we must think of taking her to London for the Season, it might do her good to attend a few small, private parties before then. What do you think?"

"I think you are right about Lucy, and I am sure I shall enjoy the Plumbrooks' parties very much. I should love to dance again. With you."

"That won't be possible," he said, stiffly. She could not have meant to hurt him, but how could she talk so?

"What, do you think I know nothing but the *ballet*? Let me tell you I am equally proficient at waltzes and country dances."

He smiled, knowing she was teasing him, but shook his head. "You know I cannot dance. I never really had the chance to learn properly, then after the accident. . . . Don't mock me with such suggestions, darling."

"I don't mean to mock you," she said. "I have been watching you, and I've noticed how your limp becomes much better after you have walked some time. Is that not true?"

"It is true," he said, wondering what she was getting at.

"Don't you see what that means? If your leg had truly healed badly, so it was a different length from the other, you would always limp."

"I hadn't thought of that."

"You are very right to keep exercising your leg, but there are other things that might help, too. One of the dancers at the King's Theatre had sustained a similar injury. He did special limbering exercises, which you might try. And his wife used to rub his leg in a special way. She called it *massage*. It certainly seemed to help him. I could try it, if you wish."

Her desire to help warmed his heart, though after three years of limping, he did not hold much hope.

"I am sure there is no way you could touch me that I would not enjoy, my dear."

"You have taught me to ride," she said, her sunny smile a noble reward for his compliance. "Now I shall teach you to dance."

After breakfast, eager to begin the course of treatment

she had described, she all but dragged him to the library where, she said, the soft carpet would provide a good surface for what she planned. She ordered him to lie down, then knelt beside him and began tentatively to rub her hands over his hip and thigh. At first he was distracted by her closeness, her womanly scent, but as she began to touch him more firmly, he began to notice new sensations in his hip.

"How does it feel?" she asked, anxiously.

"Good." He sighed. It hurt, and yet as she continued to work his muscles, he welcomed the pain. It felt as if her gentle kneading somehow brought the ache to the surface and dispersed it. Just a few minutes later, he noticed a new sensation. Or rather, the absence of one.

"The pain . . . it is nearly gone," he said, in wonder, realizing he had not felt so well in nearly three years. And now that the pain was gone, he was even more acutely aware of his beautiful wife kneeling just inches away from him.

"I am glad. The pain may return, but if we keep up this course of treatment, you may feel a more lasting improvement. Perhaps we should try some exercises now?"

He glanced over to the door. It was shut.

"Yes," he said, and pulled her down on the floor beside him.

Marcus had called her insatiable, but in the succeeding days, Juliana decided the term could as well be applied to her loving husband. After that fateful picnic, he continued to be as charming and passionate as ever, and amazingly inventive. He made love to her in her bedchamber and his, in the library, even in a secluded corner of the gardens, and taught her the many ways lovers could please each other.

It occurred to her that she might already be carrying Marcus's child, although it was far too early to tell. The prospect filled her with both fear and wonder. Although she enjoyed talking to the villagers' children and hearing their quaint views on life, she had so little experience of children. What sort of mother would she be? And how would a child affect the life she and Marcus were just beginning to plan together?

When she was alone with Marcus, encircled in his loving arms, her worries retreated. He loved her, and she knew now that she loved him. Whatever came, they would face it together. Together, they would find a way to be happy.

As for Marcus, he had never known such a blissful period. No longer burdened with debt, or troubled by pain, with a beautiful wife by his side and in his bed, he knew he was the luckiest of men.

"You are holding me entirely too closely, Marcus! It is not proper."

Marcus did not relax his hold one iota, as he twirled his wife in a small circle in the library, where they had gone after dinner several weeks after beginning their true marriage.

"You are my wife. Can I not dance with you as I please?"

She pursed her lips adorably. "Everyone will be scandalized. You know that fashionable couples do not sit in each other's pockets."

"Are you suggesting we emulate, let us say, the Bentwoods?"

"Heaven forbid! Very well, hold me as you wish. But this is still not the correct way to perform the waltz. Mind your steps, please."

"How can I, with such a beauty in my arms?" he asked, letting his gaze rove down from her face to her décolletage, where the sapphire brooch he had just given her for the second time sparkled between the curves of her breasts.

"I told you you were holding me too closely," she scolded, but her lower lip quivered with suppressed laughter.

There was nothing to do but to kiss it.

"Marcus! Do you want to learn how to waltz, or not?"

"As you wish, my lady," he said, and returned his attention to his steps.

Every movement was a joy. Juliana's treatments had dramatically reduced his pain, although he suspected that his leg would never quite regain its original resilience. He would never shine on a ballroom floor, either, but what did it matter how well he danced, as long as he could do it with Juliana? Taking the time to try to learn the steps only enhanced the anticipation of the delightful way the lesson was likely to end.

They took a few more turns about the library, until he could no longer bear the temptation of his wife's sweet form pressed against him. He guided her over against a wall, as if by accident, and silenced her protests with a kiss.

Then he heard a faint knock on the door. Annoyed, he looked toward the door, wondering what could be important enough to interrupt them, and at such an hour.

The knocking came again, more loudly.

"Come in," he said, relaxing his hold on his wife, noting with regret her bright eyes and flushed cheeks. Perhaps, once he'd dealt with the interruption, they could resume what they had begun.

"Mr. Hutton, my lord," said Critchley, in an apologetic tone, before ushering in his grandfather-in-law. Mr. Hutton looked well. There was a twinkle in his eye as he eyed Marcus and Juliana.

"Grandpapa!" Juliana exclaimed, and Marcus released her so she could greet her grandfather.

"My little Juliana," said Mr. Hutton, enfolding her in a hearty embrace before looking up at Marcus. "Good day, Amberley. Sorry to interrupt, but I've something to tell you that wouldn't have been right to put in a mere letter."

"You are always welcome, sir," said Marcus. "I trust they are preparing a room for you?"

Mr. Hutton nodded.

"Have you dined, Grandpapa? Or do you care for some tea?" asked Juliana.

"Some tea would be most welcome, my dear," he said.

After giving orders to Critchley, Juliana bestowed her grandfather in the most comfortable chair in the room, and curled up on the floor beside it, still holding his hand. Marcus took the opposite chair, glad to see the two of them so easy with each other. It had disturbed him to see them at odds over Hutton's matchmaking. They were too alike, he reflected. Strong-willed, stubborn, but amazingly generous toward those they cared for.

"So, what is it you came all the way from London to tell us, Grandpapa?" asked Juliana.

"In point of fact, I have come from Bath."

"Did you see Mrs. Frisby? Is she well?"

"Very well indeed," he said. "That is what I wanted to tell you. A few days ago I offered Mrs. Frisby my hand in marriage, and she accepted. We were married yesterday."

Juliana stared up at him for a stunned moment, then smiled.

"How delightful! But it is so sudden. Why did you not tell us, so we could have attended the wedding?"

"At our age we saw no reason to wait, my dear, and we know how busy you are here. With the estate, of course."

Marcus realized Hutton had not wanted to interfere with their honeymoon any more than was necessary.

"I am very happy for you both," said Juliana. "Dear Mrs. Frisby will take the greatest care of you, I know."

"I'm not senile, child. I don't need a nursemaid," said Hutton. "It is just that I missed her company. She says she missed mine, too."

"You should have brought her with you, sir," said Marcus. "You know you are both always welcome here."

"Thank you, m'lord. We will do that sometime. But I must be off to Bath tomorrow, so we can get back to London. Business waits for no man, you know."

"Well, I wish you very happy."

"Most kind of you, Amberley. By the way, you needn't worry about Juliana's inheritance. Of course I will arrange a generous jointure for my wife, but the greatest part of my fortune will go to the both of you and your children."

"It is of no consequence, sir," he protested. "You have done enough for us already."

Juliana was glad to see the tea tray arrive, for she knew Grandpapa's references to their money made Marcus uncomfortable. She poured out tea, then excused herself, to seek out Mrs. Critchley and tell her exactly what Grandpapa would like for breakfast. At the foot of the staircase, she met the efficient housekeeper, who had come to ask just what arrangements should be made for his comfort. After a mere five minutes, Juliana turned back toward the library. She had not gone halfway down the hall that led to it when she heard Grandpapa's voice once more. It was a shame his hearing was not what it once was, but he never could be convinced that he spoke too loudly.

"—never seen Juliana so glowing. Could she be—but I suppose it is too soon to know."

She sighed. She should have known Grandpapa would be so eager to learn if she was increasing. Marcus said something in reply, but she could not catch his words. She paused, waiting for a less embarrassing point to return to them.

"Ah well, plenty of time for that! Of course, Plumbrook tells me you're the last of your line, so of course you must be anxious to be setting up your nursery."

She stopped now, as Grandpapa's words sank in. *Was* Marcus desperate for an heir? Now that she thought about it, none of the relations that had come to the wedding had borne the name Redwyck. Why had Marcus not told her? Perhaps he'd feared she would misconstrue his motives for telling her he loved her, and so kept silent about the succession. She clung to the thought.

She wished she could hear what Marcus said in response, but if she went any further, they would see her from the doorway.

"I have some other good news for you," Grandpapa continued. "While redeeming your mortgage from that rascal Bentwood, I made a few inquiries. It seems his brother lost a fortune at some gaming hell, and Bentwood's all to pieces trying to pay it off. His wife spends too freely as well, which is why they left London a few months ago."

He paused. Juliana wondered if perhaps this was a good moment to return. Then Grandpapa spoke again.

"Well, the long and short of it is that I've bought up a good portion of his own lands, everything that was unentailed. I'd like to make a present of it to you. You're a clever lad; I'm sure you'll find a way to make it profitable."

She could not quite make out Marcus's reply, though she hoped he protested the gift.

"No, no, I insist," said Grandpapa. "Think of it as my way of thanking you for all you've done. I don't mind telling you, before you came along I was fretting myself to flinders over that granddaughter of mine. She'd got some rather wild notions in that pretty head of hers. Now I see you've given her better things to think about."

A heaviness descended on Juliana's chest as she suddenly remembered the arrangement she'd heard Grandpapa and Marcus make the morning after she had been discovered in Marcus's town house. How could she have forgotten?

But Marcus had had no choice at the time, her heart protested. He'd had to court her or see his lands and people fall under Sir Barnaby's control. This new development must be just another of Grandpapa's generous schemes. Marcus could not have known about it, could not have planned it. He loved her, and nothing else mattered.

She wrapped her arms around herself, hating herself for being so suspicious, at the same time shaken by the fear that Marcus had played her for a fool all along. All his sweet words, all his passionate lovemaking . . . were they all just part of the bargain he had made with Grandpapa?

No. It could not be true. Could it?

She realized the men had gone on to speak of estate business. It was time she rejoined them, but she could not decide what to do. Should she confront them, show her anger and hurt over the scheme they had arranged? What good would it do? It might distress Grandpapa, and possibly turn him against Marcus. No, she would have to speak to Marcus first, privately, and try to discover the truth.

She took a deep breath, forced a smile to her lips, and walked into the library. Fortunately, Grandpapa confessed that he was tired after his travels, and wanted nothing better than to be conducted to his bedchamber. She conducted him to his room and kissed him on the cheek, then went to her bedchamber, knowing Marcus would soon join her there.

She struggled to hide her agitation from Polly, who chattered as usual while helping her prepare for bed. She slipped between the sheets, but as soon as Polly had gone, she got back out. She could not start this encounter in bed, wearing only a cloud of lace and gauze.

She pulled on a satin dressing gown, set her candle down on the table by one of the tall windows, and sat down in one of the blue and yellow striped chairs that flanked the table. A moment later, Marcus knocked, as he always did, with a respect for her privacy that she had found touching.

She bade him come in, and he entered. A lump rose to her throat. He was too handsome, too utterly desirable, in a dark green dressing gown that revealed the strong contours of his neck and chest. He looked grave, no doubt wondering why she did not await him in bed, as usual.

"I trust they've done everything to make your grandfather comfortable," he said, sitting down in the opposite chair.

"Yes, of course," she said, clasping her hands in her lap, glad they were too far apart for him to touch her.

"I think he is very happy in his new marriage."

"Yes. They will be good companions for each other. I did not like the idea of him living alone in Russell Square, with only his servants for company."

They sat in silence for a moment, while Juliana tried to think how to ask Marcus about the conversation she'd overheard.

"Is something troubling you?" he asked softly. "I think I can guess what it is. Did you overhear what your grandfather said to me earlier, while we thought you were with Mrs. Critchley?"

She nodded, a little relieved by his openness.

"What exactly did you hear, darling?"

"I heard him say that—that you need an heir, or your title will die out. It is true, isn't it?"

He looked down, his expression sober. "Yes, I *am* the last of my name, and it *is* my duty to try to ensure the succession."

Duty. He'd used that word to her before, when talking of the need to provide for his dependents. Duty, after all, was why he had married her.

"But that isn't the only reason—or even the most important reason—why I said I wanted a true marriage," he said. "Do you believe me?"

"I—I want to believe you."

Disappointment flickered in his eyes.

"I suppose that is a start," he said, and sighed. "Do you have other reasons to doubt me?"

"Can you deny that you made a bargain with Grandpapa,

that he would redeem your mortgage if you convinced me to marry you?"

His face froze in an expression of guilt.

"Your grandfather did offer me such a bargain, but indeed, I never wanted to be anything but honest with you. I always had every intention of making you happy."

"So you had planned all this, even before you'd met me." She choked back sudden tears; she would not let him see her cry.

"No! It was my duty, but—"

"Yes! It was your duty," she said, jumping up from her chair. "Your duty to make me happy, to make me believe that you loved me, to—to keep me content, and busy, and b-breeding. . . ."

She stumbled away to the other side of the room, half-choking with anger, pain and humiliation at the memory of all that had passed between them. All the wanton, intimate acts she had so eagerly allowed him to teach her. Had it all been part of a scheme to win her compliance?

"Juliana!" he protested. His chair creaked, and she realized he had arisen and was coming up behind her.

"Juliana," he said softly. "I love you. The past few weeks have been the most glorious of my life. Can you not believe me?"

He put his arms around her, from behind. She tried to stay perfectly still, tried to ignore the heat of his body behind her, the strength of his hands clasped at her waist. But as always when he touched her, it was as if a fire had been lit somewhere inside her. If she allowed it to spread, it might consume her. She twisted out of his grasp and turned to face him, feeding her anger so she would not cast herself onto his chest.

"Yes, I know you enjoyed it all. No doubt you are like all the others. I know what they all said. At last, an heiress who is not an antidote. Bedding her will not be an ordeal. Well, I am glad you found your *duty* so pleasurable, my lord!"

Now he stood still, his face stark with pain. Her heart tore. Was she wrong? What had she done?

"Is that what you think it all meant to me?" he asked, his breathing labored.

"I don't know. *I don't know.*"

"If you haven't learned by now to trust me, to know how much I love you, I . . . I don't know how we can ever hope to be happy."

She looked down, aching, wondering if she had ruined everything, and yet still tormented by doubts. How could she think she loved him, if she could not trust him?

"I'm sorry, darling!" he said, his softened voice nearly melting her. "I shouldn't have said that. You've had so little time to adjust to everything. What reason have you to believe me, when you and your grandfather have given me everything? All I can give you in return is my love. Myself. Give me some time. Let me try to prove it to you somehow."

He took a step toward her, and once again she felt the heat stir inside her, confusing her, blinding her. She backed away.

"No! When you touch me, when you look at me like that, I cannot think," she said, turning away from him. "From the first time you asked me to kiss you, you've managed to seduce me into doing your will. I can't let you do so now."

"What can I do, then?"

The desperation in his voice nearly overset her.

"Nothing. I must leave you, Marcus."

Marcus stared at his wife's rigid back. Her words struck him like a blow to the chest. Did she mean them? If he took her in his arms, carried her to the bed and buried himself inside her, could he change her mind? Perhaps, if he tried hard enough, he could make her yield, melt her resistance. . . .

He took a step forward, then stopped, realizing that even if he succeeded in arousing her passions tonight, she would hate him for it later. But how could he bear to let her go?

The past weeks with her had brought him greater joy than he'd ever known. He'd forgotten that he'd done nothing to deserve his good fortune. He'd been so lost in bliss that he hadn't even noticed that she'd never said she loved him. If she left, she might decide her feelings for him were just a fleeting passion. He would have no way of proving that his own feelings were sincere.

A chill swept over him. There was no way to prove his love. Not even the legendary family charm could help him now. He had no choice but to let her go.

And pray every day that she would return.

"Very well," he said. "You are free to go. I stand by my promises. Will you at least tell me where you are going?"

Her voice was strained as she said, "To visit Catherine. She is near her time, now. We can tell everyone that she asked for me to come to her."

At least she did not want everyone to know about the rift between them. It was a cold comfort.

"And—will you return?"

He braced himself for her answer, but it cut him like a slowly twisting knife.

"I don't know."

Chapter Sixteen

Juliana traveled north in the expensive, luxurious chaise Grandpapa had bought for her and Marcus, attended by Polly, driven by a new but very reliable coachman, and greeted obsequiously at the best inns along the way. Despite all the comforts surrounding her, the journey seemed long and dreary.

Each night, slipping between the sheets of a new bed, she found herself longing for Marcus, and despising herself for missing him so badly. Her monthly courses came a few days after her departure. She told herself it made everything simpler, that she did not want his child, yet the discovery brought her no joy.

As they approached the northern reaches of Cumberland, she gave orders to the coachman to follow the route along Ullswater, and found the long, winding lake surrounded by high, wooded hills as picturesque as Catherine had described. They stopped in the village of Glenridding for a change of horses, and dinner, more for her entourage than for herself. They reached the vale of Lynthwaite just as the sun was beginning to descend behind the surrounding hills. Catherine had not exaggerated the appeal of the place, though it was wilder and more stark than the gentler landscapes of the Cotswolds. Built of the local blue-gray stone, Woodmere Hall had the look of a small fortress. How could Cat possibly be happy in this wild, remote place, caught in a strange marriage arranged by her cold, arrogant father?

As the carriage came to a halt before the house, Juliana tried to shake off her depression. It was no use reflecting on how both she and Cat had been forced into matches not of their choosing. The best they could do was to comfort each other. She hoped Cat was well, but if not, she would do her best to help.

She descended from the carriage, Polly behind her. Taking a risk, she directed the coachman to deposit their baggage on the steps, then drive on to the inn at Lynthwaite. She would not put the unknown Mr. Woodmere to the trouble and expense of keeping her carriage or any servants except for Polly. She had sent word ahead, and knew Cat would welcome her, but there was no telling how her husband would react to such a sudden visit.

The butler who greeted them gave every sign of having expected their arrival, which was reassuring. He escorted her to the drawing room where the family congregated after dinner. As they approached, Juliana heard childish laughter. She stood for a moment on the threshold, taking in the scene before her. Catherine sat upon the sofa, a big, dark-haired man beside her who must be her new husband. A small girl with dark, curly hair perched on Cat's other side, touching her rounded belly and giggling. In a nearby chair sat an older girl reading a book, while two boys sat at a table, whittling wood into objects that vaguely resembled horses.

They all looked up as the butler announced her, and she noticed that all the Woodmeres had the same deep, dark brown eyes.

"Juliana!" Catherine exclaimed, smiling broadly.

Mr. Woodmere rose and made a quick bow, before turning to assist his wife up from the sofa.

"Cat," Juliana murmured, embracing her friend as best she could despite Cat's firm, protruding belly. She felt a gentle flutter against her own stomach, and looked down in shock.

"The baby is hiccuping," explained Cat. "That is what Lizzie was laughing about when you came in."

Juliana tried to smile. Anxiously, she studied Cat, and realized her friend looked as beautiful as ever, her dark hair gleaming, her smoky blue eyes full of laughter and her complexion brighter than Juliana remembered. Even the curves of pregnancy looked somehow elegant on Cat's tall, graceful figure. She looked healthy. And amazingly happy.

"I am so glad you've come, Jule. You must tell me—" Catherine broke off, perhaps catching a hint of distress in her face. "We will talk later," she said. "Now you must meet Philip and all my new brothers and sisters."

"I'm delighted to make your acquaintance, Lady Amberley," said Mr. Woodmere, in a deep baritone voice, making her a bow. "Catherine has spoken of you often; I'm sure she will be glad of your support at such a time."

There was a warmth in his voice, and a heartiness about his smile, and all her doubts about her welcome fled. He put his arm around Cat, and Juliana made another discovery. His eyes positively shone with love for her friend, and Cat, nestling in his arm, looked happier than Juliana had ever seen her. Whatever the circumstances of their hasty wedding, it was clear that it had turned into a love match.

"Thank you, Mr. Woodmere," she replied, her surprise melting into joy for her friend.

"Need we be so formal?" asked Cat. "You and I are like sisters, so it follows that Philip is now your brother."

"I would be happy to think so . . . Philip," she said.

"Welcome to our family, Juliana," he replied.

Cat then introduced her to the little girl, Lizzie, the older one, Marianne, and the two boys, Jack and Harry, who all greeted her shyly but politely.

"Now I am feeling a trifle peckish," said Catherine, when all the introductions were done. "I think I'll ask them to light a fire in Philip's study, and bring us some tea and sandwiches. I'll be back in a trice, then we can have a nice little gossip."

She bustled away, leaving Juliana standing with her husband, as the others returned to their earlier activities. Philip watched his wife leave, still with that look of complete devotion in his expressive brown eyes. Juliana's heart turned over. It was just how Marcus had looked at *her*.

"I am truly glad you've come," said Philip, recapturing her attention.

"Is there something amiss?" she asked, catching a hint of anxiety in his voice.

"Mrs. McGinnis, the midwife, says everything is as it should be, but sometimes I wish Cathy would allow a physician to see her." He shook his head. "She insists that she is perfectly happy with Mrs. McGinnis, and does not want any fashionable accoucheur experimenting with her. She may be right."

Perhaps Philip shared her fears, that Cat might be like her mother. No wonder he looked so troubled.

Catherine returned at that point, and Juliana got up to follow her to Philip's study. Lined with books, furnished with a desk and a few comfortable chairs, it was a cozy room, rather like the library at Redwyck Hall, though smaller. A tray bearing tea and sandwiches sat on a small table in front of the hearth.

Cat poured tea for both of them, then eagerly took a few bites out of a thick ham sandwich.

"I am so ravenous these days," she said. "The baby seems to take up so much room I cannot eat my fill at one sitting. But you did not come here just to hear me prate on and on about my condition. Is there something you want to talk about, Jule?"

Juliana took a sip of her tea, then nodded. "Yes, there is. But first, you must tell me how you came to marry Philip. You wrote so little in your letters. You said you were happy, but until I saw you I could not believe it. How did it all happen?"

"It is a long story," Cat replied, "and one that is best not set down on paper. But now that we are together, I will tell you everything."

Juliana listened closely as Catherine told how her father, the Duke of Whitgrave, had sent her to Cumberland in disgrace, how she had met Philip and his family, and all the difficulties they had had to overcome. Somehow, hearing Cat's story made it easier for Juliana to tell the tale of her relations with Marcus, while Cat finished her sandwich.

When she'd finished, Cat gave her a searching look.

"So, you don't believe Marcus when he says he loves you?" she asked.

"I don't know whether to believe him," said Juliana. "When I am with him, I want to believe everything he says, but then I think about our circumstances, how Grandpapa arranged everything, and I just don't know."

"What does Pen think of him? She has met him, hasn't she?"

"She likes him very much."

Catherine looked thoughtful. She didn't need to say what they both knew: that Pen was not often wrong in her judgments.

"Has Marcus ever been less than truthful in any of his other dealings with you?" Cat continued her gentle probing.

Juliana thought about all her conversations with Marcus, and could not think of a single instance of falsehood. Except one, and she could not think it important.

"Only once," she said, blushing. "He . . . he said he had never been with another woman, but I think he said it only because I accused him of being a rake."

"He might easily have said that to spare your feelings. It might even be true."

"Do you think so? But he was so . . . so very . . ."

Cat surprised her by laughing. "Jule, if your husband loves you, he will naturally make every effort to please you as well as himself. If he is not a complete dolt, how can he fail?"

Vivid memories of Marcus, his slow, passionate kisses, his gentle hands, the fantasy they had played out on the *chaise longue* in the town house all spun through Juliana's mind. Could Cat be right?

"What do you think, Cat? Am I wrong to doubt Marcus?"

"I think things have moved rather quickly for both of you. Perhaps you just need some time to think about it, and sort out your feelings. Cheer up, dear. Tomorrow morning, we'll take a little walk together, and perhaps later, Philip and the children can take you for a ramble on the fells. There are some lovely places up there to just sit and think. It will do you good, I promise you."

The next morning, after breakfast, Juliana went with Catherine for a short walk along the brook that ran the length of the valley. Later, as the day was fine, Philip and the others led her on a steep climb up one of the nearby hills, or fells, as she learned they were called in Cumberland. Once she had reached the summit, out of breath and unexpectedly proud to have climbed to such a height, Philip showed her the stone circle that crowned the summit. The children flew kites, while she watched, sitting on a large stone that lay just outside the circle.

Cat was right. The sunshine and breezes of the open hilltop lifted her depression, allowing her to think about Marcus with a degree of clarity she had not thought possible. Mentally, she relived their time together, and found herself dwelling not only on his lovemaking, but the times they had spent riding together, discussing estate matters, heads together as they pored over a tenancy agreement and argued over its wording. Now every moment seemed precious to her.

Then she tried to picture Marcus, and how he was faring without her. All her imagination could conjure up were images of him performing all his duties as usual, but in all his quiet moments missing her, longing for her just as she longed for him. Was it wishful thinking?

She descended the hill in better spirits than before, although still undecided about what to do. She could not leave now, anyway. Mrs. McGinnis, the midwife, predicted that Catherine and Philip's child could be born any day.

On the third morning after her arrival, as Juliana took her customary walk with Catherine, she noticed a strange expression cross her friend's face.

"Is something wrong?" she asked, her stomach fluttering as she suspected the reason.

"I think, perhaps, my pains are starting to come," said Cat. "I felt something about twenty minutes ago, but it passed, so I didn't say anything. Now it has come again."

"Good heavens! What are we going to do? Should you lie down somewhere? I can run to fetch Philip, if you wish."

"No," said Cat, with a reassuring smile. "There's no need for that. We'll just walk slowly back to the house, and see what happens. Not that I could move quickly in any case, since at present my gait is rather like a duck's!"

Juliana forced a smile at Cat's attempt at a joke, then asked, "Are you in a great deal of pain?"

"No. It was just a little twinge both times. A sort of tightening across my belly. It is gone now."

"Are you sure it is all right for you to walk?"

"Mrs. McGinnis says it is good to walk, that sometimes it makes the baby come faster."

"I don't want it to come faster!"

"Don't fret, Jule. Mrs. McGinnis also warned me that first babies often take some time in coming."

Arms linked, they walked slowly back toward Woodmere Hall. All the while Juliana tried not to hurry, and prayed that Cat's baby would follow the midwife's prediction.

As the day went on, she had ample time to regret her prayers. They arrived back at Woodmere Hall and walked about its lawns while Philip, making a visible effort to remain calm, drove off to fetch the midwife. Juliana relaxed a little at Mrs. McGinnis's arrival. The cheery, capable-looking woman radiated confidence, reassuring all of them that everything was as it should be, and setting Philip firmly in his place by telling him that she had brought him and his brothers and sisters into the world with no trouble at all, and did he not think she could do the same for his child?

Catherine's pains continued to come at gradually shortening intervals. Juliana took turns with Philip and Mrs. McGinnis in walking with her friend about the grounds, and sitting with her when she needed rest. At first confident and cheerful, Cat became tired as the hours wore on, and more subdued as the pains assaulted her with increased intensity, so that she could no longer hold back the occasional moan. Mrs. McGinnis remained optimistic, although her occasional examinations of Catherine still showed she had not yet opened enough to give birth.

A little before the dinner hour, Catherine's water broke, and Mrs. McGinnis informed them that things often happened more quickly once this occurred. Philip carried Catherine up to her bedchamber, where Juliana saw the old, wooden birthing chair that Catherine wished to use in defiance of the modern fashion for giving birth lying in bed. Catherine brightened at the sight of it, but another pain-wracked hour passed with no clear progress.

Juliana went down to dinner and did her best to reassure the children, despite the anxiety gnawing at her as she thought of Cat's suffering. When she returned, she saw Philip conferring with Mrs. McGinnis outside the door.

"Now, sir, you know that first babies are often slow in coming. Especially, if I may speak so free, when the mother's the high-strung, nervous sort like Lady Catherine."

"But how long can it take?" asked Philip. "I don't know how she can bear much more of this."

"I cannot say for certain, sir. She is tired, and may soon begin to fall asleep a little between pains. That might help matters along."

"I thought you said walking was beneficial. Now you are saying she needs to rest?" he said roughly, turning his head to listen as Catherine moaned again.

"Every woman and every baby is different. Try to be calm, sir," said the midwife in a soothing voice.

"Cathy's mother died giving birth to her. How can I be calm?"

"Hush!" she said, looking at both of them now as Juliana came closer. "There's no reason to think your wife will die. It's not a cross birth, or a breech, and the babe was kicking nicely just a few minutes ago, so all's well there too."

"What if she does not give birth soon? Tell me the truth, damn you!"

A hint of strain appeared on Mrs. McGinnis's honest face. "It's too early to say that anything will happen. But if the babe comes too late after the water breaks, sometimes there is fever. Or . . ."

"She and the baby might both die," Philip completed the sentence, his rugged features contorted with fear.

"I said it's too early to worry about that yet," said Mrs. McGinnis. "Now, Master Philip, for your wife's sake, and your family's sake, you must calm yourself. Go eat some dinner, and sit with your brothers and sisters so they don't worry themselves to pieces. I'll send Jemima down to tell you if there's any change."

Reluctantly, Philip left them, although Juliana suspected he would eat as little as she had. Over the next hour, she sat with Mrs. McGinnis beside the bed, while Catherine tried to rest between the pains that caused her to moan and clutch at her pillow. When Philip returned, the midwife ordered Juliana to her bedchamber. She obeyed, knowing Cat was well attended.

Although anxious, she managed to fall asleep, but woke

with a start a few hours later. Unable to fall back asleep, she hastily dressed herself and returned to Catherine's room.

Fear gripped her heart as she saw Philip standing outside, leaning against the wall, his hands covering his face. Peering into the room, she saw Catherine asleep, lying on her side, with Mrs. McGinnis sitting nearby. Her worst fear receded as she watched Cat breathe, and saw a slight movement along her friend's belly. It was disappointing to see that little seemed to have happened while she'd been gone.

Then Juliana heard Philip whispering a prayer.

"Please God, don't take her, too."

She ached with fear for Cat, and sympathy for Philip. Now she remembered how Catherine had talked of his parents' deaths. Awkwardly, she stepped forward and put a hand on his shoulder, offering what comfort she could. He looked up, then they heard Cat's voice, faintly calling his name.

He rushed into the room, and Juliana followed behind.

"Mrs. McGinnis," said Catherine, her voice a little stronger. "I think—I think the baby is coming."

"Stay quiet, my lady," said Mrs. McGinnis. After a quick examination, she nodded her head, and said briskly, "Yes. You'll do now."

She directed Juliana to fetch Jemima and the nursemaid. Glad to have something to do, Juliana hurried away. When she returned with the two maids, she heard Catherine groaning with effort, and Mrs. McGinnis calmly advising her. She entered the room, and saw her friend seated in the birthing chair, relaxing as her pains temporarily subsided. Philip stood behind, his thick arms wrapped around his wife, as if he could somehow impart some of his own bear-like strength to her. Mrs. McGinnis sat on a low stool in front.

Juliana watched, feeling helpless and useless, until Cat bade her come over and stand by her side. She took one of Cat's hands in her own. A moment later, Cat squeezed it tightly, crying out as she tried to push according to the midwife's instructions.

"Well done, dearie!" said Mrs. McGinnis. "I can see the head, now. One or two more pushes like that one should do the trick."

Cat sighed, and Juliana sighed with her. She did not know how much more of this she could take, either.

A minute later, Cat screamed again, straining with effort. Averting her eyes from what was happening below, Juliana saw Cat's face convulsed with pain, though her eyes glowed with a look of fierce, almost primitive exultation.

"There!" said the midwife. " 'Tis a fine baby girl."

Juliana took one glance at the wet, wriggling creature in the midwife's arms, and looked away. Was that how a healthy infant was supposed to look?

She glanced back at Philip and Catherine. They looked as if they were still anxiously awaiting something. What?

Then the baby cried out, making a sound like the bleating of a lamb.

"Thank God," Cat breathed, and her grip on Juliana's hand finally relaxed.

"Is she well, Mrs. McGinnis?" asked Philip. "She cries so softly."

"Nonsense! She's a fine little lady. Not all babies caterwaul the way you did. I thought they'd hear you all the way to Keswick."

Cat giggled, and a moment later, Juliana joined in, laughing more from pent-up nerves than anything else. Then she moved aside with Philip as Jemima, Mrs. McGinnis and the nursemaid bustled about, taking care of Catherine and the baby.

Soon, Cat lay in bed, the baby quietly resting in her arms. Her face, though pale with exhaustion, seemed somehow transformed by an almost unearthly joy. Philip sat nearby, gazing lovingly at her. Once again, his expression reminded Juliana of Marcus. A lump came to Juliana's throat.

Then she looked at their daughter. She was so dreadfully tiny. Even though Mrs. McGinnis said she was healthy, many children did not survive infancy. How could such great joy depend on such a fragile source?

"Come see her, Jule," said Catherine.

Juliana came a few steps closer. They'd put a lace cap on the child's head, but silky, dark hair peeked out from the edges. Dark eyes gazed solemnly at nothing in particular, out of a face shaped rather like a muffin.

"She is lovely," she said politely, fearing to comment on the baby's size. After all, what did she know of babies?

"We are going to name her Elinor, after Philip's mother," said Catherine.

"Little Elinor," said Philip to the child, encouraging her to grasp one of his fingers in her tiny fist.

The baby began to nuzzle at her mother. Mrs. McGinnis came forward to help Catherine put her daughter to breast for the first time, and Juliana took the opportunity to bid them goodnight. Minutes later, she slipped into her bed and curled up, trembling, exhausted and shaken by the power of what she had just witnessed.

Juliana slept late the next morning. Polly came to her when she awoke, bearing good tidings of Cat and her baby. Elinor had awoken several times in the wee hours to be fed, but was sleeping now. Cat was sleeping as well, and showed no signs of the fever they had dreaded so much.

Juliana went downstairs to eat a solitary breakfast, since Philip had already taken the children out to the garden. As she finished, Cat's maid appeared with a tray in her hands.

"Lady Catherine is awake, and would be pleased if you would sit with her while she eats her breakfast," she said.

Juliana nodded, and followed Jemima up the stairs to Philip and Catherine's bedchamber. Cat was sitting up in the large, carved bed, feeding Elinor once more. Her maid set the tray on the bed beside her, and departed, leaving strict instructions to Juliana to call her if her mistress required anything.

Juliana sat down in the chair beside the bed.

"You look well, Cat," she said, relieved to see the color back in her friend's cheeks.

"I feel well, only a little tired," Cat replied, shifting Elinor up over her shoulder.

Juliana blinked as the baby let out a belch that seemed all out of proportion with her size.

"I suppose it will be a while before Elinor is ready for polite society," said Catherine, smiling at the child, whose eyelids were drooping. "Will you take her now, please?"

She gulped. "You wish me to take her?"

"It will be so much easier for me to eat my breakfast if

you do. She is asleep now. You could hold her, or just set her down in the cradle, if you wish."

Juliana looked toward the doorway, but no obliging servant appeared to relieve her of the task.

"Shall I call Jemima?" she asked desperately.

"Come, Jule. You can do this. I will show you how."

Reluctantly, she accepted the infant from Cat, taking care to support her head and neck as directed. It was all of ten feet across the floor to the cradle; she did not dare attempt to carry Elinor so far. Instead, she sat back down in the seat beside the bed. Somehow, the infant managed to stay asleep through the entire perilous operation.

"See, she is quite comfortable with you," said Cat, buttering a muffin, then taking a bite. "Holding a baby is so delightful, is it not?"

Juliana looked down at Elinor. *Delightful?* Terrifying was a better word.

"I'm such a coward!" she blurted out.

Cat set down her muffin. "Whatever do you mean?" she asked, blinking. "You are the most adventurous person I know."

"Yes, I know, I've always said I wanted adventures. But I'm a coward nonetheless," she replied, unaccustomed tears gathering in the corners of her eyes.

"What are you afraid of?" Cat asked gently.

"I'm afraid of holding Elinor. I'm afraid of going through what you endured last night. I'm afraid of how a baby might change my life. That I might become a domineering parent, like Grandpapa, or that I might . . . die and leave a child alone."

Annoyingly, her tears began to flow. Catherine reached a hand over, patting her on the elbow, all she could reach. It was comforting, and yet somehow made the tears flow even more quickly.

"I'm afraid of loving Marcus, that he might stop loving me. That he might not forgive me for leaving him. . . ."

Cat said nothing, only continued to stroke her arm soothingly.

"I'm so sorry," she said, looking up. "I should not burden you with all this, especially now."

"Jule, dearest," said Cat softly. "I know how you feel,

but you cannot allow these fears to stand in the way of your happiness. How do you think I felt last summer? I had no idea of how I might fit in with a family like this one, or be a good wife to a man like Philip. I nearly let my doubts ruin everything, but I am so glad I did not. Of course, I do worry that I might not be as good a mother as Elinor deserves. I know so little about babies! But I shall learn, and . . . and even if I make mistakes, no one will love her more than I do."

Remorse stung Juliana as tears began to flow down her friend's cheeks.

"Oh dear, I didn't mean to make you cry, too!"

"It's no matter. I've been prone to tears ever since I started increasing. Here, have a handkerchief. Jemima was clever enough to leave us several."

Cat took two handkerchiefs from the pile on the table, and passed one to Juliana.

"Look at us!" she said, wiping her eyes. "What watering pots we've become!"

"W-wouldn't Pen laugh? We always thought *she* was the one who suffered from an excess of sensibility." Cat blew her nose, then her expression became solemn. "Why are you still here?"

"What?"

"It is not that I do not enjoy having you here, but isn't it time you returned to Marcus?"

"Do you think he will want me back, after all the accusations I made?"

"Will you ever find out, unless you go back to him?"

Juliana clutched Elinor to her chest. The sensation was strangely comforting, now that she had become used to it.

"Philip forgave *me*," said Cat quietly. "You've done nothing so terrible as what I did last summer. I think you should go, Jule."

She was out of the chair and halfway out the door when Cat's voice checked her.

"Please, can I have my baby back?"

Chapter Seventeen

If the journey to Cumberland had seemed long, the trip back to Gloucestershire was endless. It seemed an age when Juliana finally alighted from her carriage in front of Redwyck Hall on a warm day, a little after noon.

"Welcome home, my lady," Critchley greeted her, a broad smile on his face. "His lordship has missed you."

Encouraged, she asked where he was, and whether Mrs. Redwyck and Lucy had returned to the Hall yet.

"We expect Mrs. Redwyck and Miss Lucinda back in two days, ma'am," he replied. "His lordship has gone fishing."

"When do you expect him back?" she asked, hoping Critchley did not notice how her voice trembled with eagerness.

"He left not long ago, and will most likely be gone for several hours. I think he has not gone far. I expect you can find him on the grounds, near our own stream, my lady," he replied, with an indulgent smile.

She was on the verge of running out after Marcus, but stopped as she saw her reflection in the mirror hanging across from the entrance. She was already nervous enough about her reunion with Marcus; she could not face him with a dusty face and a travel-stained dress.

She hurried upstairs, giving orders all the way. An hour later, she had bathed, and Polly was helping her into the same sprigged gown she had worn for that idyllic picnic when she and Marcus had begun their honeymoon. She rejected both the bonnet and matching spencer, arguing that the day was too warm. In truth, she could not bear to wait another minute.

She ran down the path along the stream, torn between eagerness and apprehension. Over the past few days she'd tried to imagine her reunion with Marcus. Would he be overjoyed, as Cat had predicted? Or had she destroyed his love with her hurtful accusations? Honor and duty would demand that he take her back into his home and even his bed. But would he still love her as he had during the precious weeks of their honeymoon?

She reached the meadow where they had had the picnic. He was there, just as she hoped. A rod and tackle lay beside him, but he was not fishing. Instead, he sat against one of the willows, staring pensively down into the water. The day was so warm that he'd removed his jacket, and the sight of him in his shirtsleeves set her heart pounding even more painfully than before. He did not see her.

Legs trembling with anticipation, she walked toward him, the soft turf muffling her footsteps so that they could not be heard over the gurgling of the stream. Finally, she stood right next to him. His gaze shifted to her feet, then he lifted his head, his eyes slowly traveling up her body to her face. At first he looked stunned, as if he could not believe she was there, then his eyes blazed.

"Juliana," he said, hoarsely, getting to his feet. "You've come back."

Juliana exhaled, not realizing she had been holding her breath. Marcus dragged her into his arms and kissed her fiercely. She kissed him back with equal hunger, pressing herself against his chest as he molded her against him, half-lifting her off her feet until their hearts beat wildly against each other.

"You've come back," he repeated, his voice husky. "I—I had almost given up hoping. How I've longed for you. . . ."

"I'm sorry!" she said, her voice even more unsteady than his. "Can you forgive me for all the horrid things I said to you?"

"There's nothing to forgive. You had every reason to doubt me. I—I only hoped you loved me enough to believe me when I said all I wanted was your happiness."

"I do love you," she said, tightening her hold on him. "I thought I left because I feared losing my independence, but it was more than that. I was afraid of how loving you would change my life, and how I would feel if you didn't love me, or if something happened to you. Or to our children. . . ."

"You are not afraid now, darling?"

"I am terrified," she admitted, "but when I saw how happy Cat and Philip are, with their family and their new baby, I knew I had to come back. That loving you is worth the risk."

He answered with another kiss, strong and deep and demanding. She kissed him back, moaning into the velvet warmth of his mouth as his hands roved down her back and waist. Then he lifted her off her feet again, and swiftly lowered her down onto the soft grass, coming down to lie beside her.

This time, it was no slow seduction. He pulled down her sleeves and bodice and kissed her breasts hungrily, while with the other hand he raised the skirt of her dress. She moaned as he touched her intimately, and found her more than ready. Feverishly, she tried to help him with his own buttons, then once again felt the sweet weight of his body over hers, and the remembered rapture of their joining.

They reached their peaks together. Marcus continued to hold Juliana tightly as she laid her head on his shoulder. She had never been so happy.

"Darling, what is wrong?"

She opened her eyes to look into her husband's anxious hazel ones, and realized that tears were streaming down her cheeks.

"Nothing is wrong," she said. "It is just that I missed you so badly. It is so lovely to be with you again, to be home. . . ."

He brushed away her tears and smiled.

"Home . . ." she murmured. "Do you know, I never felt as if I truly belonged anywhere before. I think that was at least part of my reason for wanting to travel."

"I'm glad you have come to think of Redwyck Hall as your home," he said. "But darling, I have every intention of keeping my promise to take you to Paris. In fact, now that I have engaged a proper steward, we could plan a more extended tour—including Rome and Venice, perhaps?"

"That sounds lovely, Marcus," she said, and turned her head to trail little kisses along his jaw.

"I have some other news you might enjoy hearing."

"What is it?"

"Last week, I was obliged to go to London, and I had the pleasure of dining with your grandfather."

"How is he, and dear Mrs. Frisby?"

"Both of them are very well. While we were having dinner, your grandfather said he is having some doubts about the integrity of the man he has in Venice, dealing with the glassmakers there. I suggested that we might, in the course of our travels, stop by the office in Venice and discover if his suspicions are correct."

"What did he say?"

"He thanked me, but said we were not to trouble ourselves and just enjoy our tour."

Juliana rolled her eyes. "I see. Now that I have *your* protection, he has no objection to my traveling."

"Perhaps. Does it matter?"

"No," she said. "In truth, it is a great concession for Grandpapa not to object to our plans."

She gazed back at Marcus. He, too, looked happier than she'd ever seen him, the lines of care and pain in his face softened by the joy she had given him. She stretched to kiss his forehead, and cried out when he took advantage of her position to caress her breasts. He pushed her down onto her back once more, and continued to kiss and stroke her, this time with tantalizing slowness. She stared up at him, amazed by the strength of her desire, by the look of renewed passion in the depths of his eyes.

"S-so soon, Marcus?" she asked, faintly.

"I was too hasty before, dear wife," he said, teasing her with his clever fingers. "This time we shall proceed more slowly."

She sighed, and abandoned herself to the joy of his lovemaking. There were, indeed, many advantages to marrying a Redwyck.

Allison Lane

"A FORMIDABLE TALENT...
MS. LANE NEVER FAILS TO
DELIVER THE GOODS."
—*ROMANTIC TIMES*

BIRDS OF A FEATHER
0-451-19825-5
When a plain, bespectacled young woman keeps meeting the handsome Lord Wylie, she feels she is not up to his caliber. A great arbiter of fashion for London society, Lord Wylie was reputed to be more interested in the cut of his clothes than the feelings of others, as the young woman bore witness to. Degraded by him in public, she could nevertheless forget his dashing demeanor. It will take a public scandal, and a private passion, to bring them together...

To order call: 1-800-788-6262

S556